BERGENFIELD PUBLIC LIBRARY, NJ
P9-DMT-860

# Under Cold Stone

**Books by Vicki Delany**

Constable Molly Smith Series

*In the Shadow of the Glacier*

*Valley of the Lost*

*Winter of Secrets*

*Negative Image*

*Among the Departed*

*A Cold White Sun*

*Under Cold Stone*

Other Novels

*Scare the Light Away*

*Burden of Memory*

*More Than Sorrow*

# Under Cold Stone

## A Constable Molly Smith Mystery

Vicki Delany

Poisoned Pen Press

First Edition 2014

10 9 8 7 6 5 4 3 2 1

Library of Congress Catalog Card Number: 2013941463

ISBN: 9781464202339 Hardcover
9781464202353 Trade Paperback



Poisoned Pen Press
6962 E. First Ave., Ste. 103
Scottsdale, AZ 85251
www.poisonedpenpress.com
info@poisonedpenpress.com

Printed in the United States of America

*To Cheryl Freedman, friend*

# Acknowledgments

Banff is a real town, located in Banff National Park, Alberta, Canada. The Banff Springs Hotel and Chateau Lake Louise are real places, as fabulous as described, but all the events that take place in those hotels are nothing but products of my imagination. All other locations, people, and events are strictly fictional.

I'd like to thank my cousin, Pamela Manning, for providing valuable insights into the challenges of living in Canada's oldest national park, and Cheryl Freedman for editorial advice. Some I accepted, some I rejected, so all mistakes are mine alone. Thanks also to Rick Blechta and Rose Benoit for use of their names, and to Barbara Peters for the elk battle.

And, as always, to the many police officers who gave of their time and expertise to help me get the Canadian policing as right as I could. Again, all errors are strictly mine.

Toad, that under cold stone
Days and nights has thirty-one
Swelter'd venom sleeping got,
Boil thou first i' the charmed pot.

—William Shakespeare
*Macbeth*, Act 4, Scene1

# Chapter One

## A CAFÉ. BANFF, ALBERTA. FRIDAY MORNING.

The scent of warm baking and fresh coffee was enticing enough to have Lucky Smith willing to endure the café's long line. She rubbed her hands against the chill and shuffled forward. Another couple of paces and she'd be through the doors at last.

Paul Keller had taken one look at the orderly crowd of tourists and locals in search of caffeine and cookies and said he'd meet up with Lucky later. He wanted to check out the sports store a few doors down the street. Lucky's interest in fishing equipment was about the same as Paul's interest in five-dollar, custom-made chai, so they arranged to go their own ways for the afternoon and meet back at the hotel in time to dress for dinner.

Dress for dinner. Such a quaint concept. But it did suit this vacation, their first as a couple, and the historic Banff Springs Hotel in which they were staying. Lucky was a firm believer in not spending time in your partner's pocket. Paul took his coffee black and liked Tim Horton's just fine—although in this town the Tim's could have quite the line-up for coffee and donuts—and his passion was fishing. Lucky thought a chai latte one of the finest benefits of civilization, and she couldn't imagine anything more boring than fishing—unless it was discussing the merits of various types of fishing equipment with the store clerk.

She was almost inside. She should have worn a coat, but as she'd planned to spend her day getting a start on her Christmas shopping and exploring the town, she'd thought a thick hand-woven sweater would have been sufficient.

The Rocky Mountains in October. As a mountain resident herself, Lucky should have remembered how changeable the weather could be.

The person in front of her, a fashionably dressed woman pushing a chair containing a dozing toddler, made it to the doors. The chair holding the child was, Lucky thought, almost large enough to house a third-world family. When did children's chairs become homes on wheels, anyway? When she was a young mother, more years ago than she cared to remember, Lucky had a push chair for her children that folded up into the size of an umbrella. A seat on wheels with a handle. That was all. This one had plush seating, padded sides, a folding canopy, two cup holders (for the parents, not the child). Wide enough to fit toys, drinks and snacks, and shopping bags, as well as a toddler. With an extra bag slung on the back in case of an emergency purchase.

The woman wrestled her child's mobile home over the ledge and into the shop. Lucky held the door. The young mother didn't bother to thank her. Lucky considered saying something but bit her tongue. She was on vacation, after all.

Deep in thought about the lack of manners these days, she was almost knocked off her feet as a man shoved against her. She stumbled and fell into the door. The man attempted to force his way past Lucky, but she thrust her arm out, blocking the entrance. "There's a line."

He was in his thirties, tall but scrawny, with scraggy blond hair and hostile blue eyes that bored into her. Thin lips, a scab in the right bottom corner, formed the words: *Fuck off, lady*.

She blinked in surprise. "There's a line up here," she repeated, "please wait your turn."

"Where are you from?" he snarled.

"I doubt that's relevant." Her heart started beating faster. She studied his eyes for any sign of current drug use. His pupils were normal sized, the whites slightly red but more perhaps from a late night than overindulgence. His eyes would be an attractive dark blue if they didn't overflow with aggression and a sense of entitlement.

The young mother glanced over her shoulder to see what was going on, and then she dipped her head and shoved her child further into the café. Lucky couldn't blame her. She had a child to care for.

Lucky stepped forward to stand on the threshold, blocking the entrance. The man lifted his chin and thrust his chest out. He was considerably taller than she—at five foot nothing, most people were—and loomed over her.

*Bitch*, he mouthed.

She broke eye contact to glance around, seeking some support. The young couple immediately behind her had their arms wrapped around each other, heads close, eyes for nothing but the objects of their affection. The head of the man behind them was bent, thumbs moving rapidly as he tapped out a message on his smartphone. The line snaked down the sidewalk: Couples chatted and people listened to their iPods or sent vitally urgent messages on their own phones. The space in front of Lucky was now clear. She did not move. No point in standing her ground and risking confrontation if the rude man would then slip in behind her.

A second man, shorter but beefier, stood slightly behind the first. "What's your problem?" he asked, his voice low, deliberately pitched not to carry. "I'd guess time of the month, but you're too old for that."

"Never too old," the tall one said.

Lucky was no longer worried about being cold. Sweat ran between her shoulder blades and she could feel dampness on her forehead. She almost stepped back. Let the bullies pass. Not worth fighting over.

But that wasn't Lucky Smith's way. If he'd even bothered to say excuse me before pushing through, she would have let it go.

"There's a line up," she repeated. "You'll be served in your turn, like everyone else."

"Hey." The texting man snapped his phone shut and returned to the real world. "Let's move it. Haven't got all day here." He was also young, and large, and looked as though he spent a good part of his day in the gym.

The two men hesitated. Then, with another whisper of "bitch," the taller one broke away. His friend looked at Lucky for a long time. She returned the stare.

"I'll see you around sometime." He leaned over, and she could smell stale beer, unwashed clothes, and far too much testosterone. He licked his fleshy lips. "Maybe there won't be so many people around then."

He caught up to his friend, slapped him on the back, and they disappeared into the throng wandering the street.

Lucky exhaled. Her legs wobbled. She reached out a hand and leaned against the door.

"You okay?" the young female lover asked.

"Yes. I'm fine. Thank you for asking."

"Well, in that case," her boyfriend said, "will you keep moving?"

# Chapter Two

**TOCEK-SMITH HOME. OUTSIDE TRAFALGAR, BRITISH COLUMBA. FRIDAY AFTERNOON.**

Molly Smith eyed the turkey. It did not eye her back.

It was frozen solid and had no head.

Now, what was she supposed to do with it? The Internet said the safest way to defrost a turkey was to leave it in the fridge. Unfortunately, it also said that this twenty-pound beast would take five to six days to fully defrost. She didn't have five to six days. She had forty-eight hours.

Her mom had left her with instructions for cooking the turkey as well as recipes for her favorite side dishes and desserts. She'd said to go to the butcher to order a fresh, organic, free-range turkey. Her mom hadn't told her to put the order in a month ahead of time, and when Smith showed up this morning—Friday—to buy one, expecting to pick it up on Saturday, she was told she was too late. All those birds who had only days ago been happily pecking in the weeds of their spacious enclosures surrounded by green fields overflowing with organic produce ripening in the sun were accounted for.

She wasn't too disappointed. A free-range turkey was always nice, but plenty of people bought a factory-farm-raised bird from the supermarket, and they seemed good enough. Unfortunately, the supermarket in Trafalgar didn't stock fresh turkeys, only frozen ones.

She wondered if Adam would mind having his Thanksgiving dinner on Tuesday.

He wouldn't. He'd told her he didn't see the point in preparing a big feast for just the two of them. But she was determined to do it right.

She'd propped her iPad on the kitchen table. Back to the Internet to search for plan B. Okay, apparently you could defrost the turkey in cold water. That method seemed to suit a cook who had nothing at all to do for an entire day as the water should be kept cold and constantly refreshed. Smith was scheduled to begin a twelve-hour shift in two hours. It might have been doable if she still had her apartment above Alphonse's bakery on Trafalgar's main street, to which she could slip every few hours to replace the water. But now that she was living a good half-hour outside of town, it was unlikely her shift supervisor would approve of her driving back and forth all night.

She twisted the square-cut diamond ring on her left hand. She could tell Adam that as they were going to her mom's sister's place in Seattle for American Thanksgiving at the end of November, she'd decided one huge turkey dinner a year was enough. Two, if you counted Christmas, and Molly's mother, Lucy Smith, whom everyone called Lucky, always did a turkey at Christmas. A fresh, free-range, organically fed turkey.

But then what would she do with this monstrous slab of frozen beast?

Ah, what the heck. They were young and healthy. A bit of improperly defrosted turkey wouldn't kill them. She wiped out the sink, dropped the heavy bird into it, and ran cold water.

It would be just the two of them for dinner on Sunday. Adam Tocek and Molly Smith. Their first Thanksgiving together and she wanted to cook a traditional turkey dinner with all the trimmings. Lucky had given her the family's favorite recipes—stuffing (not *dressing*!), butternut squash casserole (sweet with a hint of maple syrup), mashed potatoes, gravy, roasted Brussels sprouts, and pecan pie. She eyed the pile of grocery bags spread out across the counter. Even if she did have time to defrost the turkey in the fridge, she'd have trouble finding room.

She put away the groceries and thought about her mom. Lucky and Paul Keller had gone to Banff to spend the holiday weekend at the Banff Springs Hotel. Lucky had balked at first, not wanting to be away at Thanksgiving. But it was the shoulder season in town—between the departure of summer hikers and kayakers and the arrival of skiers—so things were slow at the store, Mid-Kootenay Adventure Vacations. Besides, Lucky and Paul had never been away together, and he was anxious to treat her to a luxurious, although short, vacation.

At the beginning, Smith had been unhappy about her mom's new relationship. Paul Keller was Chief Constable of Trafalgar. Smith's dad, Andy, had died two years earlier and the chief was divorced, so that wasn't the problem. It was just that her mom was, well, her mom, and Keller was her boss. But they seemed good for each other—the office staff gossiped about how nice it was now that the chief wasn't so cranky all the time—and Lucky was happy. All of which was good enough for her daughter.

She checked the recipes one more time to make sure she hadn't forgotten to buy something important. She was on afternoons this week, would get home at three on Sunday morning, nap for a few hours, and then get up and start cooking. Fortunately, Sunday was the start of four days off, so she didn't have to squeeze the preparation and then the meal into between-shift time.

Adam wasn't a bad cook—heck, he was a lot better cook than she was—but he was working all weekend and as the Royal Canadian Mounted Police dog-handler for the district, he could be called out at any time, with no notice, so she'd volunteered to do it all.

She headed upstairs to get ready for work. She showered, washed her hair and tied it into a ponytail, put on her uniform, struggled into her equipment-laden belt, went to the gun safe and retrieved her Glock. Last of all she slipped off her engagement ring and tucked it into its box in the table on her side of the bed. She never wore the diamond to work.

Back downstairs, she drained the sink and added fresh cold water. She studied her efforts—the bald white turkey looked mighty unappealing. Then, feeling like a proper fifties-era housewife, she shifted her gun belt, settled the weight of the Glock into a better place on her hip, and left for work.

# Chapter Three

**BANFF SPRINGS HOTEL. BANFF, ALBERTA. FRIDAY AFTERNOON.**

Lucky's heart was no longer in Christmas shopping. The incident at the coffee shop had upset her, more than she might have expected. Not only the men's shocking rudeness but the obliviousness of everyone else to what was going on. If the man had struck her, would anyone have torn their attention away from their iPods and phones long enough to notice?

She abandoned her shopping expedition and walked back to the hotel. She hadn't even had that cup of chai, but left the café before she reached the counter and, taking care to go in the opposite direction from the two men, pushed her way through the crowds. It was a Friday, the start of Thanksgiving weekend, and the town was packed with tourists. The jagged snow-covered mountains—Norquay, Sulphur, Cascade, Rundle—stood stark and beautiful against the clear blue sky. These mountains were a good deal taller, sharper, and much younger than the ones surrounding Trafalgar and usually they took Lucky's breath away. Now, she scarcely noticed them. She'd slipped into a toy shop, the windows bright and colorful with stuffed animals, but soon realized she was paying more attention to who might be coming through the doors after her than possible gifts for Ben and Rebecca, her grandchildren.

Confrontation wasn't new to Lucky Smith. She was a passionate, strong-minded woman. She'd cut her teeth on radical politics back in the '60s and hadn't slowed down since. She'd been reluctant to enter into a relationship with Paul Keller, a police chief no less, fearing their divergent political opinions would be too divisive. Instead, she found that they both enjoyed a good, respectful argument. This incident, today, had upset her. Perhaps it was the senselessness of it, the naked hostility two men in their thirties had shown to an older woman who simply expected them to display a modicum of manners.

As she walked up the long sweeping hotel driveway, the view momentarily relieved her of her funk. Built in 1887, The Banff Springs was nicknamed "The Castle" and resembled something one might find perched on a wind-swept crag overlooking the North Sea. Nestled in the mountains, deep in the forest beside the fast-moving Bow River, the hotel had been built in memory of the Scotland for which the town had been named. Lucky stopped walking and simply stood for a few moments, admiring the grand old building. Gray stone, white trim, towering turrets, the surrounding forest and looming mountains. The Banff Springs Hotel had been built as a destination for railroad magnates, royalty, and silent movie stars in an era when travel was considered luxurious and people knew the meaning of grand. She imagined her tormenters of earlier getting short shrift if they tried butting in line here.

She laughed at herself. Funny how finding oneself on the *right* side of class and income barriers, if only for a few days, made even Lucky Smith want to pull up the drawbridge and keep the hoi polloi out. The handsome young doorman, dressed in the hotel's smart green-and-brown livery, held the door open for her, giving her a smile full of straight white teeth. He had clear skin, shiny black hair, and was tall and fit. The staff name tags indicate where they are from. His said, Harry. Australia. Lucky reminded herself that the people who'd built this hotel, and worked in the kitchens and cleaned the bathrooms in the early days, were not attractive young people on a world-traveling adventure. No doubt it was a much different place "below stairs" in those days.

She returned Harry's smile and walked into the lobby. Simply being here made Lucky feel special. Special and pampered. The lobby was huge, aged stone, highly polished wood, acres of white marble dotted with carpets in a red-tartan pattern, gleaming chandeliers. Smiling staff and prosperous happy guests. A waiting elevator took Lucky swiftly to the fourth floor.

By the time she got to their room she was feeling a good deal better. She felt better still when she saw that in her absence the bed had been made, towels fluffed and rehung, magazines stacked, the desk and dresser tidied, and everything wiped down. A silent army of staff made the hotel work so flawlessly.

Lucky hadn't travelled much in her life—something she regretted. She and Andy had owned a store, and that didn't lead to having a lot of spare time for vacations. Nor money, either, with the store to run, employees to pay, children to raise and to send to university. Most of the family's vacations were to visit relatives in Washington State. Lucky had never been to Europe, never been outside North America. She went to the windows, tall and deep-set, and looked over the rooftops of the hotel and across the green forest to the river and the snow-covered mountains beyond.

She could, she thought, get used to living like this.

She had no idea what Paul must be paying for the room. It might be the shoulder season, same as at her store, but this was Thanksgiving weekend. When he'd proposed the holiday, she'd gulped and insisted on paying her share and been secretly relieved when he refused.

She kicked off her practical walking shoes and hung her sweater in the closet. She was back earlier than expected, and Paul would be a while yet. She'd treat herself to afternoon tea in the lounge. No doubt after that she'd be too full to enjoy dinner, but this was a vacation, after all.

# Chapter Four

**LIGHTHOUSE KEEPER RESTAURANT. BANFF, ALBERTA. FRIDAY AFTERNOON.**

She absolutely hated this awful job. The only thing that made it bearable was the money, and that six-top had just stiffed her on the tip. Sensing big spenders, Tracey had largely ignored the two old folks who demanded milk—real milk not as served in the plastic container—for their tea, and then couldn't decide if they wanted salad or soup and fussed over how well the bacon in the club sandwich was cooked. Instead she'd focused her attention on the six well-dressed, expensively groomed American tourists.

This place was, to put it mildly, a dump. It was called the Lighthouse Keeper, and happened to be in a good location just off Banff Avenue, so occasionally the better class of tourist didn't realize they were slumming it until they were inside. This bunch had looked around, lifted their noses in the air, and turned as if to leave. But one of the men said he was starving and this place was as good as any. Besides, there wasn't a wait for a table. He plunked his fat ass down and yelled at Tracey to bring him a menu. His friends reluctantly joined him. They ordered quickly with no questions. Exactly the sort of customers she liked. A couple of beers, glasses of wine, appetizers for the table, then burgers or steaks and fries for the men, and fish with salads for the women. She bustled about, pouring water, unasked, bringing drinks, taking the food order, smiling, smiling, smiling, while the old lady tried to get her attention to complain that the tea was cold.

And then, after all that, the old folks left twenty percent and thanked her and the snotty tourists left five. A five-percent tip. She felt like running into the street after them and throwing it at their feet. But money was money—even five percent—and pride was expensive.

Tracey McMillan carried the dirty dishes into the kitchen. At three o'clock in the afternoon the restaurant was empty. The back door was propped open and she knew Kevin, the cook, was outside grabbing a smoke in the alley. Her feet ached, and she pulled up a stool. She took off her shoe and rubbed at her toes.

She'd been working since seven. Less than an hour to go. Tracey hated breakfast and lunch shifts: cheap meals, not much liquor, people in a hurry, hung-over from the night before. A couple of times she'd been called in at the last minute to take a dinner shift when one of the other staff had been sick. They were a lot busier, but the tips sure made up for it. She needed better and more hours, but Kevin, the owner as well as the cook, said she had to work her way up.

God, she hated this place. Hated this town. She'd been better off back in Smith's Falls, Ontario. Prospects were no better there, but at least a person could afford to live in Smith's Falls. Banff was lovely to look at but so overrun with wealthy tourists the rents were sky-high no matter what sort of dump you lived in. The town was located smack dab in a national park, so no one was building cheap apartment complexes for the workers.

If it weren't for Matt, she'd be outta here. Back to Smith's Falls, dragging her tail between her legs, asking her mom to take her in, just until she got back on her feet. Mom would roll her eyes, light up another fag, take a swig of rye, and say, "Come on in, honey."

Matt. He was great guy if only he'd drop the chip on his shoulder. Angry at the world, most of the time. But not angry at Tracey, not often anyway. She loved him, she really did, but she wasn't sure what his feelings were for her. She knew she wasn't a babe. She was only nineteen to Matt's thirty-three, which was good, but no matter how much she starved herself she could never be fashionably skinny. She had an overbite that she hated, although Matt said it was cute, and thin hair the color of dog shit. She'd dyed her hair blond once, but that made it look like it belonged to a dog with a stomach disorder. She'd had a roommate a while ago, who worked in a spa and allowed Tracey to use some of her expensive makeup and hair products. Those had put color on her face and bounce in her hair. But the roommate moved on, taking all her stuff with her, and Tracey had never been able to allow herself to pay more than she could afford for frivolities.

She wasn't like so many girls here, with their shiny hair, glowing complexions, perfect teeth, and trim bodies. They came from all over the world to work in Banff. Not many of them, Tracey thought bitterly, needed the job. They were here for the experience and probably paid as much in rent, maybe more, than they earned in wages. Tracey had applied for jobs at some of the good hotels. She never even got a reply. No doubt they wanted girls named Tiffany from New York or Marie-France from Paris or Pippa from London. Not Tracey McMillan from Smith's Falls, Ontario.

Still, that was the way it was, and no point getting mad over it. At least she had a boyfriend. Better than her mother could say. It would be nice, though, if she and Matt could live together. Like every other working-class schmuck in Banff, they stitched together a strange assortment of living arrangements. Matt bunked in with three guys in an apartment whose only advantage was that it wasn't too far from the center of town. Talk was that the old apartment buildings on that street were going to be demolished for another luxury hotel. Where the hell the workers were supposed to live then, no one seemed to worry about. At least Matt had his own room, small as it was. Tracey was crashing with a couple of girls who were friends of friends of Matt. She slept in the living room on a pull-out couch that had seen far better days. Her roommates worked days, and usually went to bars or parties in the evening. They might come in at all hours, bringing guys home to continue the party. Tracey would crawl deeper under the covers and try not to hear the blare of the TV or noises from the girls' bedrooms.

Matt promised that he and Tracey would get their own apartment soon. Once skiing at Sunshine opened in November he'd be able to supplement his bartending job and start bringing in better money. Tracey glanced at the calendar on the wall. Another month, at least, until the snow fell and the skiers arrived. She'd give Matt until then. And then a month to get some money together. Either they had an apartment, or at least a room in an apartment, by then, or it would be Christmas in Smith's Falls for her.

She loved Matt. But she couldn't continue living like this.

The kitchen door opened and Martina and Julianne bounced in, laughing. They didn't bother to share the joke with Tracey. She struggled to get off her chair and put her shoe back on. Time to leave this dump. She had one hour to get home and change and be at her other job at Global Car Rental by five. Put in a four-hour shift there and be back at the restaurant in the morning at seven.

What a miserable life.

# Chapter Five

**TRAFALGAR CITY POLICE STATION. TRAFALGAR, BRITISH COLUMBIA. FRIDAY LATE AFTERNOON.**

Sergeant John Winters stretched back and wiggled his toes. He had his shoes off and his feet on the desk as he flipped the pages of a six-month-old edition of *Blue Line* magazine. Almost quitting time, but he had nothing to go home to. Eliza was in Saskatoon, visiting her mother and sister. Ray Lopez, the only other member of the Trafalgar Police Service's General Investigative Section, had the Thanksgiving weekend off to spend with his family. Someone had to mind the store, so Winters had nobly offered to stay behind. Not that he didn't like Eliza's mother, he did, a great deal. But he didn't have much to say to the old woman, and Eliza's sister Jennifer could be a right bitch when she got into the dinner wine. Which she did before, during, and after dinner. The result, he'd always thought, of jealously over the younger, prettier, richer, far more successful sister. John Winters never thought of himself as much of a catch, particularly not for a woman like Eliza, so beautiful she'd been a top-ranked international model in her youth. Not only was she still beautiful in middle age but also a wizard on the stock market, with a head for business that matched that of Warren Buffett.

But even John Winters, small-town cop, was a pretty good catch compared to the series of men who passed through

Jennifer's life, sometimes leaving a baby behind for her to remember them by.

"Working hard?" Barb Kowalski came into the GIS office with a stack of reports to be read and signed.

Winters grinned at the chief constable's assistant. "It seems as if every scumball and troublemaker in town has gone to Mom's for Thanksgiving."

"Think we'll get lucky and they'll decide not to come back?"

"Be careful what you wish for," Winters said. "We'd all be out of a job."

Barb laughed. She'd worked for the police for thirty years, longer than anyone else here, and she knew that was unlikely to happen. Trafalgar was a tourist town, but one that catered to young adventure vacationers. Too early for skiing, too late for kayaking, kids only back in school for a month so not too restless yet. The town could be quiet the second weekend in October, Thanksgiving weekend.

"I have enough paperwork to last me well into my retirement even if we never get another call," Winters said. "It's the calm before the storm, I fear. People are starting to make noise about the Grizzly Resort starting up again, and it's rumored there'll be protests next week."

"That place. Never anything but trouble. As an employee of this department I won't tell you what side I'm on, John, but in my spare time, I might be found wishing they would go away and leave us alone."

"I have a meeting on Tuesday with the Mounties to go over what we might expect."

There'd been trouble before around plans to turn a parcel of pristine wilderness into vacation homes. The development had been put on hold and for the past couple of years only a single security guard kept watch as the forest crept back to claim its territory. Now, new owners had bought the land, heavy equipment was moving back in, fences were being repaired, and security was increased. Trafalgar sits in the middle of the B.C. wilderness, eight hours or more in either direction to the nearest Canadian big city, four hours to a small city. If Trafalgar residents wanted to go to the mall, they need a passport: The nearest mall is across the border in Spokane, Washington, two hours away. Plenty of people moved here specifically to escape the city and unchecked development. They were not happy, to say the least, at the news. On the other hand, good jobs in Trafalgar were scarce and the development would bring plenty of those, plus business to the shops on Front Street.

Once again, fault lines were splitting the town. It would be up to them, the Trafalgar City Police, as well as the RCMP, to try to keep the peace.

"As you say," Barb said, "keeps us employed. I'm taking advantage of the chief's absence, and I'm off now. You won't tell him I left early, I hope."

Winters glanced at his watch. "You'll be cheating the town out of ten minutes, Barb. Can you live with the guilt?"

She tossed the papers on his desk with a snort. "I'll get over it. Particularly the next time I work straight through lunch because the chief forgot to tell me he needs the budget to show the mayor this afternoon. At first I thought our dear leader was getting senile. Instead, I've decided he has happier things on his mind."

"Lucky guy."

Barb laughed. "In more ways than one." She lowered her voice and leaned slightly toward him. "Something I've been meaning to talk to you about. I know you and Paul get together over beers now and again to talk about the department. Has he ever said anything to you about, well, maybe thinking of retirement?"

"No. Why do you ask? Do you think he's considering it?"

"Wondering, that's all. He's well past the age for a full pension. After Karen left him, he was lonely, that's no secret. Lost without the routine of living with another person. I assumed he'd abandoned retirement plans because he needed the job. Not for the money, although the divorce probably cost him, but for something to do. Now, well…now that he's with Lucky I thought he might be thinking of traveling, having some fun. Going fishing."

"I've no idea, Barb. It might be that this jaunt to Banff puts the idea in his head."

She was silent for a moment. She glanced over her shoulder, but no one was standing at the door or coming down the hallway. "I'd appreciate it if you give me a heads-up if you do hear anything, John. You know I can keep the chief's secrets."

He nodded. She wouldn't have lasted thirty years as a civilian in the police department if she couldn't keep her mouth shut. And, on occasion, her ears.

"It's just that, well, I've decided to retire when Paul does. I'm too old to train another chief constable. I'd like you to keep that to yourself, if you could."

He smiled at her. "You know I will."

"Thanks. I'm off home. Looks like I'll only owe the taxpayers five minutes now. Stay safe, eh?" And she left.

Five o'clock on the Friday of a long weekend. The office was quiet. His computer beeped to tell him he had an incoming message. He opened it eagerly. A retirement announcement from the RCMP detachment in Castlegar.

He sighed and went back to his magazine.

# Chapter Six

**GLOBAL CAR RENTAL. BANFF, ALBERTA. FRIDAY LATE AFTERNOON.**

The man blinked behind thick glasses as he waved his hands in the air. His wife flipped frantically through a small book, seeking the right words.

Tom shrugged. "You broke it, man. You gotta pay. You got insurance, right?"

The man babbled incomprehensibly as he gestured to the car's windshield. A tiny chip in the glass.

"Rock," his wife said, finding the word she wanted. "Rock."

As if Tom Dunning cared what hit their car.

They were a middle-aged couple who'd decided to cut themselves free from the herd of their tour group and take a day for themselves. Rent a car, drive into the mountains, admire the scenery, get off the main road, maybe see some wildlife. They were dressed in expensive outdoor gear bought specifically for this trip, clothes their tour company had told them would be appropriate for the Canadian wilderness. The wife's earrings were gold hoops, the chain around her neck also gold. She had a nice-sized rock on her finger and her pink nails were freshly groomed. The man looked like he'd had a manicure too. Tom didn't have much time for men who visited spas.

"Five hundred dollars," Tom said. He shrugged, trying to look sympathetic. "Sorry, that's what it costs for a new windscreen."

"Five hundred dollar!"

"You got insurance, right?"

"Insurance, yes." The man's head bobbed in agreement. The wife continued flipping through her phrase book.

"Claim it from them."

"Small," the man said. He held his hands close together as if trying to indicate the size of the chip. "Small."

Tom could see the size all right. That was kinda the point. "Sorry," he said again.

The man continued to argue, a stream of broken English amongst the rapid Japanese. He could argue till he was blue in the face, didn't matter. Tom had the credit card details, a signature taking responsibility for the vehicle.

Enough of this. Tom turned and headed back to the building that housed the Banff office of Global Car Rental. The Japanese man began to follow, but his wife grabbed his sleeve. She said something, sounded pleading. Telling him to drop it. He argued for a moment and then stomped away, the wife scurrying after.

"What was all that about?" Tracey asked as she put her purse under the counter. She was a nice girl, Tom thought, and young. Could even be pretty if she bothered to put on some makeup and wore clothes that didn't look like they were bought at the secondhand shop. He might have considered screwing her, just to get one up on Matt, but he had a good thing going with Jody, and right now Tom didn't feel like upsetting that particular apple cart.

"They got a stone in the window. Didn't want to pay."

"It won't be much, right?" Tracey said. "Looks like a small chip."

"Right," Tom said. "Twenty or thirty bucks." Leaving four hundred and seventy dollars pure profit for him and the boss to split with Barry the mechanic who'd provide a receipt for the cost of an entire windshield replacement.

# Chapter Seven

**BANFF SPRINGS HOTEL AND LIGHTHOUSE KEEPER RESTAURANT. BANFF, ALBERTA. SATURDAY MORNING.**

"I," Paul Keller announced to Lucky Smith, "am in the mood for a full greasy-spoon breakfast."

"Breakfast," she groaned. "After that dinner, how can you even think about breakfast?"

"Man's gotta keep his strength up." He pulled her close.

She tucked her head into the crook of his arm, and ran her fingers across his chest. "You're a dirty old man."

"Not unless I get some breakfast into me." He threw off the covers.

"Neither one of us," Lucky said, "needs the calories."

Paul crossed the room to open the drapes, and then headed for the bathroom. "We'll work it off on the trails." His head popped back around the door. He gave her an exaggerated wink. "And in the bedroom."

Lucky stretched across the king-sized bed, delighting in the lingering warmth from Paul's body. Sunlight streamed through the windows. She ran her fingers across the crisp sheets, enjoying the feel of the rich, smooth fabric.

Yesterday, she'd had a perfectly delightful afternoon tea in the hotel's Rundle Lounge, sipping Earl Grey, munching on light-as-air blueberry scones covered in jam and clotted cream, thin sandwiches, and delicate pastries. All while she tried to ignore the outrageous price of forty dollars, never mind the unnecessary calories. She'd paid with her credit card, too guilty to put it on the bill for Paul to take care of. She'd brought her book to read while she relaxed, but scarcely turned a page, so captivated was she by the stunning view of the Bow Valley outside the floor-to-ceiling windows as well as the parade of fashionable tea-drinkers, most of whom looked as if forty dollars for tea and sandwiches wasn't at all out of the ordinary.

And then, not long after, a stroll through the hotel grounds having done little to work off the unnecessary meal, Paul had arrived back at the hotel, laden with new fishing equipment, and escorted her to dinner. She'd bought a dress for this trip, spending far more than was her norm, and felt young and pretty in a black calf-length wool dress topped with a sparkling gold jacket. She'd worn the gold and diamond earrings her son Samwise had given her a few Christmases ago. The outfit would have been stunning with sexy high-heeled gold sandals, but as she wasn't really young and pretty and occasionally got a bad twinge in her right hip, she had to be content with plain black flats.

They dined in the Castello Restaurant, and Lucky felt she had to do the meal justice. She was quite virtuous passing on an appetizer but couldn't resist ordering the lamb. She loved lamb and ate it at almost every opportunity. Paul had a Caesar salad followed by the rib eye. Lucky had never been much of a drinker, and Paul was more a beer guy, so they simply had one glass of wine each.

And now he wanted a full breakfast?

She reminded herself that they were on vacation. After breakfast they planned to drive to Lake Louise to have a look around another historic railroad hotel and see the famous glacier, and then head up to Lake Moraine—instantly recognizable to all Canadians for having been featured on the back of the twenty-dollar bill for many years—where they'd go hiking.

Tomorrow, Sunday, Paul wanted to try some fishing, and Lucky planned on joining a guided excursion to Johnston Canyon and the ink pots.

Paul came out of the bathroom and she slipped in to shower. Soon, dressed in sturdy hiking clothes and boots, armed with cameras and maps, they left the hotel. On his wanderings the day before, Paul told her as they drove into town, he'd seen a suitably cheap-looking restaurant that had hearty breakfasts on the menu.

It was, inappropriately for the mountain setting, called the Lighthouse Keeper and decorated to resemble an East Coast fishing village. The oars, fishing nets, and lobster trap decorations were tattered and cracked, the wood floors stained, the bottles behind the bar covered with a sheen of dust. The scent of stale grease and spilled beer hung over everything.

Paul rubbed his hands together in glee. "Perfect." Lucky felt a rush of affection, and placed her hand lightly on his arm. He smiled down at her.

"Table for two?" the waitress asked, not bothering to show much interest in the new arrivals. With her long sad face, bored eyes, and lifeless hair she reminded Lucky of some of the young mothers who passed through her child nutrition classes at the women's support center. The beginnings of a round belly spilled over the waistband of her faded black pants, the result of a diet consisting mostly of fast food burgers and pop. She grabbed menus and led the way to a table for six in the center of the room. Only one other table was occupied. They mustn't get very busy at this time of day, not if Paul and Lucky could be casually shown to the biggest table.

Lucky scanned the menu. "I'm not very hungry, Paul. I only want tea. Why don't you get an extra side of toast and I'll have some of that?"

The waitress was soon back with Lucky's tea and coffee for Paul. Paul placed his order: fried eggs, bacon, sausage, hash browns, extra toast. He got to his feet. "Be right back."

Lucky poured tea and ripped open a package of milk. She was stirring her drink when she heard a voice behind her. "Well, well, if it isn't the back-of-the-line lady."

Startled, she looked up to see the two men she'd encountered the day before—the ones who'd tried to push their way ahead of her into the coffee shop. She'd told Paul about the incident as they dressed for dinner last night and he muttered something about jerks everywhere. She hadn't thought about it since.

She certainly was thinking about it now. The men loomed over her table, smirking. "Surprised to see you slumming in a joint like this," the taller one said.

"Looking for some rough fun?" The second one touched her green scarf, hand woven, pure wool, which she'd hung on the back of her chair.

"Don't know about fun," the tall one said. "Not for you anyway, lady." His hand shot out, and he snatched up her tea cup.

She leapt to her feet, as hot liquid splashed against her sweater. Paul was nowhere to be seen. The patrons at the other table had stopped eating and were watching. The waitress stood frozen at the door to the kitchen, her eyes wide and her hands to her mouth.

"Call the police," Lucky ordered in a good loud voice.

The shorter man laughed, a laugh without humor. "We don't need any cops, Tracey. Chill, we're just being friendly-like to a visitor to our nice town." There was something familiar about him, Lucky thought. Something about the shape and color of his brown eyes and he way he held his head and shoulders.

The waitress plucked at the man's sleeve. "Matt, please, I don't want any trouble. Barry, get out of here."

Barry, the taller one, took a step back. "No trouble. We came in for breakfast but don't much like the company. Let's go, man."

Matt didn't move. Lucky reached into her pocket and pulled out her cell phone. "If you won't call the police," she said to the waitress, "I will." The man's eyes narrowed. His hand shot out and he grabbed Lucky's arm. He gave it a twist. "We don't need any goddamn interfering cops. Say you're sorry for disrespecting Barry here, lady, and then we'll let you go." With his other hand he plucked the phone out of her hand. Lucky yelled.

The waitress screamed. Matt released Lucky's arm and then he was out of her space and spinning around. Paul Keller, eyes narrowed, face red with anger, had him by the collar of his jacket. Spittle flying, Paul bellowed, "You filthy little punk." He grabbed the man's other shoulder and shook. "How dare you put your hands on her?"

Lucky's phone had flown across the room. She scrambled after it. Paul might be a police officer and he had once been used to subduing drunks, but these days he was an out-of-shape, overweight man with a desk job who smoked too much and exercised too little. No match for a man young enough to be his son. She grabbed the phone, flipped it open, punched in 9-1...But before she could finish the sequence, she glanced back at the men. To her surprise the younger fellow's shoulders were slumped and his hands lifted in surrender.

The man at the other table tossed bills down and, almost pushing his wife, slipped away. The waitress' eyes were wide and frightened. The cook, dressed in a stained white jacket and striped gray pants, had come out of the back, alerted by the raised voices. He gripped a phone, Lucky was pleased to see. Barry, the taller one, had disappeared.

Paul released his grip and took a step back. He was breathing heavily and his red face dripped sweat. "What the hell's the matter with you? Harassing women in a public place. Apologize, right now."

"Or what? You gonna arrest me?"

"I have grounds to. Uttering threats, attempted theft, drunk and disorderly."

"Chill, man. I'm not drunk and I didn't steal anything. I wasn't threatening, just having fun."

"Some fun."

Lucky's head spun. This conversation was almost surreal. She looked, really looked, at the young man. Noticed his beefy frame, the way the ridge of his eyebrows hooded his brown eyes, his full lips. She looked at Paul Keller.

Oh, dear God, no.

"Nice to see you too, Dad," Matt Keller said with a sneer that turned his handsome face ugly.

# Chapter Eight

**LIGHTHOUSE KEEPER RESTAURANT. BANFF, ALBERTA. SATURDAY MORNING.**

Lucky knew Paul was estranged from his only son, Matthew. He had been for quite some time, long before the divorce from Karen. The boy, Paul had told her, had a wild streak and a quick temper he couldn't control. He'd hoped that as Matt got older, out of the tempestuous teenage years, he'd calm down. But that never happened. Matt quit school at seventeen and wandered from one dead-end job to another. He seemed to stay out of trouble, mostly, and for that Paul was grateful. It was all too easy, as Paul Keller well knew, to start down the slippery slope of not having much money but a sense of entitlement that led to crime and eventually prison. The boy kept in touch with his mother and she passed his news on. Matt was pretty much a ski bum these days, drifting from one resort to another, picking up jobs as ski patrol or a ski instructor in the winter, waiting on tables or tending bar in the off-season.

It hadn't helped, Paul had confided in Lucky, that he, Matt's father, had been a police officer. In a small town like Trafalgar, the boy felt humiliated every time one of his friends had an encounter with the police or if his dad was the one to answer a call to a house party out of control. The family moved to Calgary when Matt was seventeen, and he refused to go with them. Father and son had argued, angrily, bitterly, said words that could never be unsaid. Karen blamed Paul for her son's failure; Paul didn't see it that way. The kid simply didn't have the fortitude to make something of himself. Paul had only seen Matthew a few times over the years since: a Christmas at Karen's sister's, at Paul's father's funeral, at the wedding of his daughter Cheryl. The latter had been only a year ago, and Paul thought it was well past time to bury the hatchet. To reconcile. Matt had not agreed. If anything, he seemed angrier at his father than ever. He blamed Paul for the divorce, which seemed odd considering that the boy hadn't lived with his parents for sixteen years now.

But when families fell out, sense and reason had little, if anything, to do with it.

"Sit down," Paul ordered now, in a voice Lucky hadn't heard since their younger days when Constable Keller and Mrs. Smith could often be found on opposite sides of the barricades. Figuratively, and occasionally, literally.

Matt dropped into what had been Lucky's chair.

"I don't want any trouble here." The cook lifted his phone. "Matt, go home."

"I'll take care of it," Paul said.

The cook glanced between the men. "Now that Barry's scarpered, Matt won't cause any more trouble." He shook his head, his long gray hair confined in a net, and went back to the kitchen, mumbling. The waitress slid up to their table. She put a hand on Matt's shoulder and he shrugged it off with a growl. The girl winced.

Paul pulled over a chair but did not sit down. "First of all, apologize to Mrs. Smith. Then you can tell me what you think you're doing harassing people at this time of the morning. At any time of the day."

Matt lifted his head. He studied Lucky. He was a good-looking young man, with high cheekbones and thick black lashes guarding brown eyes that could have been attractive if they had a touch of warmth in them. "So," he said with a lazy drawl, "this is *her*. Mom told me you'd taken up with some fancy lady. I thought she meant someone...*younger*."

Paul's face flushed and for a moment Lucky thought he'd strike his son. She said, quickly, "I remember you, Matthew. You used to come into the store to look at the ski equipment. You skied with my daughter, Moonlight, didn't you?"

Matt's eyes widened, and then he dipped his head. "Mrs. Smith. Yeah, I remember. Sorry, I didn't recognize you there."

"Would that have made a difference?" Paul was still standing, looming over his son.

The policeman, Lucky thought, not the father. She pulled up a chair and sat down. "We've all changed," she said, "over the years. It's nice to see you. Are you living here, in Banff? Still skiing, I hope. Moonlight gave up competition. I was sorry about that, she was very good. Not good enough, she said."

"She wanted to be the best," Matt said as a shadow of a smile touched his mouth. "And she usually was. I've a job at Sunshine as an instructor soon as the hills open. What's Moonlight doing?"

"She's a…uh…still living in Trafalgar. She doesn't like to be called Moonlight anymore, but Molly, which I must say I do not like."

Matt nodded. Lucky glanced at Paul. She jerked her head toward the empty chair, indicating that he should sit down. He did so, but his posture was no less aggressive. Hands clenched, back straight, a vein prominent in his neck.

Tracey, the waitress, hovered at Matt's shoulder, twisting her hands together. Obviously they knew each other. A girlfriend?

"Your father and I are here for the weekend." Lucky felt like the only living human at a vampire's wake, chattering away, trying to ignore the currents whirling in the air. "We're staying at the Banff Springs for a special treat."

Matt's eyes flickered toward his father.

Lucky briefly considered suggesting Matt and Tracey have dinner with them tonight. She usually tried to smooth troubled waters whenever she could. But, in the back of her mind, she realized she didn't want to spend any time with Matt. He might be Paul's son, but he had been rude and threatening to her. Besides, it wasn't any of her business, although if her relationship with Paul continued on its course, it might be some day.

She leaned over and picked her bag off the floor. Got to her feet. "I didn't want breakfast anyway and the tea's cold now."

"I'll get you another," Tracey said.

"No. Thank you. Paul, why don't I walk to the hotel? You and Matt have lots of catching up to do."

Paul pushed his chair back. "We've a full day planned, and I intend to enjoy it. If," he said to his son, "you want to go for a drink or something later, we're at the Banff Springs until Tuesday morning." He handed Tracey a green twenty-dollar bill.

Paul stalked out of the restaurant. Lucky followed. She glanced over her shoulder. Tracey was kneeling on the floor beside Matt. The boy's eyes were on his disappearing father.

# Chapter Nine

**LIGHTHOUSE KEEPER RESTAURANT. BANFF, ALBERTA. SATURDAY MORNING.**

Tracey rested her hand on Matt's back. When he didn't pull away, she dared to slide closer, her knees scraping against the old wood of the floor. "Was that your father?"

Matt didn't look at her. "Yeah. Great guy, eh? If he hadn't been with Mrs. Smith he probably woulda sucker-punched me."

"You know the woman, too?"

He shrugged. "She owns a shop back home."

"In Calgary?"

"Nah. I grew up in a miserable dump of a town in B.C. The folks moved to Calgary when I was in grade twelve. That's when I split."

"Oh." Tracey didn't know much about Matt's life before they met. She knew he didn't get on with his cop father, rarely saw his mom and his sister. This guy here today, Matt's dad? He didn't look so bad. He was angry, but who wouldn't be the way Barry was hassling his girlfriend? Matt, she thought with a twinge of disloyalty, was far too quick to follow Barry. One day, he'd follow Barry into real trouble, if he didn't watch out. Barry had the sense to leave as soon as the woman threatened to call the cops and Kevin came out of the back. Kevin, they all knew, was an ex-con and he wasn't going to allow any trouble in his place. Barry usually had the sense to drop it when things started to get out of control, but not Matt.

"You want something to eat?" Tracey said. "Your dad paid but they didn't have their breakfast."

"Nah." His head was turned away from her, so she couldn't see his face. She touched the back of his neck. Hot. Hot and wet.

"I guess you didn't know your dad was in town, eh?" She slid her arm around his shoulders like a fawn testing to see if the meadow was safe to enter.

"No. Didn't know he'd taken up with Mrs. Smith, either. Mom said he'd met some lady, but not who it was. Funny that Moonlight's still in Trafalgar. Probably married with two-point-five kids and a job at her mom's store. She was younger than me, but one hell of a skier. I figured she'd do better."

Tracey felt a twinge of jealousy. Matt's voice was almost longing as he caressed the name on his tongue. *Moonlight, what a lovely name*. Much nicer and more interesting than boring old Tracey.

Matt shrugged Tracey off. "I gotta go."

"You working tonight?"

"Yeah."

"I might pop in later, when I get off at the car rental." Matt worked as a bartender at a fancy wine bar some nights.

"Suit yourself."

Tracey would have liked him to show more enthusiasm at the prospect of seeing her but that was just Matt. He kept his emotions to himself. She couldn't afford to go out drinking often, and certainly not there, but she'd order the cheapest drink available and make it last until the place got busy and Matt told her to get lost because they needed her seat.

The door swung open and Tracey struggled to her feet. Customers. Four guys dressed in safety vests and heavy, dirty beige overalls with orange stripes on the pants. Construction or road workers. She didn't feel much like smiling, but made an effort. They nodded to her and headed for a table at the back.

Tracey went to the front counter to get menus. She wasn't paying any attention to the new arrivals; instead she was worrying about Matt. She was glancing over her shoulder, to where he sat with his head in his hands and his shoulders slumped, when one of the men tripped over a crack in the wood floor and stumbled forward with a curse, crashing into an unoccupied table. Startled, Matt's head jerked up.

And Tracey could see that he was crying.

# Chapter Ten

**CHATEAU LAKE LOUISE. LAKE LOUISE, ALBERTA. SATURDAY NOON.**

Chateau Lake Louise was a grand old railroad hotel, younger sister of the Banff Springs. The building faced Lake Louise, emerald green, deep, cold water fed by the glaciers of Mount Victoria, framed by towering mountains.

The drive from Banff had been tense, to say the least. Paul gripped the steering wheel as if it were his son's throat and Lucky stared out the window, scarcely seeing the panorama of dark trees and snow-tipped mountains sparkling in the sun.

He parked the car and they walked toward the majestic white stone building, so perfectly situated. Lucky slipped her hand into Paul's, and was grateful that he didn't snatch his away. He said little as they rounded the hotel and the famous view of the lake and glacier spread out in front of them. The gardens had been neatly tucked away for the winter, the canoes taken out of the water, and the lake wasn't yet frozen over, but the scene was still spectacular. The lake front was crowded with chatting, laughing groups, and more cameras than Lucky had ever seen in one place, people posing and smiling while their friends clicked away. This might well be the most photographed spot in Canada.

"Let's get a picture, Paul." Lucky dug in her bag for her own camera. Without waiting for him to agree, or not, she waved at a couple about their age. "Would you mind taking our picture, please?" She handed the man the camera, an inexpensive compact, and showed him the button to snap the shot. Then she half-dragged Paul to a spot she thought would make a good background. She rested her gloved hand on his arm, and felt some of the tension melt out of him. He slipped his arm around her shoulders and her for-the-camera smile folded into a real one.

"One more," the cameraman said in a heavy German accent.

Lucky and Paul posed again, and when she glanced at him out of the corner of her eye she was pleased to see him smiling. She took her camera back, thanked the couple, and she and Paul walked into the hotel.

They took their time wandering around, enjoying the old architecture, the modern elegance, and the sense of history that filled the halls and public rooms. Lucky wanted to pop into some of the stores, maybe look for Christmas gifts. One glance at the price tags and they were scurrying back out.

"I'd like to get some postcards," she said as they passed the bookstore.

"Postcards?" Paul repeated. "We'll be home before they get there."

"I know. But I like sending postcards." She rifled through the rack. Plenty of majestic mountain and wildlife scenes, some illustrating the rich history of the hotel. Lucky laughed heartily, and Paul left the display of old fishing posters to see what was so funny. She held up a card: a scene from a silent movie, altered to show, behind the film's lovers, three uniformed Mounties kissing their horses. "For Adam," Lucky said.

Paul grinned. "They don't call them the horsemen for nothing."

"I keep wondering if Norman's expecting to be a groomsman at the wedding," Lucky laughed, referring to Adam Tocek's police dog.

"They won't want him wearing his ordinary working vest. I suppose the Mounties could do up a splendid dog jacket in red serge."

"Pants with a yellow stripe down the leg? Two legs or four do you think?"

"Hat might be hard to fit. He'll keep trying to toss it off."

They laughed again, and Lucky went to pay for her purchases.

"I never did get breakfast," Paul said, once she'd joined him in the hallway. "And I'm starving. Let's have an early lunch before we carry on."

She agreed and they followed the signs to the Poppy Brassiere. Paul's appetite was back in full force and he ordered the substantial Rocky Mountain breakfast, but Lucky asked for tea and a muffin. Paul handed the menu to the waitress, and when she was out of earshot, he said, "Perhaps we should have stayed at that dive in Banff. Heck of a lot cheaper."

She didn't know whether that was an opening for her to ask about Matt, his son, but before she could venture into those troubled waters, Paul asked how the plans were going for Moonlight and Adam's wedding, and Lucky had to admit that as far as she knew there were no plans. They'd gotten engaged. Moonlight sported a beautiful diamond ring and had moved into Adam's place in the mountains. Nothing more had been mentioned.

"Young people today…" Paul's eyes twinkled.

Lucky roared with laughter. "Indeed. Can't imagine what the world's coming to. Andy and I got married in a registry office and the next day we left for Canada." Andy and Lucky had crossed the border into British Columbia when Andy got his draft notice. He'd not seen nor spoken to his unforgiving father again. His mother had had to slip into Canada to visit, pretending she was going to see friends. Both Andy and his father were dead now, all hope of reconciliation gone. "My mom was dreadfully disappointed, but my older sister had been married in a fancy church wedding. I suspect Dad was relieved at not having to shell out for another big bash."

The stop in Lake Louise lifted Paul's spirits and they enjoyed their day at Lake Moraine. Banff National Park might seem crowded with tourists, but as soon as you drove off the highway, stepped off the paved paths, turned a corner and were out of sight of the majestic hotels, you were reminded that this was a true wilderness area. Prominently displayed grizzly bear warnings mark the beginnings of the hiking trails.

Lucky and Paul took the easier, flatter path along the lake. The trail was rough, scarcely maintained, and they clambered over boulders and around fallen trees. At this high elevation, patches of fresh snow filled the darker recesses of the woods and the bite of approaching winter was in the air. The famous Ten Peaks, all of them over 10,000 feet, filled the sky above. The lake, a stunning shade of pale green, lay to their left, and the forest, ancient and primeval, to the right. Quiet and still, the scent of pine trees, disturbed earth, icy-fresh water. "Do you want to talk about it?" Lucky said at last.

"No," Paul replied.

Despite the horrible start, it turned into a lovely day. The hike invigorated them both and, to Lucky's extreme delight, on the drive down the mountain they spotted a group of elk at the side of the road. Paul slowed the car, and Lucky leaned out the window to take pictures. They both knew better than to get out of the car. Mother elk could be as protective of their young as any other species.

They had dinner in the German-style pub on the lower level of their hotel. Then it was back to the room where Paul watched a hockey game on TV and Lucky settled into her novel. The lights were switched off and they were curled up together by ten o'clock.

# Chapter Eleven

**TRAFALGAR CITY POLICE STATION. TRAFALGAR, BRITISH COLUMBIA. SATURDAY EVENING.**

"Still here?" Six o'clock and Molly Smith was beginning Saturday afternoon shift.

Sergeant John Winters swung his legs off his desk. "Catching up on some reports."

"You having Thanksgiving dinner tomorrow or Monday?"

"Neither. Eliza's gone to Saskatoon to visit her mother. She bought a roast chicken from the supermarket, so I'll have to make do with that. Won't be the first time."

Smith hesitated. He could read the thoughts crossing her mind. She felt sorry for him, alone on the holiday. She should invite him to her house. To the house she shared with Adam Tocek, where they were having a proper festive dinner. She didn't really want him there—they were co-workers, not friends and he was her superior. But still, she should be polite and ask.

"Would you like to have dinner at our place tomorrow night?"

He considered saying yes, just to see the expression on her face. "No, but thanks for the offer, Molly."

Relief.

# Chapter Twelve

**GLOBAL CAR RENTAL. BANFF, ALBERTA. SATURDAY EVENING.**

Tom Dunning left Tracey to lock up the office. Jody was waiting for him at her place. She'd have pizza and beer on hand. He could probably talk her into leaving the food until later. Tell her some romantic drivel about how he'd been thinking of her all night and just couldn't wait. Girls like that sort of stuff.

He had been thinking of her. But not because he particularly wanted to gaze into her dark eyes or hear all about her day. When he'd phoned and told her to pick up pizza and a movie, she'd started to grumble. She wanted to go out. Alistair's band was playing at a bar and everyone said they were good. And that new movie, that romantic comedy with Jennifer Aniston, would be gone by the end of the week.

He considered telling her to shut the fuck up and do what she was told, but Jody wasn't that much of a pushover. She'd only let him go so far. Not that he cared for her one way or the other, but he wasn't ready to move on quite yet.

After he screwed her and she was feeling all soft and romantic, he'd promise to take her to the bar tomorrow night. And then make up some excuse when the time came.

Tom hated live music. Jody was always whining about wanting to go to bars or shows. He'd let her take him to hear some long-haired chick play her guitar and wail about damage to Mother Earth. That hadn't been so bad, but he still wouldn't go out to hear rock. Tom liked rock music as much as the next guy. He just couldn't stand to see it being performed.

He'd had enough of that when he was a kid. His dad, Mad Mike Dunning, had played guitar in a band. Tom and his sister had grown up on the road, touring every little dump of a town—and there are a lot of dumpy towns among the wheat of the Canadian Prairie or the rocks, trees, and lakes of Northern Ontario. A childhood of lousy motels, greasy food, Mom trying to keep up their education. Then the band hit it big and for a couple of years the hotels were a lot better, and they traveled in planes and tour buses rather than a twenty-year-old Kombi. The groupies got better too, younger, thinner, sexier. Tom's mom pretended not to notice.

Over all those years, the good times and the bad, the one thing Tom remembered the most was his dad shouting at him to play. He'd been given a guitar and told to play, Goddamnit!

But Tom had a problem. He had no musical ability whatsoever. He was completely tone-deaf. He couldn't identify one note from another or remember how to create a particular sound if his life depended on it. No matter how much his dad yelled at him and called him a slacker, he couldn't read the music or make the notes sound like they should.

Slaps to the side of the head and screamed insults did nothing to help.

His younger sister could play. She was good, very good. But she was a girl, and as far as Mad Mike was concerned, major rock bands didn't have girl guitarists. Their dad might have forgiven her if she could sing, but in that she was also a disappointment.

Tom inherited his lack of musical ability from his mother, and as the band began sliding down the charts, Mad Mike Dunning took out his frustration on his wife. Tom's mom died in a car accident when Tom was twenty-one, working construction in Toronto. His sister had married a musician and they played country music in the same sort of dives and dingy bars where their dad had started out.

Tom went to his mom's funeral, didn't speak to his dad, and left town the next day. His sister had been on tour and couldn't make the funeral.

Over the years, Tom saw pictures of his dad occasionally, heard a couple of times that the band was planning a big reunion concert.

It wouldn't happen. The singer, the only truly talented one of the bunch, had died of an overdose, and Mad Mike himself now weighed about three hundred pounds and had a nose that belonged on Rudolph the Red-Nosed Reindeer.

It gave Tom a not-inconsiderable degree of satisfaction the time he saw a picture of his dad on an online gossip site, passed out and being loaded into the back of a cruiser, his pants so far down he was mooning the camera. The headline read: "How Low Can He Go?"

Still, Tom couldn't bear to listen to live rock music.

It was time he moved in with Jody. He was doing okay with his cut of the take from the car repairs and the other stuff that was going on at Global, but he didn't like wasting money. He rarely spent any time at the apartment he shared with three other guys. He was sick of being surrounded by Alistair's equipment and the posters of rock bands he insisted on sticking to the walls. Tom spent most nights at Jody's, so why not move in? Her roommate, a stuck-up bitch from Vancouver, wasn't a bad piece. Get her alone one night when Jody was out, and he could show her what she was missing.

Might even be able to talk them into a three-way.

It wouldn't be for long, anyway. One thing he'd learned from good old dad was to know when it was time to move on. Barry was starting to complain that he deserved a bigger cut. Complain to the wrong people and someone, someday, might squeal to the cops on Global Car Rental. Tom Dunning intended to be nowhere around when that happened.

Before he left, he might even do the squealing himself.

# Chapter Thirteen

**REDS WINE BAR. BANFF, ALBERTA. SATURDAY NIGHT.**

Tracey regarded Reds Wine Bar with a mixture of bitter hatred and yearning envy. She detested the place, but hoped one day it would be the sort of bar where she could hang out without feeling awkward and out of place.

Tonight, she perched on a stool at the far end of the bar. She sipped her wine; to her dismay the glass was emptying too fast. The place was filling up and she'd have to leave as soon as she finished her drink. She couldn't take a seat that could be used by a tipping customer. Matt wouldn't like that.

She watched him while he worked. Handsome in a white shirt and black tie, pouring drinks, taking money, joking with customers and the other staff. She'd phoned him after finishing at the restaurant, while changing to go to the car rental job, to check he was okay after the encounter earlier with his dad. By the time she'd taken the orders of the four construction workers into the kitchen and brought out their coffee, Matt had left the restaurant. They'd been busier than usual for the rest of her shift and Tracey had been almost run off her feet. She got some good tips, though, so that made it okay.

Matt had sneered at her on the phone, dismissive of her concern. He had a few bad things to say about his dad, and hoped they wouldn't run into each other again. But Tracey had seen the look on his face this morning, and she knew it was nothing but bluster. Her heart ached for him.

A group of women swung into the bar, all sporting expensively cut and colored hair, short tight dresses, high heels, makeup, and bright red nail polish. With much tossing of heads and giggling, drawing all eyes to them, they pulled stools into a circle. They found themselves one short. They eyed Tracey, taking in the cheap shiny blue dress, the plastic jewelry, the shoes that hadn't been new even when they were new to her. But mostly taking in the fact that she, Tracey, was *alone*.

She lifted her head and stuck out her chin. She wasn't alone. She was with her boyfriend. He might be working, but that didn't matter. She wasn't *alone* like a loser who didn't have a date on a Saturday night.

Some people had to work for a living. Her mother, on one of the few occasions she'd been sober and employed, had told Tracey to be proud she was working class. Proud to work hard, to earn a decent living, not a rich bitch mooch like these girls. She'd tried to be proud. That hadn't lasted long.

Matt laid cocktail napkins in front of the new arrivals, giving them a huge grin of welcome. The smile he rarely had for Tracey. He told them tonight's specials were listed on the blackboard behind the bar or they could see the menu offering wines by the bottle or glass. The women smiled and preened. One of them was so thin you could, Tracey thought, use her hips for clothes hangers and her tits to measure walnuts. Tracey glanced at the woman's face, and upped her estimate of her age. Lines radiated out from the corners of her eyes and mouth, and the skin on her throat was as wrinkled as the right sleeve of her ivory blouse, which the iron had missed.

A long-haired, long-legged, bleached blonde leaned over, giving Matt a good view of her more- than-ample breasts, and asked him breathlessly what he'd recommend. Her lips were as red as her sharp fingernails and Tracey imagined those nails turning into claws, reaching across the bar and grabbing Matt by the front of his shirt.

He grinned and glanced down the scooped neck of the woman's dress, not long enough to be offensive, briefly enough to let her know he liked what he saw. He never looked at Tracey like that. Not that Tracey had boobs like that in any event. Fake probably.

Matt rattled off the names of a couple of bottles. The blonde waved her hand in the air, her talons glistening, and said, without asking the price, that they'd have a bottle of Chardonnay from the Okanagan Valley to start. Tracey, because she had no one to talk to, had spent her time reading the wine list. That was one of the more expensive whites.

"A good choice." Matt pitched his voice pitched slow and sexy.

Tracey swallowed a hefty mouthful of her wine. Only a dribble remained.

She counted up the tips she'd made today, balanced that against her share of the rent due at the end of the month. Perhaps she could treat herself to another drink.

Matt brought glasses and the Chardonnay and made a big deal out of uncorking the bottle. Tracey didn't know why they bothered. Screw caps were so much easier. He poured a mouthful of wine into the blonde's glass. She swirled it around, sniffed it, sipped it, never taking her eyes off Matt.

He didn't take his eyes off her either.

"Very nice," the blonde purred, and Matt poured for them all.

What the hell was Tracey doing here? She had nothing to offer a guy like Matt. He was good-looking, older, from a middle-class family. Tracey's father had run off before she was born, and her mother drank too much and couldn't hold down a job. She worked two jobs and could barely pay the rent on a couch in someone's living room. That bottle of wine these women were throwing back without tasting it cost more than Tracey earned in a shift at the car rental company.

Acid stirred in her gut and she felt tears behind her eyes. One of the girls glanced at her, and didn't bother to cover her sneer.

She waved to Matt. "Could we possibly get another stool? My poor feet are simply aching after all the shopping we did today."

Matt glanced at Tracey. She lifted her glass and thrust out her chin. "I'll have another."

Surprise crossed his face, but he only said, "Let me see what I can do."

"You are *such* a dear," the girl cooed. Her friends giggled. Tracey was beginning to hate that giggle.

Prompted by Matt, a man brought over a stool and the girl wiggled her amble rump onto it. She shouldn't be wearing that dress—not with *that* butt.

Matt handed Tracey her drink. He started to say something, but one of the waitresses called for him.

The bar was filling up. It was a small space, meant to be intimate. The lights were low, the tables illuminated by candles, the music soft jazz. Rich people with good teeth, good hair, nice clothes, drank wine and beer, nibbled on canapés, and laughed and chatted. Tracey was starving. She hadn't eaten since breakfast, but she couldn't afford anything they served here. It was all small bites, meant to be shared. Small bites but big prices. She'd go to McDonald's later, grab a burger and a pop.

The blonde who'd ordered the wine burst into over-loud laughter and threw her arms out. Her glass tipped and Chardonnay sloshed down the front of Tracey's dress. The friends tittered and the blonde turned her head. "Oh," she said, in a voice that said she didn't give a shit, "sorry about that." Her eyes were watery and her speech slurred, and Tracey figured this wasn't their first stop of the night.

She could have made a huge deal out of it. Insisted the woman pay for her dry cleaning bill. Not that Tracey had ever once in her life taken her clothes to a dry cleaner. If it couldn't be washed in the Laundromat or the sink, she didn't buy it.

She let it go. If the woman objected, wanted to get into an argument, Matt would hustle Tracey out so fast her feet would barely touch the ground.

What the hell. She didn't belong here anyway. She tossed back the rest of her wine and slid off her stool. A woman, older than most of them here, gray hair sprayed into a helmet, pearl necklace, hands glittering with diamonds, hip-checked Tracey and grabbed the seat.

She hesitated at the entrance, wanting to get a last glimpse of Matt. He was laughing with one of the waitresses. The woman was married, but Tracey didn't care for the way she eyed Matt.

"Excuse me," someone said, trying to come in. Tracey slipped away from the lights and laugher of the bar and into the dark night.

# Chapter Fourteen

**BANFF SPRINGS HOTEL. BANFF, ALBERTA. SUNDAY EARLY MORNING.**

Lucky didn't recognize the ringing at first. Confused, she struggled out of sleep to find Paul sitting up, the bedside phone clenched in his hand.

"What?" he said. "Where?"

Lucky's heart leapt into her mouth. Moonlight: a police officer, a dangerous job. When her daughter first started working for the police, Lucky found it hard to sleep when the girl worked nights. She lay in bed, thinking of all the bad things that could happen, even in peaceful Trafalgar. But Andy, Lucky's late husband, Moonlight's father, reminded her that people could be, and sometimes were, killed crossing the street. The police were more protected than most. Lucky didn't stop worrying, but she did start sleeping better. Then, when Moonlight got engaged to Adam, Lucky realized she'd have two cops in the family to worry about.

She could tell by the look on Paul's face that this wasn't a wrong number or a hotel employee calling to check if everything was all right. "Yes, I know. But where exactly is that? Calm down, take a breath, and give me the address."

Her thoughts tumbled all over themselves. If one of his officers was hurt or, God forbid, dead, wouldn't they call Paul on his cell phone, rather than go through the hotel switchboard? She scrambled across the bed and grabbed her own phone, which she'd laid out on the bedside table. She flipped it open, and fell back with relief. No calls, no messages. The battery was charged and it had a full complement of bars indicating the strength of reception. If something terrible had happened, both Moonlight and Adam had her number.

She glanced at the clock. Two forty-five.

"Call the police as soon as you hang up. 911." Paul threw off the covers. "Give me fifteen minutes."

"What's going on? Paul, who was that?"

The bathroom door closed behind him. Lucky leapt out of bed. Fifteen minutes. If Paul was going to be somewhere in fifteen minutes then it couldn't be a problem back home. And it couldn't be the RCMP with bad news from Trafalgar if he'd told the caller to contact the police. She pulled her nightgown over her head. It was new, another something special she'd bought for this weekend, all peach satin and cream lace. Long and flowing, not skimpy and sexy. Lucky Smith had long ago ceased to be able to get away with skimpy and sexy. She was pulling on her jeans when Paul came out of the bathroom and began throwing on his own clothes.

"Paul, please, tell me."

"That was Matthew. His roommate's dead."

"Why? How?"

"Matt says he got home, found the fellow dead."

"How awful." Lucky thrust her arms through her sweater.

"I'm going over there. You don't need to come."

"But I want to. Perhaps I can help."

"No. This is bad, Lucky. Bad. The death wasn't an accident. He was knifed. Murdered."

Lucky lifted her head. She looked Paul in the eye. "Then all the more reason for me to come. You're not going because you're a police officer. You're going because you're his father. You need me, Paul, even if your son doesn't."

# Chapter Fifteen

**BEARTRACK TRAIL. BANFF, ALBERTA. SUNDAY EARLY MORNING.**

Not wanting to wait for the elevator, Paul galloped down the stairs, Lucky following. The night staff threw them startled looks as they dashed across the deserted lobby, but Paul didn't slow down to explain. He had a GPS in his car and shouted an address to Lucky as he pulled out of the parking garage. Lucky punched in numbers while Paul drove down the hill toward Banff townsite, and then through dark quiet streets. Shortly after three o'clock a few lights were on in bars as the staff cleaned up or enjoyed a drink. The last few stragglers made their way home past closed shops and restaurants.

Lucky Smith was a mountain woman. Born and raised in Seattle, adulthood in the B.C. Interior, the one time she'd travelled to Kansas to attend a cousin's wedding, she'd been overwhelmed by the simple vastness of it. The open spaces, the distant, visible horizon, the sky that went on forever. Wedding over, she escaped back to the mountains, seeking comfort and safely in their familiar bulk.

Tonight, although the sky was clear, the surrounding mountains cut off the glow of the moon and most of the stars. Lucky shivered. So beautiful during the day, at night these mountains seemed ominous, looming over them, closing them in. Trapping them.

No need to get fanciful. That would be no help to anyone. She glanced at Paul. In the light from the dashboard she could see his face set into serious lines. He didn't look angry, simply determined.

"Turn left," she said, "and then an immediate right. Arriving at…" the efficient British accent announced from the GPS.

"Are you sure you gave that thing the right address?" Paul slid the car to a stop against the curb.

Lucky read it back to him. "That's what you told me."

The street was empty. The address they'd been directed to was a three-story apartment block on a street of similar buildings. Street lamps cast pools of faint yellow light onto the sidewalk. A black cat leisurely crossed the road, paying Lucky and Paul no attention. Paul opened his door and light filled the interior of the car.

"What's the matter?" Lucky asked.

"This is a small town. The police should have gotten here faster than we did. There's a flashlight in the glove compartment. Give it to me." She did so and he climbed out of the car.

Lucky opened her door.

"Stay here," he ordered.

"But…"

"But nothing. Matt didn't call 911. That means something… someone might have prevented him. Do you have your phone?"

"Yes."

"Call 911. Give them the address. Tell them we have a report of a homicide. Tell them who I am. And, Lucky," he bent down and stuck his head into the car, "you will stay here. This is now a police action."

"Paul, wait for the Mounties."

But he was gone. He headed for the building at a trot, slipping in and out of the shadows, slightly bent at the knees and waist. Lucky made the call and was told the police were on their way. She watched as Paul approached the front door. He didn't stand in front of it, knocking, like anyone else would. He stood to one side, back against the wall. His hand reached out, gripped the doorknob, and turned it. The door swung open, an interior light came on, and Paul slipped into the vestibule, moving fast and keeping low. A row of mailboxes and buzzers lined the wall, illuminated by the weak light in the entrance. Paul punched a button, repeatedly. No one seemed to be answering and Lucky breathed a sigh of relief. He couldn't get in. He'd have to wait for the police. Like all Canadian police officers, Paul Keller carried a gun to work but never when not on duty.

She waited, heart pounding, itching to get out of the car, to go to Paul, but, knowing that this time, for once, she had to do as she'd been told. It was only a matter of moments until she heard a siren, another, and the street was washed in white, blue, and red lights. Lucky told the 911 operator the police had arrived, and snapped her phone shut. She stuffed it into her jacket pocket and jumped out of the car. She flagged down the first vehicle. "Over there," she shouted to the officer, a woman not much older than Lucky's own daughter. "Chief Constable Keller's waiting for you."

Paul shouted and waved, and two officers ran to join him in the vestibule. Another took a post outside the door. Lights began coming on in the neighboring houses and apartments, faces appeared at windows, and a few people ventured outside to stand on their front steps and watch the excitement.

When Lucky looked back at the apartment building, the two Mounties and Paul were gone. Someone must have buzzed them in.

More cars, white with the logo of colored stripes and horseman with a lance, arrived, followed by an ambulance. A crowd began to gather, coats thrown hastily over pajamas, bare feet stuffed into shoes, laces untied. Uniformed officers ordered people to keep back and spoke into radios at their shoulders. Yellow tape was being unrolled and tied around the spruce trees fronting the property.

No shots rang out; no one screamed in terror or cried out in pain. Lucky took a deep breath, summoning her courage, lifted her head, and marched purposefully across the small patch of browning grass toward the door, as if she had reason to be there.

"Sorry, ma'am." The Mountie guarding the door stopped her. "I'll have to ask you to stay behind the tape."

"I'm with Chief Constable Keller," she said, her eyes fixed on his face. She wondered if he was old enough to shave yet. He hesitated. His radio spat out something incomprehensible amongst a burst of static and he turned, waving Lucky through.

She slipped inside. The inner door had been propped open. A single weak bulb hung over the hallway, and a staircase, dark and narrow, led up. A Mountie was talking to a group of women at the end of the hall, their apartment doorways open. No need to wonder where to go: The voices of the police overhead were loud and footsteps pounded the floorboards. Lucky dashed up the stairs.

Uniformed men and women stood at the first door on the right, facing into the room. Lucky slipped up behind them, cursing her lack of height. An officer turned and thrust out an arm. "You can't come in here."

"I'm with Chief Constable Keller."

The police parted. Paul's face was pale and lines that hadn't been there yesterday dragged down the skin. Lucky glanced around him, into the room. She soon wished she hadn't.

A man lay on the floor, close to the door. He was on his back, his arms flung out to the sides, looking at, but not seeing, the light overhead and the water-stained ceiling tiles. At first Lucky thought someone had spilled a bucket of red paint onto the dull beige carpet. Her hand came to her mouth as she realized he lay in a pool of blood. Blood covered his throat. Paramedics packed up their equipment. They were in no hurry.

Lucky gasped, and Paul grabbed her arm. He pulled her into the hallway. "I told you to stay in the car."

"Matt?" she asked.

Paul shook his head. "No sign of him. Damn fool must have run after calling me."

Footsteps on the stairs. A man, dressed in jeans and a light windbreaker. Shorter than Paul but powerfully built. Silver and gray hair cut short, gray eyes set in deep folds of skin, a lined face full of gray stubble. "Chief Constable Keller?"

Paul held out his hand. The men shook.

"Sergeant Edward Blechta. I'd say it's a pleasure, but not in these circumstances. My dispatcher told me you called this in. Do you know the victim?"

"No. My son," Paul sighed, deeply, looking every one of his fifty-eight years, "phoned me at my hotel. Said he'd come home to find…this."

"Your son? Where's he now?"

"I don't know."

Blechta's tired gray eyes studied Lucky, and he did not smile. "You are?"

"Lucy Smith. I'm Chief Keller's…"

"Friend," Paul finished.

"Friend. People call me Lucky."

"Are you?"

She flushed. "I mean that's my nickname. Lucky Smith."

"Not so lucky today," Blechta said. "If you have no reason to be here, Ms. Smith, I'd like you to leave. Chief Keller, I'm going to have a look at the scene. Then I have some questions for you."

Paul said, "As long as Lucky's here, she should have another look at the body."

"Me?"

Paul lifted one hand, but he didn't touch her. For the first time, she noticed drying blood on his tips of his fingers. "You might recognize him, Lucky."

"I don't know anyone in Banff. We only arrived on Thursday."

Paul gave her a weak smile. "Take a deep breath. Look at the face and tell us what you see."

Blechta nodded. "Might as well get it over with."

The uniformed officers moved aside as, first Blechta, then Lucky and Paul, entered the apartment. Lucky looked everywhere but at the thing on the floor. The furnishings in the living room were old and shabby, with the exception of a huge flat-screen TV against one wall. The TV was on, showing a group of suit-clad men sitting around a table, hockey team logos on the wall behind them. The sound had been switched off. The couch and chairs were a muddy brown—probably as much stain as fabric—and tattered. Once, a cat had been at them. The coffee table was plywood with a smear of veneer and a substantial gouge in the center. Old sheets were tossed over the curtain rods to make drapes, so thin in places they did nothing to keep the glow of the streetlights out, or private activities in. A haphazard assortment of posters advertising music acts hung on the walls. A guitar and microphone stand and what Lucky thought might be amplification equipment were in one corner, a stack of cardboard boxes in another. She could see into the kitchen: nothing but a jumble of beer cases and dirty pots piled high in the sink.

The scent of food past its expiry date, spilled beer, and unwashed dishes filled the apartment. All of it overlaid by the distinctive smell of coffee mixed with skunk. Pot.

It was like so many other transient apartments Lucky had been in for her work with the youth center and the women's support center, although untidier than most. Lucky's clients were mostly female; they might not be neater than the guys who lived here, but they usually made an attempt to clean up when she was expected.

"Lucky," Paul said gently, "have you seen this man before?"

She swallowed, tried to still her stomach and breathe calmly and steadily, and then she looked down. The face was unmarked by violence, but the glassy eyes and frozen expression could only mean death. A fly, a shiny fat black bluebottle, the sound of its buzzing loud in the quiet of the room, flew past to settle on the man's face. He made no move to wave it away, so Lucky leaned over to do so. Paul grabbed her arm. "Eyes only, Lucky, please. Don't touch anything."

She nodded, and tried to swallow and not to think about flies crawling across the face, and where they had come from at this time of year.

To her surprise, she did recognize him. The tall lean body, the unkempt blond hair. The sneer was gone now, replaced by a look of shock. Shock and fear and pain and something she didn't recognize but thought might be an awareness of death.

She glanced away, and then she saw a knife lying on the carpet. It looked like an ordinary kitchen knife, the blade about six inches long. Covered in blood.

Her stomach moved and she put her hand to her mouth. Paul's arm slipped around her, and he led her out of the apartment into the hallway. Blechta followed. The officers had stopped what they were doing and watched her.

"Take your time," Blechta said.

Lucky swallowed. "It's him. The man who tried to push in front of me at the coffee shop Friday. I saw him again, yesterday morning, at the restaurant. You saw him too, Paul."

"I thought it was him, but I wasn't sure. I was concentrating on…on Matt at the time."

"Matt being your son?" Blechta said.

"Yes."

"Barry's this man's name," Lucky said. "That's what the waitress called him."

"Ms. Smith you can go back to your hotel. I'll want to talk to you about what you know about this man, but…"

"I don't know anything about him, except that he was rude to me, very aggressive. Perhaps I shouldn't have…"

"Don't start making excuses for the punk now he's dead, Lucky," Paul said. "He was a bully, plain and simple."

"I want to hear more about this bullying," Blechta said. "But that will have to wait. Chief Keller…"

"Paul."

"Paul. I'm going to have to ask about your son. Does he have a car?"

"I don't know."

"Constable Donohue."

"Sir?"

"Take Ms. Smith to her hotel."

"I'd like to stay," Lucky said.

"I'm sure you would," Blechta said. "But you can't."

"Ma'am," the young officer said, "if you'll come with me."

Paul gave her a weak smile. She reached out and touched his face. Constable Donohue shifted his feet.

"I'll need your son's full name, DOB, and a description," Blechta said to Paul. A door opened at the end of the hallway, and a tousled head popped out, eyes wide with interest. "Novak, didn't I tell you to keep those people inside?"

As Lucky and her escort made their way down the narrow stairs, they squeezed past people heading up, laden with equipment. They nodded to Donohue and ignored Lucky.

# Chapter Sixteen

**BANFF SPRINGS HOTEL. BANFF, ALBERTA. SUNDAY EARLY MORNING.**

If the night doorman at the Banff Springs Hotel was at all surprised to see Lucky Smith delivered to the hotel in a police vehicle, he was far too well-trained to show it. "Good evening, madam," he said politely, holding the car door while she clambered out.

At least she hadn't been stuffed in the back, behind the partition, where the doors didn't open from the inside.

It was approaching five o'clock. Lights in the lobby were dim and no one was around except for a single woman behind the registration desk pecking at a computer. The elevator doors slid open the moment Lucky pushed the button, and she made her way down the quiet hallway to their room. The restaurants were closed, but room service delivered snacks twenty-four hours a day. Before so much as taking off her jacket, Lucky picked up the phone and ordered tea and a selection of whatever sandwiches were on hand. She wasn't particularly hungry, but she had no intention of going back to bed. She had no idea how long Paul was going to be. Whatever time he got back, he'd probably appreciate having food on hand.

She would have liked to have been allowed to stay with Paul. He had to be frantic with worry over Matt. The boy had phoned his father when he needed help. That was good. What had he told Paul? He came home and found his roommate dead on the floor?

Might that not have been the entire truth? Had Matt been responsible? Was he hoping his dad, the police chief, could get him out of trouble?

Lucky pushed the thought aside. The boy had panicked. Run into the night. Perhaps he feared the killer was still hanging around. They did that, sometimes, didn't they?

Why then, had Matt not come forward when his father arrived, followed by the police?

Was he being prevented from doing so? It hadn't looked like there'd been a fight in the apartment, but it was such a mess, and Lucky hadn't spent time studying the details. Perhaps the killer had come back, or hadn't left, and forced Matt to go with him. Had Matt been dumped in the wilderness for the bears and the wolves to find? Or had he changed his mind after phoning Paul and gone willingly with the killer?

Lucky Smith was an optimist, always had been. She generally thought well of people and she wasn't often disappointed. But now, try as she might, it was impossible to conjure up a positive scenario out of this mess.

Either Matt was a killer, an accomplice to a killer, or dead.

All these thoughts, and probably worse, would be running an endless loop through Paul's head. Was it harder, she wondered, to face what might have happened, or be happening, to your own loved ones when you were a cop and had seen it all before?

Lucky had seen Paul working as an active police officer in their younger days, before he moved to Calgary. But she'd largely forgotten that side of him, now that he wore a white uniform shirt, starched and ironed, and spent his days behind a desk, attending city council meetings, mixing with the public, essentially doing a bureaucratic job. Paul had switched into cop mode, cool and efficient, before he'd so much as hung up the phone with Matt. The training never left them.

Lucky could increasingly see it in her own daughter, in Moonlight, and didn't like it. When they went for a coffee at Big Eddie's or lunch at George's, mother and daughter, a chance to catch up on each other's gossip, Moonlight might be dressed in summer shorts and a bright t-shirt with long tanned legs and sports sandals, or in ski clothes straight from the hills at Blue Sky, but she would sit with her back to the wall, facing into the room, and her eyes never stopped moving, checking everyone out, looking for trouble.

Moonlight had told her that being a police officer was just her job, a job she happened to love very much. But Lucky was beginning to realize it was more than what she did. It was becoming who her daughter was.

A light tap at the door dragged Lucky out of her thoughts. She told the waiter to put the tray on the table and gave him a hefty tip. When he'd left, closing the door silently behind him, she poured her tea and took it to a chair by the window.

Her thoughts drifted to Barry, the dead man. A bully all right, and like most bullies quick to turn and run as soon as someone stood up to him.

Had someone stood up to him this time and he found himself with nowhere to run?

Lucky stared outside, her tea getting cold, as dawn began to creep across the mountains and light spread over the world.

# Chapter Seventeen

**TRACEY'S APARTMENT & BEARTRACK TRAIL.
BANFF, ALBERTA. SUNDAY MORNING.**

Not accustomed to drinking much—she knew from her own mother where that road led—after two glasses of wine on an empty stomach and then a dinner of burger and fries, Tracey had not had a good night. She lay awake worrying about Matt, worrying about everything. That he'd decide he'd be better off with one of those rich bitches from the bar, that she'd lose one of her jobs, that she'd be kicked out of the apartment if her roommates decided they wanted the sofa back.

It seemed as if she'd only just fallen asleep when the front door flew open and light flooded into the apartment along with a woman's giggle and a man's drunken laughter. Tracey groaned and pulled the blankets over her head.

"Quiet," Amanda shouted. "My roomie's asleep."

"Huh?" The man tripped over the rug and stumbled into the low coffee table. A candlestick fell over, rolled onto the floor. Tracey burrowed deeper.

Amanda and the unknown man staggered through the living room. Fortunately, they had sufficient presence of mind to shut the door to Amanda's bedroom behind them.

Tracey flopped onto her back and stared up at the ceiling. She had to get out of this place.

A man's groan, and Tracey pulled her pillow over her head. Somewhere outside sirens sounded, racing to some tragedy or another. She tried to get back to sleep but sleep didn't want to return. At last, she gave up, climbed out of bed, and went into the kitchen to make a cup of tea. Thankfully, all was quiet behind Amanda's door. Crystal had been in the living room watching TV when Tracey came in, but she soon said good night and went to her own tiny bedroom. Tracey sat at the kitchen window with her tea and watched the dark quiet street come to life while tears ran down her face.

She arrived at the restaurant as Kevin was flipping the sign on the door to open. "Surprised to see you this morning," he said.

That was probably the longest sentence Kevin had directed at her since she'd been hired. "I've got a shift, don't I? Did I make a mistake on the schedule?"

"Nah. I figured you'd have more important things on your mind."

"Like what?"

He studied her face, and her stomach flipped. Kevin was one ugly man. Short and bowlegged, nose broken more times than probably he could remember, skin pitted with the remains of teenage acne, gray hair too thin to be worn long, and small black eyes that didn't seem to reflect light. He had a good-sized pot belly, being overly fond of tasting his own cooking as well as eating up the leftovers, but his arms bristled with muscle. He rarely said much, other than to issue orders or complain about the waitresses' work habits, but he wasn't a bad boss. He'd spent a lot of years in prison, armed robbery, rumor said, and he was determined to never go back. He worked hard at his business, and expected everyone around him to work hard also. Staff had been fired for slacking off or calling in sick when they weren't.

"What?" Tracey said.

"Trouble over on Beartrack Trail last night. Lots of cops, ambulance. Detectives and forensics. The coroner."

Beartrack Trail. The street where Matt lived. Tracey reminded herself that plenty of people lived on Beartrack Trail. "Nothing to do with me. How do you know, anyway? Your place is in the opposite direction."

"Pays," Kevin said, "to keep in touch with what the cops are up to."

"Overdose, probably. Or some stupid drunk who fell and cracked his fat head open. No loss to anyone."

"Tracey."

"What?"

"They were at Matt's apartment."

Kevin's face had settled into kind lines of the sort she'd never seen before, and that, more than his words, made fear rise into her throat. Her heart pounded.

"Matt? You mean Matt…"

"It's Barry."

"Thank God." Her laugh came out as more of a snort. "Then definitely no loss to anyone. We weren't exactly *friends*, Kev."

"You still don't understand, Tracey. The cops can't find Matt. They say he's done a runner after killing Barry."

Before she knew what she was doing, Tracey was out the door and down the street. It was about one kilometer to Matt's apartment. This early on a Sunday morning, the town wasn't busy, a handful of eager tourists looking for breakfast before going out for the day, some locals having a morning run. The sky was dark, threatening rain.

She called Matt's number. It went to voice mail. She left a message, trying to sound cheery and only a bit concerned. He hated it when she whined or complained.

By the time she arrived at Beartrack Trail her heart was about to give out. She skidded to a halt as she rounded the corner. The street was full of police cars, both marked and unmarked. Officers patrolled the grounds and yellow tape had been strung from the trees in front of number 214—Matt's place. A small crowd had gathered on the opposite sidewalk to watch. Tracey walked slowly toward them, her legs numb and her heart frantic.

"You can't go in there," a Mountie said.

"My friend…lives there."

"You'll have to see your friend later."

"Is…is someone hurt? Dead?"

"I can't say anything at this time." The Mountie turned at sounds coming from inside the building. The door opened. Officers came out. People pushing a stretcher.

"Get out of the way." The Mountie jerked his head at Tracey, who stood in the center of the path. The bored politeness had left his voice.

She stepped aside. An ambulance was not waiting, no one hurried, the body on the stretcher had a cloth pulled up over its face. The only sound Tracey could hear was the roaring of blood in her own ears. The crowd stopped talking and stood respectfully, watching as the stretcher was maneuvered down the sidewalk to an unmarked black van. An older man took off his hat.

Tracey took a step forward. Then another. She reached out her hand. Someone grabbed her arm and she was pulled roughly back. A man dressed in jeans and a blue jacket, gray hair cut short.

"Out of the way," he said to her. His voice was not friendly and his eyes were narrow with suspicion. "What's your name?"

"Tracey."

"Tracey what?"

"McMillian."

"Do you have reason to believe you might know this person, Tracey? Or have any knowledge of what went on here?"

"No." Kevin had said it was Barry dead. Not Matt. And Kevin had good sources; he made it his business to know what was going on in town. Besides, Tracey assured herself, this…body… was tall. Taller than Matt.

"Sorry." She turned and fled back the way she'd come.

When she was around the corner and out of sight of the police, she tried Matt again. Again it went to voice mail. She left another message, saying she'd been to the apartment and was worried.

What had Kevin said? The police were looking for Matt.

They couldn't possibly suspect Matt had *killed* Barry? They were friends and Matt didn't have a mean bone in his body. It was a mistake, obviously. Just a mistake.

Matt might not even know Barry was dead, not if he hadn't been home last night or this morning. The reason why Matt might not have come home after work, she tried not to contemplate.

She had to find him. Where could he be? Not at Reds. It was only open in the evening. The ski hills weren't operating yet. He liked to go hiking, into the wilderness. He camped out sometimes, went by himself for a few days into the mountains when he had time off work. Once you got out of town and off the highway, cell phones didn't work.

Hadn't he told her he picked up a few extra shifts this week when one of the other bartenders had sprained his ankle?

He wouldn't skip work to go camping.

Unless the fight with his father had upset him so much he needed to get away.

He hadn't seemed upset last night. He seemed to have forgotten all about his dad being in town.

Matt's dad.

He was a cop.

Tracey pulled her phone out of her pocket once again. Matt wouldn't thank her for interfering, but if he was in trouble, in bad trouble, serious trouble, how could she simply go back to Kevin's and wait on tables as if everything was okay?

She punched in 411. Asked for the Banff Springs Hotel.

# Chapter Eighteen

**TRAFALGAR CITY POLICE STATION. TRAFALGAR, BRITISH COLUMBIA. SUNDAY MORNING.**

John Winters finished his magazine. He took his feet off the desk. Dave Evans and Dawn Solway came in the back door and walked past his office, heading to the lunch room. Winters started to rise. He could use a coffee himself.

His phone rang and he checked the display. The boss.

"Aren't you in Banff?" Winters said.

"Yes. And that's the problem. Look, John, I have something I need you to do for me."

"Shoot."

To John Winters' increasing surprise and dismay Keller explained that his son, Matthew Allen Keller, was a suspect in a homicide. Matt had called his father to say he'd discovered a body, and then fled the scene. The Mounties were hunting for him now. The Banff RCMP were being polite to their visiting colleague, but not letting him in on much that was going on.

"I want a record-check on Matthew. I want to know if he has a vehicle, any other known place of residence. Everything you can find."

"Do you think that's wise, Paul? Let the locals handle it."

"He's my son. It might not be wise to get involved, but it's what I have to do. I guess I also have to call Karen. Not looking forward to that."

"Okay," Winters said. It wasn't as if he could tell his boss he was too busy with his own cases. "I'll see what I can find out. What's the name of the victim? I'll dig up what I can on him, too."

"Barry Caseman. I don't have his DOB, but I do know where he lived." Keller rattled off an address.

"I'll be in touch."

"Thanks."

"And, Paul, good luck."

Winters hung up, and turned to his computer.

# Chapter Nineteen

**TOCEK-SMITH HOME. OUTSIDE TRAFALGAR, BRITISH COLUMBIA. SUNDAY MORNING.**

This wasn't supposed to be so hard.

Molly Smith struggled to lift the pastry into the pie plate in one piece. It kept coming away from the countertop in sticky clumps. She tossed another handful of flour into the bowl, and rolled it all up into a ball again.

Now it was so dry it wouldn't hold together.

She glanced at the magazine article she'd cut out and stuck to the fridge with a souvenir magnet from their summer trip to Las Vegas to see "Love," the Cirque De Soleil Beatles show. The well-manicured hands in the photo held a marble rolling pin with one smooth round of pasty wrapped around it. In the next picture the pastry was folding perfectly into the bottom of the glass dish.

Smith's mom made pie all the time. She tried to remember how Lucky did it. Come to think of it, didn't Lucky use store-bought pastry these days?

Enough of this. She grabbed the lump of dough, threw it into the pie plate, where it landed with an uninspiring thud, and began stretching it and smoothing it out with her fingers. Pecan filling bubbled on the stove and Adele was singing on the iPad.

Sylvester wandered in from the family room, where he'd been enjoying a morning nap. He eyed her meaningfully and she obediently opened the back door. Sylvester was Lucky's dog and usually went to one of Lucky's many friends on the odd occasion she went away. No one could be found to take him this time, and so he'd come to Molly and Adam's place. She'd been nervous as to how Norman would react to this invasion of his territory, but the police dog didn't seem to mind as long as Sylvester kept away from his food bowl.

The fat white turkey squatted in the sink, ready to be stuffed. It seemed to have thawed okay. She'd been able to wrestle the giblets and neck out. Good thing the Internet instructions said to do that. Why on earth would anyone put a plastic bag *inside* a turkey, anyway? She eyed the bird as she pounded pastry. Nothing more unappetizing than a naked uncooked turkey.

There. The recipe said to put the prepared pastry into the fridge for half an hour before adding the filling and baking it.

Why was all this taking so darned long, anyway?

Flour was sprinkled on the floor at her feet as though a snowstorm had blown through. Her fingers were coated in it along with sticky pieces of dough. She rubbed her hands together under the tap, leaving traces of flour all over the faucets, and put the prepared pastry into the fridge.

As she dried her hands on a dish towel, she checked her stack of recipes. Apparently you weren't supposed to stuff the turkey until just before it went into the oven, but it was fine to make it ahead of time. First, she should start peeling and chopping squash. The squash casserole had to go into the oven before the turkey; not enough room for them both in there. It should be okay to cook the squash and the pie at the same time.

Forgot the pie filling. It was boiling rapidly, spitting sticky goo all over the stove top like lava from an erupting volcano. She thrust the wooden spoon into the pot and began to stir. Some of the guck had stuck to the bottom. She dug the spoon harder and scraped the pot. She switched off the heat and wiped her forehead with a sigh as she surveyed the disaster of a kitchen.

It was a wonderful kitchen. Adam had bought the house from an older couple looking to downsize and move closer to town.

They'd been known far and wide for their parties, and the house had been built to accommodate that. The cupboards and island were painted fresh white and the cabinets inlaid with sparkling glass windows. The floors were pale hardwood, the countertops granite, the faucets pewter. The sink was square and deep. Wide French doors opened onto a spacious wooden deck and a view of sweeping lawn leading to the forest enclosing the property and tree-covered mountains beyond.

Right now, every pot and pan they owned was either on the stove or in the sink. Flour and pasty crumbs littered the countertops as well as the floor; the kitchen composter overflowed.

And she'd only just started.

Smith dropped into a chair at the kitchen table. It was ten o'clock. She'd finished work at three a.m., been curled up in bed with Adam by four. He'd risen an hour later and headed out the door with Norman for his day shift, trying to be quiet. She'd slept a bit more, and answered her alarm at eight. Somehow in the two hours since, she'd turned the kitchen upside down yet had only managed to slice onions, celery, and apples for the stuffing, make the pastry for the pie, and overcook the filling. Adam was due to get off work at six this evening. She'd told him dinner would be at eight. She planned to get everything ready, put the turkey in the oven, set the table with flowers and candles, and then nap for a couple of hours.

She eyed a bag of bright red cranberries on the table. She should have bought canned cranberry sauce, but her mom always used the fresh ones. Was she supposed to peel them or something? She found the recipe. It didn't say anything about that.

This cooking business was harder than it looked in the glossy magazines.

For a moment she considered calling her mom. No, she wouldn't phone for help. Her mom was on vacation—a romantic vacation. Smith hated to think she might interrupt something, uh, romantic.

Her phone rang and she leapt to answer it. Maybe it would be someone inviting them to dinner. She checked the display.

"Hi, Mom. Happy Thanksgiving."

"Oh. Same to you, dear."

"Are you having fun? Is the hotel putting on a special dinner tonight?"

"I think so."

"Mom, are you okay? Is something the matter?"

"I hope I'm not disturbing you, dear. I know you were working last night, but I was hoping you'd be up."

"I am up. I'm making pie. It's going really well. Is something the matter?"

Lucky let out a long breath. Smith's hand tightened on the phone. Her mom was easy to read and something was definitely wrong. Had she had a fight with Keller? As bad as it was, her mom dating her boss, it would be worse if they had a nasty breakup.

"Paul's son, Matt. Do you remember him, Moonlight? He remembers you."

"Vaguely. He skied, I think. Mom, what's happening?"

"Matt's in trouble. Paul's with the police and he hasn't come back. I'm getting very worried. I wanted to hear your voice."

"What sort of trouble?"

"We think he witnessed a murder."

"Oh, my gosh."

"Either witnessed it or came upon it shortly after it was done. He's disappeared. I called Paul a few minutes ago, but he didn't have time to talk."

"If I leave now, I can be in Banff by nighttime."

"I'm not asking you to come, dear. It's too far. What about Adam? What about your special dinner?"

"The dinner can wait."

"It might be all sorted out before you get here."

"Then you can call and tell me to turn around." Smith had turned the oven on to preheat for the pie. She switched it off. "If you don't want me to come, Mom, say so. Otherwise, I'm on my way."

Her mother's voice was so soft Smith could barely hear. "I need you, Moonlight."

Smith put the pot lid on the pecan pie filling, thrust the turkey into the fridge, swept chopped onions into a bowl, and called Sylvester. The old dog came slowly, ignoring the impatient pleas for him to hurry up. What was she going to do with Sylvester? No time to try to find someone to look after the dog. Adam could easily spend more than twelve hours straight at work if something came up. Sylvester would have to come along. She phoned Adam as she threw clothes into an overnight bag, and explained what little she knew. Adam said he'd call the Banff Mounties and find out what was going on.

He told her to drive carefully on the mountain roads. The seven-hour trip from Trafalgar to Banff was not an easy one. The highway was good, but it went over mountain passes and even this early in the year there could be snow and ice at the higher elevations.

By ten-thirty Smith and Sylvester were on the road.

# Chapter Twenty

**GLOBAL CAR RENTAL. BANFF, ALBERTA. SUNDAY MORNING.**

Tom watched the cop car pull up outside the office. Two officers got out.

This could not be good. He told himself to calm down, no telling why they were here.

He made no move to go outside and greet them. Let them come to him. Keep them as far away from that beige Corolla at the back of the lot as possible.

"I wonder what they want?" Jody looked up from her fashion magazine. The Corolla had just been delivered and checked in. Jody had accepted the keys and done the paperwork. Tom had pretended to check the vehicle for damage, and parked it in a distant corner. He'd been told it was coming, told it was a *special* car and he was not to clean it or let anyone near it. It would be picked up on Tuesday.

The bells over the door tinkled and the two cops came in. The man approached the counter, while the woman stood back, her eyes flicking around the small room, checking out Tom and Jody.

"Help you?" Jody asked.

The cop ignored her. "You Thomas Dunning?"

"Who wants to know?"

"I do. And don't be funny about it."

"Yeah. I'm Dunning."

"You live at 214 Beartrack Trail? Apartment 23?"

"Yeah. What's this about?"

"Were you at home last night?"

Tom threw a look at Jody. She returned it with a shrug. "No. I wasn't. I don't sleep there every night."

"Where were you last night, between say midnight and three a.m.?"

"At my place," Jody said.

"And you are?"

"Judith Wong. I'm called Jody."

"Is that right, Tom?"

"Yes."

"You didn't go home this morning? Change your clothes maybe, have breakfast?"

"No, I didn't. I keep some stuff at Jody's place."

Tom felt the tension flowing out of his neck and shoulders; his hands released fists he hadn't been aware he'd made. If the cops were asking what he'd been doing last night, then this had nothing to do with the Corolla or the car repair business. It had to be about Barry. The dumb fuck. What the hell trouble had Barry gotten himself into now? Had he cut some drunken college chick out of the herd, told her he had the best stuff back at his apartment? And did she, this time, have the guts to call the cops when it was all over and she woke up? He reminded himself not to look relieved at the direction this conversation was taking. He stared the cop in the eye and stood his ground. Let them fight for what they wanted.

"You share the apartment with Barry Caseman and Matthew Keller?"

"Yes." Yup, Barry was in trouble for sure. Good thing he was paid up on his rent.

"We're sorry to have to tell you this." The female cop spoke for the first time. She didn't sound at all sorry. "Mr. Caseman was found dead in your apartment this morning."

Tom didn't have to pretend to be shocked. "What the hell?"

"Oh, my God," Jody said. "Are you sure? What happened?"

"Is Matt okay?"

"Why wouldn't he be?"

"Matt must have been there, wasn't he?"

"When was the last time you saw Matthew Keller?"

"Yesterday morning. He and Barry asked if I wanted to go to the Lighthouse Keeper for breakfast. I didn't. They left. Matt's girlfriend works there so he hangs around sometimes hoping for a free meal."

"What's his girlfriend's name?"

"Tracey," Jody said. "Tracey McMillan. She works here in the evenings."

The female cop wrote something in her notebook.

"You didn't see or speak to Matthew Keller since then?"

Shaking heads and a chorus of "No."

"The landlord tells us there's a fourth resident of that apartment, Alistair Campbell. Do you know where we can find him?"

"Alistair's a musician. Does gigs around the area. He comes, he goes. I don't keep track of them, you know."

"Do you have a number for Mr. Campbell?"

Tom pulled out his phone, called up the contact list. Gave them Matt's also. The female cop wrote the numbers down.

"If you hear from Matt Keller, tell him to call our office immediately." She handed over her card.

Tom threw it on the counter. "Yeah, sure."

"Make sure you do," the male cop said. And then, with dark looks and no farewells, they left.

Tom and Jody were silent as they watched the police leave. Tom let out a long sigh. They might not be interested in the Corolla, but he wished it would get picked up. The sooner the better.

"Poor Barry," Jody said.

"Fuck Barry. I want to know what the hell trouble Matt's gotten himself into." Tom left the office as he began making phone calls. The boss needed to know the cops were poking around.

# Chapter Twenty-one

**BANFF SPRINGS HOTEL. BANFF, ALBERTA. SUNDAY MORNING.**

A handful of people were up and about, walking the hotel grounds wrapped in raincoats or carrying umbrellas. It was a gray morning. Low-hanging clouds and drifting traces of mist concealed the mountains above, and the river below was a band of silver.

Lucky had opened her book, but hadn't read a word. She'd demolished all the sandwiches, including the ones she intended to save for Paul. She scarcely remembered eating them. When under stress Lucky Smith did tend to eat mindlessly. She thumped her more-than-adequate belly in disgust.

She was accomplishing nothing at all sitting here staring out the window.

Moonlight was on her way, and the thought gave Lucky a warm glow. She was going to have to be strong for Paul; she needed her daughter to be strong for her.

Funny how roles changed over the years. When Graham, Moonlight's first fiancé, had died, Moonlight had fallen apart, but her parents, Lucky and Andy, had been there, strong and understanding, wrapping the young woman in their love until she was able to struggle back to her feet. Then came the shock of Andy's sudden death, and Lucky and her children supported each other in their grief. Now it was Lucky's turn to reach for help. No one dear to them was dead this time, and hopefully no one would be, but worry could be as debilitating as grief. Lucky had phoned her son, Samwise, in Calgary, to fill him in on what was happening. Calgary was only an hour and a half from Banff, and he'd offered to come down, but Lucky caught the hesitation in his voice and said no, not yet. It was Moonlight Lucky needed now, and Samwise had his own young family.

It would be many hours still before Moonlight arrived.

Lucky took her raincoat out of the closet and, making sure her cell phone was deep in her pocket, headed out the door. She needed a walk, to do something, rather than sit and stare out the window and wait for the phone to ring.

How, she wondered, not for the first time, did they ever manage to live without cell phones? In the old days, she would have had to stay in and sit by the phone, all day if necessary, waiting for it to ring. The thought brought a smile to her face as she remembered doing precisely that. Waiting in her dorm room while her girlfriends went to a party, sad and lonely and so hopeful because a guy by the name of Andy Smith she'd met in class that morning had asked for her number. Keeping the door open when she went to the bathroom, lifting the phone off the hook occasionally to make sure it hadn't stopped working.

He hadn't called, and she'd gone to bed in tears. The next morning her roommate said she'd seen him at the party, long straight blond hair, Fu Manchu mustache, tie-dyed shirt, bell-bottom trousers and all, wandering through the house, searching for something and looking very disappointed.

Easy to laugh now, but that night had felt like the end of the world.

The lobby was busy, people checking out, others preparing to head off for the day. A family group, four generations by the look of it—baby snug in its mother's pouch, young children freshly scrubbed and brushed and dressed in holiday clothes, a proud octogenarian leaning on a young man's arm, laughing and chatting as they headed for the restaurant.

Today was Thanksgiving Sunday. She and Paul had reservations tonight for the Banffshire Club, the hotel's premier restaurant. She should probably cancel them. The restaurant would be full and want to know if they weren't coming.

She'd hold off a few more hours. Maybe the case would be resolved, Matt would be found safe and no longer under suspicion. She could phone Moonlight to tell her to go home, and Lucky and Paul could continue with their vacation.

And maybe, she thought, winged pigs will swoop through the lobby at any minute.

She didn't know if she'd be able to get a signal on her phone if she headed out on some of the more remote hiking trails, so she took her time wandering the hotel grounds. She pulled gloves out of her pocket and wrapped her scarf tightly around her neck. The air was mountain-fresh, crisp and full of the scent of pine and mulch with a taste of winter soon to come. Lucky stood still, back straight, and took deep refreshing breaths, scooping her arms up above her head and dropping them, hands together as if praying, down her front. She performed the movement ten times, and then continued her walk. She followed the signs and the neat path through the woods that led to the golf course. She hadn't seen anyone carrying clubs so the course must be closed for the winter and would be a nice place to stroll. Plus, she couldn't imagine those golfing businessmen types going anywhere they couldn't get reception for their array of smartphones and other gadgets.

Lucky jumped as the quiet of the foggy morning was broken by a loud, high-pitched, almost unworldly squeal. It was repeated, then followed by a crash, sounding like someone had dropped a truckload of silver trays onto a ceramic floor. What on earth? People began running past her. Not in fear but in excitement, faces wide with pleasure, urging children on.

Lucky began hurrying also, driven by curiosity, and she emerged from the woods into a grassy, groomed clearing as the sounds came again, shaking the trees and the ground itself. Two huge male elk faced off on the green, heads down, hair bristling, pawing and snorting. Their impressive multipoint antlers were wider than their shoulders and almost doubled their height. A herd of small brown-and-black females stood on the sidelines, watching the fight along with Lucky and the excited tourists and hotel staff.

The smaller of the males once again bellowed the challenge. They charged. Antlers clashed together and locked. Birds flew out of trees, children shouted in delight, cameras snapped.

More people were arriving, everyone sensibly keeping their distance not only from the fighting bucks but also from the group of females.

Lucky studied the females. Did they care, she wondered, who won and who lost? Or did they go along with the winner, accepting their fate as it came, in the same way so many human females had had no choice but to do down through the ages?

The animals' faces showed nothing, and Lucky turned back to watch the battle. One was a good deal older than the other, larger, stronger, combat-scarred. Poor old guy, having to fight off the young ones every year. Lucky thought of Paul with a smile. Not that young men were fighting for her attentions, but some life remained in her old guy yet and she'd been pleased that she'd invested in an expensive nightgown.

The older elk was pushing the younger back now, and Lucky cheered him on.

Then, with one last clash of their antlers, the young one broke away, and was almost instantly swallowed up by the trees. The victor stood on the field of battle for a few moments, breathing deeply, and then he headed slowly toward his harem. They drifted away, making scarcely a sound as they, too, disappeared into the forest.

"Wow," a little boy said, "that was great."

"Do again tomorrow?" one of a pack of Japanese tourists asked Lucky. "Same time?"

People did sometimes think this was Disneyland.

Lucky continued her walk, feeling much better. Life, after all, went on.

When she got back to her room, her face tingling from the cold, her always-wild mop of hair curling in the damp, the first thing she noticed was the red light on the bedside phone. Mood shattered, she cursed herself as she grabbed for it.

She shouldn't have gone out. She should have stayed in. Anything could have happened.

"I'm...uh...I'm looking for Mr. Keller? Is this the right room?" The voice was low, hesitant, every sentence ending in an upturn, a question. "We met yesterday, although you probably don't remember me? It was in the Lighthouse Keeper, the restaurant in Banff? I'm...uh...I'm Tracey, Matt's...girlfriend? I'm real sorry about what happened yesterday. Matt's not like that, really. I've just been to Matt's place, to his apartment." A long pause, then, "He's dead. No! I don't mean Matt's dead, but Barry is. Matt, he isn't answering his phone. I don't know what to do. I'm worried. I thought you'd want to know, that's all. He told me you're his dad. Maybe I shouldn't have called. I'm sorry to bother you. Bye. Oh, if you do know where Matt is, tell him to call me, please. He's got my number, but in case he's lost it, here it is again. I'm running out of battery power, though. If I don't answer he can call me at..."

She rattled off a series of numbers and hung up, after another apology for bothering them.

Poor girl.

Lucky replayed the message, this time with a pen in her hand and hotel notepad on the table to jot down the number. Without thinking, she dialed.

"Lighthouse."

"I'm looking for Tracey?"

"Hold on a sec."

Several long moments passed, and then, "Hello?" said a very hesitant voice.

"Is that Tracey?"

"Yes."

"This is Lucky Smith. I was with Paul Keller yesterday."

"Oh, right. I remember."

"You left a message for Paul at the hotel. He's not here at the moment. Can I help you?"

"Have you heard from Matt? Do you know where he is? Is he okay?"

"I'm sorry, but no, not since..."

"Since what?"

Noise in the background. A man talking, dishes clattering.

"Why don't we meet?" Lucky said. "I can come to you. Are you at work?"

"Yeah. I didn't know what else to do."

"I'll be there as soon as I can."

Lucky hung up without waiting for the girl to agree. Or not. She should call Paul. But then he might tell her to stay out of it.

She had to be doing something.

# Chapter Twenty-two

**TRAFALGAR CITY POLICE STATION. TRAFALGAR, BRITISH COLUMBIA. SUNDAY NOON.**

John Winters did not like what he was learning. Matthew Keller had been in and out of trouble for years. Most of it minor: one drinking and driving offense, bar fights, drunk and disorderly, possession of marijuana. He'd done a short stretch in jail for taking part in a bar brawl in Whistler in which a police officer was cut with a broken beer bottle. Fortunately, for Matt, the officer wasn't sure which of the combatants had struck him, so Matt got off on the more serious charge of assault PO. He was released about a year ago, and didn't seem to have been in any trouble since.

Not trouble the police were aware of at any rate.

Winters wondered how much Paul knew about this. He could have run the same checks as Winters did, easy enough. But a lot of cops, sensibly, didn't want to be checking up on their kids. Winters had suspected Keller was estranged from his son. The only evidence the boss even had one was the photograph that used to be on his desk—taken about ten years ago of Karen and two teenagers. When Karen left the marriage, Keller had removed the picture and replaced it with one of his daughter, Cheryl, on her wedding day.

He wondered if a photo of Lucky Smith would one day take a place of pride on the chief's desk. Molly would be mortified.

The latest address he could find for Matt Keller was the Banff one Paul had given him. Matt owned a car, a 2001 Honda Civic, which had no outstanding fines, but to dig much deeper, into bank accounts say, Winters would need a warrant. That, he wouldn't be able to get just doing a favor for a friend. The most recent mention of employment showed that Matt worked at a bar in Banff called Reds. About a month ago there'd been a theft at the bar when a woman's purse was taken. Matt wasn't suspected, but he was named on the police report as a witness. Winters continued reading. No one had been apprehended; the purse itself was found in a back alley the following day, credit cards and U.K. passport in place, four hundred dollars in cash missing.

He brought up the RCMP database and began reading about the killing in Banff. Police and border guards throughout Alberta and B.C. had been requested to be on the lookout for Matthew Allen Keller. No warrant, yet, thank goodness.

Next, Winters looked into what he could find on Barry Caseman. And he found plenty. Small-time hoodlum. A couple of convictions for theft, one for sexual assault when he'd grabbed a woman's breast in a bar, another sexual assault charge that was dropped when the woman left town and refused to come back to testify. A trail of fights and D&Ds. Caseman was an automobile mechanic, but he seemed to have trouble holding down a job and drifted from one party town to another. At the moment he was employed at a garage in Banff.

Make that used to be employed.

The death of Caseman probably wouldn't turn out to be much of a mystery. No doubt he'd insulted someone's girlfriend, gotten himself into a brawl with a guy who didn't intend to forgive and forget, or invited a buddy back home for a beer and found himself on the losing side of an argument.

If not for the disappearance of Matt Keller, who had called for help, it would be a simple matter of finding some guy wiping down his knife blade or bragging around town that no one messed with him.

It was too soon for much forensic evidence to have been entered into the file. Nothing on blood types found at the scene, other than Caseman's. No fingerprint reports yet, which probably wouldn't mean anything significant in any event. Matt Keller lived there, along with Caseman and two others, according to interviews with the neighbors, and it sounded like the sort of place people dossed down when they'd been kicked out of their own apartments or were passing through town.

The knife used had been left beside the body. It appeared to be a standard kitchen knife, covered in plenty of prints, and forensics was running computer searches for matches. Winters checked, but the report didn't say if the knife matched others in the apartment. The officer in charge of the investigation was a sergeant by the name of Edward Blechta. Winters had never run into him. He hoped the guy had enough empathy to cut Paul Keller some slack.

"Yeah?" Keller said, answering Winters' call.

Winters outlined what he'd found. Keller grunted in acknowledgement.

"Caseman sounds like a piece of work," Winters said. "Trouble looking for a place to happen."

"I had the pleasure," Keller said. "And it wasn't."

"Your son's been staying out of trouble for the past year."

"Smartening up, maybe."

"Any sign of him?"

"No. And that isn't good. His phone, the one he used to call me, was found in the apartment. Our hotel was the last number called. Two incoming calls since, messages left. The ringer was off, and the phone under a table, so we didn't hear anything. When we returned the call, it went straight to voice mail. No name, a standard message. Blechta's trying to track the caller down as well as get the phone company to let us into Matt's voice mail box."

"Might be significant if someone tried to get Matt and isn't picking up now."

"True. But cell phones can be unreliable in the mountains."

"As well I know."

The background chatter faded, and Winters guessed Keller had sought some privacy.

"You ever heard of this guy, Eddie Blechta?"

"No."

"See what you can find, will you, John? I want to know what sort of cop I'm dealing with here."

"Will do." Winters looked up at a knock on his door. Jim Denton, the dispatcher. He mouthed, *a call.*

"It'll have to wait, Paul. Looks like I've got work to do."

"When you can get to it."

"We've got your back here if you need anything."

"Thanks, John." The chief's voice broke. "I appreciate it."

"Trouble at the Grizzly Resort site," Denton said. "A couple of carloads of protesters have arrived."

"That's not our call. The location's out of town. Do the horsemen need help?"

"No, but another bunch *is* heading our way. There's a matching demonstration forming in front of the offices on Front Street. Armed with protest signs and bullhorns."

Winters swore under his breath as he reached for his jacket.

# Chapter Twenty-three

**LIGHTHOUSE KEEPER RESTAURANT. BANFF, ALBERTA. SUNDAY NOON.**

The Lighthouse Keeper was almost full when Lucky Smith entered. A woman called out, "Be with you in a sec," as she crossed the room carrying plates piled high with pancakes and sausages, eggs and potatoes and toast. The place was warm and redolent with damp wool drying, strong coffee, and hearty, greasy breakfasts.

"Table for one?" the waitress asked, reaching for a menu. She was about Lucky's age with a worn face and wary eyes and an inch of gray roots in too-black hair twisted into a rough bun.

"I'm looking for Tracey. Is she around?"

"I'll get her."

The waitress went through to the kitchen and Tracey came out almost immediately, carrying a coffeepot. She headed for a table, poured refills, asked if everything was okay. Only when her duties were finished did she approach Lucky.

"Mrs. Smith? Thanks for coming."

"Can you talk? You're busy, and I don't want to take you away from your work."

"Kev said it's okay if I take my break now." By the look on the older waitress' face, it was not okay with her but she said nothing. The door opened, and a group of four came in with a wave of cold, damp air. Lucky and Tracey slid past them onto the street.

"You're going to freeze." Lucky nodded to the girl's t-shirt, black, long-sleeved, with a picture of a lighthouse on a rocky point facing an incoming storm printed on the front.

"I'm okay." Tracey dug in the pocket of her baggy pants and came up with a pack of cigarettes and matches. Without asking permission, she lit up. She shifted from one foot to another, and glanced up and down the street while she sucked smoke into her lungs. Her fingernails were chewed to the quick.

"Why the lighthouse motif?" Lucky asked, trying to take some of the tension out of the air.

"Huh?"

"In the restaurant? It's all about lighthouses and fishing villages. We're a long way from the ocean. Everything else around here is about mountains."

"Oh. Kev, the owner, he's from Newfoundland. Hasn't been back since he was a kid, says he has nothing to go back for. I think he misses the sea sometimes." She was smoking rapidly, barely exhaling one puff before dragging in the next.

"How long have you worked here?" Lucky asked. She had no desire to engage in small talk, but this nervous girl seemed to need time to gather her courage to say what she needed to say.

"Two months. It's okay, I guess. I'd like to get better hours, though. I work at a car rental place in the evenings." The streets were busy with cars and the sidewalk with pedestrians. The women moved away from the restaurant doorway as two men came out and a couple went in.

"How long have you and Matt been together?"

"Two months. We met right after I got to Banff. I hate it here. I wish we could go someplace else, but Matt has a job at Sunshine lined up for when the season starts." Nothing was left of her cigarette but the filter. Tracey threw it to the ground and crushed it under her foot. Her running shoes were heavily scuffed, the laces shredding at the edges.

"Matt?" Lucky said.

The girl's wide brown eyes filled with tears. "Have you heard from him?"

"No." Lucky assumed Paul would not want her telling Tracey that Matt had called his father, asking for help. The police, he'd once told her, exchanged information in one direction only. Lucky wasn't with the police, and she was free to say whatever she liked, but she decided to wait and see what she could learn. "What do you know about what happened, Tracey?"

"Nothing. Nothing at all. And now my damn battery's died. He knows I'm working this morning. He can call me at the restaurant if he wants. I hope…I don't know what I hope."

"Do you have any idea where Matt might have gone?"

Tracey shook her head.

"A friend's place?"

"Maybe, but I can't think who. Matt doesn't have many friends other than Barry and Tom and Alistair, the guys he lives with." Tracey chewed at a hangnail on her thumb. It came away with a spurt of blood. "He might…"

Lucky waited. The girl sucked at the beads of blood. "Might…"

Her voice was low. She watched cars driving past. "Might have gone to a hotel with a girl, when he got off work last night. Girls on holiday, with money to spend, they hang around the wine bar some nights." She fumbled in her pocket and pulled out the pack of cigarettes and a lighter.

"Does he go with them often?"

Tracey shook her head. She lit the fresh cigarette with trembling hands. "No. I don't know! I don't know what he does. They're so much prettier than me. They've got loads of money, are looking for a good time. Why wouldn't he?" She started to cry. "Look, I'm sorry I called you. That's probably what happened. He's shacked up with some rich bitch and doesn't even know Barry's dead."

Lucky looked at the tear-streaked face, and debated what to say. Matt had not gone with a woman last night. He'd come home, probably as soon as he got off work, found his roommate dead, phoned his father. And then he disappeared. She reached out and touched the girl's arm. Startled, Tracey turned and looked at her through eyes red and wet, full of disappointment and sorrow. Lucky gave what she hoped was an encouraging smile.

"Matt phoned his father last night before three. From the apartment."

"He did?"

"Yes. That's all I can tell you. When we arrived he was gone."

Tracey wiped at her eyes with the back of her hand.

"He didn't pick up a woman at the bar, and he did go straight home. So where might he be now? Think Tracey."

"Hey, Trace!" The older waitress stood in the open restaurant door. Warm air and the scent of frying bacon and plenty of grease swirled around her. "You gonna be all day? I need help in here."

"Back in a minute." The second cigarette joined the first on the wet sidewalk.

"One minute. Or I'm complaining to Kev. I can't work this whole place by myself."

"I have to go," Tracey said. "Kev's okay, but he doesn't like slacking off."

"You're hardly slacking off."

"Whatever. I missed the start of shift going around to Matt's place."

Lucky pulled a pen and notebook out of her purse. She ripped a piece of paper out of the book and scribbled on it. "Here's my cell number. Call me if you think of anything. Please. Even if you only want to talk."

Tracey took the offering, and turned it over in her hands. "Matt does a lot of hiking and camping. He likes to go into the backcountry by himself, sometimes for days at a time. If he needed to get away for a while, he might have done that."

"If you hear anything from him, please let me know. Tell him his father is very worried."

"I will. Nice meeting you, Mrs. Smith."

Lucky watched as Tracey slipped back into the restaurant. A cold drizzle had started to fall as they stood on the sidewalk talking. Lucky was wrapped in her raincoat, but the girl wore nothing but her restaurant uniform. She seemed to love Matt Keller, perhaps a good deal more than he loved her. Poor thing.

But Lucky wasn't here to interfere with anyone's romantic relationships. She flipped her phone open and called Paul. He answered immediately.

"Anything?" she asked.

"No. Hold on a sec."

She waited. The mountains surrounding the town had been swallowed by low-hanging clouds. The rain was picking up and pedestrians scurried for cover.

"Okay," Paul said. "I wanted to go some place private. I'm now in the men's room. They've put a BOLO out on Matt. I told them he called me precisely because he didn't kill that man, but they're, shall we say, keeping their options open."

"Any other suspects?"

"No one in particular, but this Caseman guy was a real lowlife. I doubt finding suspects will be a problem."

Lucky laughed without mirth. "Good thing I was with you last night. I might have considered doing some damage to him myself. Have you tried phoning Matt?" Stupid thing to say. As if that wouldn't have occurred to the police. But Paul answered her question anyway.

"His phone was left in the apartment. His car's parked outside on the street."

"I might be able to help. I've had a chat with Tracey."

"Who the hell's Tracey?"

"Matt's girlfriend, apparently. At least she thinks she is, although I got the impression she's not very secure in the relationship."

"Lucky..."

"Sorry. She's a waitress at the restaurant. The one where we ran into Matt yesterday. She called me earlier, called you, actually, at the hotel, looking for Matt. She's been calling him, but he doesn't answer. She doesn't know where he is, but she says he's a keen backcountry camper. Goes into the wilderness by himself when he needs some down time. I thought…I thought that might be a possibility."

"I swear, Lucky, you can get more out of people in a casual conversation than any officer in the interrogation room. They've been trying to get ahold of someone who phoned Matt this morning, but they're not answering, and the phone company hasn't come back yet with a name or address."

"Her phone battery died. I get the feeling she's not too well organized at the best of times."

Paul chuckled. "Trust Lucky. Where's this girl now?"

"At the Lighthouse Keeper."

"Okay. Officers will be there shortly. It might be nice if you happen to be hanging around, if you think this Tracey trusts you."

"Is it important, do you think, about the camping?"

"It might well be, my love. It might well be."

# Chapter Twenty-four

**HIGHWAY OUTSIDE INVERMERE, BRITISH COLUMBIA. SUNDAY AFTERNOON.**

Smith pulled over at a rest stop to let Sylvester have a break. The dog ran about, head down, nose twitching, searching for exactly the right spot, while she made a call. So far the drive had been easy. The road on the mountain pass between Salmo and Creston had been recently groomed and cleared of snow, visibility was good, traffic light. The weather was supposed to stay dry for the remainder of the day until she crossed the Yoho Pass into Alberta.

"I'm outside Invermere, Mom, and thought I'd check in. I should be there in another two hours or so, all going well. Any updates?"

"A few, although no sign of Matt. Acting on a tip that Matt's a keen wilderness hiker, the police had one of his roommates check his things. He says some of Matt's camping and hiking equipment might be gone."

"They think he's gone into the wilderness, then?"

"Looks like that's a possibility. The roommate couldn't be sure. He said he hadn't been in Matt's room for weeks, and it's possible Matt sold some of his stuff. He was always short of money. They all are while waiting for ski season to begin. Paul was relieved to hear it. If Matt had time to get his things…"

"Then he wasn't coerced into leaving. What did this roommate have to say about the death? Was he there?"

"His name's Alistair and he's a musician of some sort. He played at a bar last night and the band members went to someone's place after closing for a few drinks and to hang out. He came home to find the police crawling all over his apartment. The other roommate says he spent his night at a girlfriend's."

"All possible, Mom. How's the chief doing?"

"The Mounties are letting him tag along, although they're not telling him much. As long as Paul's kept in the loop, and kept busy, he'll be okay."

"And you, Mom? How are you?"

"I'm fine, Moonlight. I'm dreadfully worried about Paul, but I don't have a personal involvement in this. I've only met Matt once since he was a child and it wasn't a very promising encounter. I'm glad you're coming, dear. If I have to support Paul…"

"You need someone to support you. See you in a couple of hours. I'll call as I'm coming into town and you can tell me where to meet you. Oh, I'll need someplace to stay. Is town very busy, are there likely to be any motel rooms free?"

"I'll check you into the Banff Springs."

Smith sputtered. "I can't afford to stay there."

"My treat. I'm heading back to the hotel now. There doesn't seem to be much more I can do." Lucky let out a long sigh. "I just want this to be over."

"I know, Mom. I know."

"Bye, dear."

Smith put her phone away. Sylvester was sniffing at the base of an overflowing garbage bin. An eighteen-wheeler sped past, kicking up mud and slush, heading north. Sylvester. For a moment she'd forgotten she'd brought the dog. He could hardly stay in her room if she was at the Banff Springs. He was too big to be smuggled into the elevator, and not well enough behaved to keep quiet, in any event.

She'd worry about what to do with the dog when she got there.

# Chapter Twenty-five

**FRONT STREET. TRAFALGAR, BRITISH COLUMBIA. SUNDAY AFTERNOON.**

Tensions were building, along with the size of the crowd, by the time John Winters arrived at the Grizzly Resort offices on Front Street. Protesters carrying homemade signs in support of the area's bears were spilling off the sidewalk into the street and Dave Evans was trying, unsuccessfully, to order them back.

A patrol car came down the hill and pulled to a stop in the center of the nearest intersection, forcing traffic to find its way through the backstreets.

Winters estimated about twenty people were part of the protest. Almost as many had simply gathered to see what was going on. He recognized a good number of them. The environmentalists were there, as could be expected, plus those who took part in just about any protest that happened to be going on—also as expected. This was not a spontaneous demonstration, not if a second bunch had driven up to the construction site itself.

He thought it strange, however, that it was being held on a Sunday afternoon, and Thanksgiving Sunday at that, when the town was about as quiet as it ever got and people were gathered around their holiday dinner table. Good thing Lucky Smith had gone away for the weekend. Now that Lucky was dating the chief of police, things could get a bit hairy if they had to detain her. Which had been known to happen. Lucky was a passionate activist and these days the environment was one of her main concerns. Paul Keller would tell his officers to make no exceptions for Lucky, but they'd have to try to guess whether he meant it. Would Lucky tone down some of her more public activities, Winters wondered, to save the chief embarrassment? They could only hope so.

He wasn't too concerned about the locals. The usual mixture of young idealists, long-haired, long-bearded, and older folk, well-groomed, neat in good outdoor gear, who cared about maintaining the place they had chosen to call home.

But there were a couple he didn't recognize. One of them, a man, was standing off to one side, watching. He was in his thirties, short black hair, thick beard, well-muscled under a leather jacket. A Toronto Blue Jays ball cap was pulled low over his forehead. He saw Winters studying him, and stared back, through eyes cold and unfriendly.

"You don't have a permit to block the street." Al Peterson, in charge of the uniform shift, addressed the crowd. "Get back on the sidewalk immediately."

The older women obediently moved. They urged some of the younger protesters to follow. A few glanced around, seeking someone to tell them what do to. John Winters obliged. He wasn't in uniform, but everyone in town knew who he was. "Come on, Paula," he said to a young woman, clad all in black with hair dyed the color of midnight, black nail polish, and an assortment of strangely placed piercings. "You have to get off the street."

"We've the right to protest, Mr. Winters. We have to stop that development. It's prime…"

"Yes, I know. I also know that you are allowed to protest, provided you do it peacefully and at no inconvenience to others. But you need a permit to block the street and your group doesn't have one. It would be within the law for us to remove you. You don't want that, do you, Paula?"

A woman approached. Winters had never seen her before. Lean and fit, moderately attractive with short, spiky red hair, dressed in jeans and an over-large sweater. "These streets belong to everyone, at least until they're sold to the highest bidder along with everything else in this country. You don't have to move," she said to Paula. She carried a hand-painted sign with a rather good drawing of a rearing grizzly bear and the words This is What a Grizzly Looks Like.

People, who seconds ago had been heading obediently toward the sidewalk, stopped.

Winters sensed no hostility in this crowd. These people were his friends and neighbors; they had a legitimate concern and were here to make their point. But all it took was one hothead, one outside agitator, to turn a peaceful protest ugly. He kept one eye on the woman's hands. The sign was mounted on a wooden stick about two feet long. It might have a blunt edge, but it could turn into a formidable weapon. Winters sensed, as much as saw, Al Peterson standing behind him.

"I'm John Winters, Trafalgar City Police. I don't know you."

"That's right. You don't."

"I've told you my name. What's yours?"

All around them people shifted. Some of the older ones were growing uncomfortable at the possibility of a confrontation. A few women lowered their own signs and slipped away.

The red-haired woman eyed the watching crowd. Most faces were not sympathetic. "Robyn Winfield, if it's any of your damn business."

"Which it might well be. New to town, Robyn?"

"Been here a couple of days. Nice place. Trying to keep it that way. Out of the hands of the money-grubbing developers."

"You're welcome to make your concerns known publicly, Robyn. As long as it's also legally."

"Legal." Winfield spat in the road, missing the toe of Winters' shoe by less than an inch. The shot had been well aimed. "The rich make laws to suit them and then tell you bunch of patsies to arrest us for breaking them."

Winters turned back to Paula. "Where's Beowulf?" he asked, referring to her young son.

Lashes thick with mascara blinked. "A playdate at my friend Colleen's place."

"That's nice. I'm sure he wants you to pick him up on time. Which you'll be able to do, Paula, if you stop blocking the road."

"Sorry, Mr. Winters." She lowered her head and pushed through the crowd.

"Anyone else not wanting to move?" Winters asked. He looked people he recognized directly in the eye. No one met his stare. One by one the crowd broke up. Most simply left, carrying their homemade signs. A young man tried to start up a chant, "Mountains for bears," but his voice drifted off when no one joined in.

Soon, only Robyn Winfield was left standing in the street.

She looked at Winters with narrow hostile eyes. And then, with an exaggerated bow, moving slowly to make her point, she climbed onto the sidewalk. She leaned her sign against her leg, and there she stood, toes hanging over the edge of the curb, arms crossed over her chest.

Winters considered asking Winfield for some ID. Make sure that was the woman's real name, and then run a records check. But, he decided, that would be unnecessarily provocative.

He had no doubt he'd have plenty of other opportunities to check up on Robyn Winfield.

The protest was over. A handful of people propped their signs against the doorway to the offices and in a few minutes no one remained but Dave Evans, ordered to stay for a while to ensure they didn't return to start the demonstration up again. Even the silent, watching man had slipped away unobserved.

Winters headed back to the office. Tensions were running high in town now that the resort was once again under construction. Everyone needed to let off some steam. Nice of them to do it on a quiet Sunday in October. Nice of the counter-protesters, those anxious for the jobs the resort would bring to the area, to stay away.

John Winters had absolutely no doubt things wouldn't be as easygoing next time.

# Chapter Twenty-six

**BANFF SPRINGS HOTEL. BANFF, ALBERTA. SUNDAY AFTERNOON.**

Lucky arrived back at the hotel with little idea of what to do while waiting for Moonlight to arrive.

About all she could reasonably do was wait. Lucky didn't like waiting. She wanted to be with Paul, but was well aware that Blechta was barely accommodating Paul Keller's presence in his investigation as it was. When he interviewed Tracey at the Lighthouse Keeper, Blechta and Tracey had sat at a table in the kitchen, and Paul and Lucky had been ordered to wait in the dining room. An officer flipped the sign on the door to closed. The cook, who, Lucky learned, was also the owner, had not been pleased. But he had the wary eyes of a man who'd learned not to mess with the police, and said nothing. He and the older waitress had taken tables at the other side of the room clutching mugs of coffee. They sat in silence until Blechta came out and told them they could reopen the restaurant.

Lucky wanted to stay behind to offer Tracey what support she might need, but one look at the cook, whose scowl was increasing every minute his place of business was closed, had her slipping out in Paul's wake. Blechta told one of his uniformed officers to, once again, escort Lucky back to her hotel.

Paul. Theirs was a strange relationship, a meeting of opposites in many ways. She'd found out only a few months ago that

Paul had been in love with her for many years; she'd never had the slightest idea. Andy hadn't liked Paul Keller, but Lucky put his animosity down to old-hippie verses old-cop. Only now, with the clarity of hindsight, could she see that Andy's dislike had been much deeper, more personal than she'd realized. She remembered the time Moonlight had gone missing. It was after the girl had become a police officer and John Winters had taken her disappearance very seriously. How angry Andy had been, to come home and find Paul Keller sitting at his kitchen table, sipping coffee and eating Lucky's homemade squares. Lucky had put Andy's overreaction down to worry. Now, she realized, Andy had been jealous.

He'd never had the slightest reason to be: Lucky had loved Andy passionately and unreservedly all the years they'd been together. Still, it was nice to know he'd loved her equally in return.

Now, Andy was gone and Lucky was with Paul Keller, after all. She wondered, as she looked out the window of the patrol car at the outline of the mountains, barely discernible in the low-hanging cloud, what Andy would have to say about that.

He would, she was sure, be nothing but happy for her.

Funny that she could find love with two such different men. Paul had none of Andy`s spontaneity, his sense of fun and adventure. Not a bad thing, really, at her age. Spontaneity was well and good for the young. Andy would have surprised her with this trip to Banff the morning they were due to leave. Paul had involved her in every detail of the organization.

Andy's death had devastated her, but it was fun to find a new partner in your old age.

For the sex, if nothing, else. She must have laughed out loud for the officer half-turned in his seat and said his first words since she'd gotten into his car. "Here on vacation?"

"Yes."

"Weather's supposed to clear tomorrow." He turned off the road onto the long sweeping driveway to the hotel. Lucky felt a twinge of guilt, thinking about sex when poor Paul was out of his mind with worry.

The same doorman as earlier greeted her arrival. As he had done this morning, he held open the door of the police car for her, his face expressionless. Rumors would be swirling "downstairs" about her. She briefly wondered what they'd think she was. A not-very-efficient undercover cop? A visiting dignitary travelling incognito?

A rich old broad who couldn't hold her liquor most likely.

She was thinking once again about Paul Keller and sex as she walked into the lobby. A woman stood up from a high-backed, ornately carved armchair, and the thought died as thoroughly as if Lucky'd been drenched in an icy shower.

The woman stood there, her body stiff, watching Lucky with cold, unwelcoming eyes, waiting for her to approach. Which she did. "Karen. It's nice to see you."

"I heard you'd taken up with my husband," Karen Keller said. "I should have known."

"Only after you didn't want him anymore." Lucky was sorry the minute the words were out of her mouth. No need to respond to rudeness with more rudeness.

Karen was a petite woman, almost as short as Lucky, but much slimmer. She looked good, her makeup expertly applied, her hair, highlighted in shades of caramel, cut in a neat chin-length bob. She wore a brown wool pantsuit accented by a red and gold scarf and gold jewelry. She looked, in short, as if the past year had been kind to her. Lucky suddenly felt old and dumpy in her calf-length, brightly colored skirt, hiking shoes with black socks, practical raincoat. She'd been woken at three and hadn't so much as looked at herself in the mirror since. She could practically feel her hair frizzing in the damp air.

"You're here because of Matt?"

"First the police called me, to ask if I'd heard from him, and then Paul. I'm living in Calgary, and was able to get away immediately." Not even expensive makeup and jewelry accents could hide fresh lines of fatigue and worry.

"Why don't we go for a cup of tea and I'll fill you in on what I know."

Karen hesitated.

Out of the corner of her eye, Lucky saw a man heading toward them. "We're checked in," he said to Karen. "I've sent the bags and coats on up." He turned to Lucky. "You must be Lucky Smith. I'm Jonathan Burgess. It's a pleasure to meet you." He held out his hand, and Lucky took it, thinking Karen hadn't done too badly for herself. She could hardly remain antagonistic to Lucky for being with Paul, when Karen had brought along a paramour of her own. Jonathan was a tall imposing man, probably in his early sixties, with thick gray hair lightly gelled, and pale blue eyes. He was dressed in gray slacks ironed to a knife edge and an oatmeal sweater over a collared blue shirt. His wide smile was full of capped teeth, his hands manicured. Lucky pegged him as a lawyer, an oil company executive perhaps. Or, God help them, a politician.

He put his arm lightly around Karen's shoulder, marking his territory. "Fortunately Karen and I were brunching together when she got the call, so I was able to bring her. She's wasn't in any condition to drive, as you can imagine."

*They were brunching, were they? What was wrong with having brunch, or plain old breakfast?*

Not Lucky's problem. She returned the smile. "I suggested we go for tea. You'll be wanting to know what's happening."

"I want to see Paul," Karen said.

"He's tied up with the police right now."

"He can free himself to talk to me. Why am I not surprised Paul happened to be on the scene? That's why Matt ran off. Paul was always after him, night and day, to…"

"Karen," Jonathan said, his voice soft. Soft but strong. "Tea's an excellent idea. We didn't finish brunch. They do a nice afternoon tea here, I've heard."

Lucky upped her opinion of Jonathan. Right now, he was exactly what Karen needed.

They made it into Rundles Lounge with minutes to spare before tea service ended for the day. Jonathan made a big show of thanking the staff for letting them in, and studying the menu in detail. Karen watched Lucky, her eyes narrow with hostility, and Lucky pretended to be admiring the view. Only a few tables were occupied, people still chatting although their teacups were empty and nothing lay on their plates but scatterings of crumbs.

Jonathan ordered a bottle of Champagne. Lucky didn't think that at all appropriate—they were scarcely here for a celebration. Perhaps Jonathan was used to drinking Champagne. Karen didn't seem to notice.

"Always liked this hotel," Jonathan said, making neutral conversation while the waitress laid out the place settings and the people at the next table argued amongst themselves over who was going to pay the bill. "Although I prefer Lake Louise. I worked as a bellhop at the Chateau a couple of summers in the early seventies. It was only open three months of the year back then, in the summer months. Banff was a sleepy little town in those years. Nothing at all like it is now. Can't fight progress."

Lucky also remembered that sleepy little town. These days if you restricted yourself to the Banff townsite itself, as a lot of tourists did, you might not even know you were in a national park. The town wasn't allowed to grow anymore, but still it stretched at its seams, pushing the animals further and further back. Occasionally, an animal wouldn't be pushed, and there were regular sightings of elk or even the occasional black bear, in backyards or on the streets. Grizzlies, thoroughly dangerous, were rare, but even they ventured too close for comfort sometimes. People said they came here to see the animals, but most of them didn't really. If a bear ventured into a residential street or onto hotel grounds, it would be tranquilized and removed or chased away. Never mind the highway. That one of Canada's busiest highways, the Trans-Canada between Calgary and Vancouver, went right through a national park and a protected wilderness area, seemed to Lucky to be a travesty.

Whenever talk of developing the Grizzly Resort property outside of Trafalgar came up, the example of Banff was mentioned as a worst-case scenario. Still, as Jonathan said in such clichéd terms, you couldn't fight progress. Although a good many people, including Lucky herself, tried to.

"What is it that you do, Jonathan?" Lucky asked sweetly.

"Real estate," he replied, "and various other business interests."

She felt like asking him how much money he'd made from the destruction of sleepy little towns but decided she had more important things to worry about today. She checked her watch—four o'clock. Moonlight should be arriving soon.

The Champagne was brought to the table, and great ceremony went into opening and serving. Jonathan tasted it, pronounced it excellent, and the women's glasses were filled.

Karen had scarcely taken her eyes off Lucky, but she said not a word while the waitress fussed. Finally pots of tea and a three-tiered platter of elaborate sandwiches, blueberry scones, and pastries were served and they were left in peace. "I want," Karen said, her voice brittle with barely controlled anger, "to know what is going on." She gripped her Champagne flute so tightly Lucky feared it might shatter. Karen was not wearing a wedding or engagement ring, but she did sport a healthy-sized emerald on her right hand.

Lucky saw no reason not to tell Matt's mother everything she knew. She'd preferred to speak to Paul first, but she'd been ambushed by Karen and hadn't had the chance to slip away and call him. She left out the part about the encounter at the coffee shop and only mentioned that she and Paul had run into Matt at the Lighthouse Keeper and told him where they were staying.

Karen groaned.

"Matt isn't suspected of having killed this fellow, is he?" Jonathan asked.

"I don't know what the police are thinking."

"Of course he's not suspected," Karen snapped. "He did the right thing and called for help. I can't believe Paul let him down, again."

"That's hardly fair," Lucky said. "We went around to Matt's place immediately."

"Paul should have phoned the police first."

"Paul told Matt to do it."

"Which he was obviously unable to do, probably because the killer was still there. Paul should have realized that." Karen threw back her glass of Champagne and poured herself another. Bubbles danced in the crystal flute: the only cheerful thing at their table.

"No point in throwing around accusations." Jonathan slathered jam and clotted cream onto a scone. He, at least, was enjoying the fancy food.

Lucky stuffed an open-faced smoked fish sandwich into her mouth, without tasting a thing. "You were not there, Karen," she said, when she could speak again. "So don't try and second-guess those of us who were."

"If I wasn't there, it's because...."

Lucky pushed her chair back and got to her feet. "Enough. Clearly, you have unresolved issues with Paul, but don't attempt to discuss them with me or to interfere in what is, after all, a very serious situation."

"I don't need you to lecture me. I am well aware my son could be in considerable danger."

"In that case I'd advise you to act accordingly. Thank you for the tea, Jonathan. Nice to meet you."

Lucky stormed out of the lounge as the waitress watched, open-mouthed. Lucky's stomach crawled up into her throat and she felt a wave of heat wash over her. Her knees wobbled and she leaned against a table to keep herself upright.

The table was decorated with pumpkins and squash, artfully arranged colored leaves, and assorted pinecones. Thanksgiving. She should cancel their dinner reservations.

"Are you all right, madam?" A bellhop approached, his handsome young face creased in professional concern.

"Perfectly fine, thank you."

"Can I help you to a seat?"

"I'll be okay in a minute. Thank you."

"If you're sure," he said before answering a summoning bell from the concierge.

She had to call Paul. Let him know Karen was here, and she was not about to be helpful. Her phone rang. Moonlight.

"I'm about fifteen minutes away, Mom. Where are you?"

"At the hotel. Oh, dear, I forgot to book your room. I'll do that now and wait for you in the lobby."

"Change of plan. I'm going to meet the chief at the police station first. I'll come to the hotel later."

"When you do, we're in room 615."

"Okay. I have Sylvester."

"You have what?"

"Sylvester's with me."

"Really, dear. Why on earth did you bring the dog?"

"Because I didn't know what else to do with him."

"You can leave him in the car for now. He's usually quite happy in the car."

"I'll be there when I can."

Karen and Jonathan came out of the lounge. Karen crossed the lobby with quick, angry steps, her heels rapping the gleaming marble floors. Jonathan spotted Lucky. He gave her a look, and then hurried after Karen.

# Chapter Twenty-seven

**RCMP DETACHEMENT. BANFF, ALBERTA. SUNDAY LATE AFTERNOON.**

Drops of rain began to fall as Smith joined the Trans-Canada Highway, and by the time she reached Banff it was coming down in sheets. With the time change, it was almost six o'clock and lights had been switched on in homes and stores to break the gloom. She'd been through Banff many times and knew the view was spectacular: jagged mountain peaks snowcapped all year, deep green forest, wide, racing rivers. Today she could barely see the cars in front of her, never mind admire the scenery.

She used her GPS to direct her to the police station on Lynx Street. Most of the streets in Banff were named after animals. She wondered if someone living on, say, Squirrel Street, felt less important than anyone with an address on majestic Elk or mighty Wolf.

She parked in the street, told Sylvester to guard the car, and walked up the steps to the front door, hands over her head to protect her from the worst of the rain. She announced to the buzzer that she was Constable Molly Smith, here to see Chief Constable Paul Keller, and she was admitted. A uniformed officer told her to take a seat in the waiting area.

Keller came out almost immediately, looking as though he'd aged a decade in the couple of days since Smith had seen him last. "Molly," the chief said with a tight smile, "your mother told me you were on your way. Good of you to come."

"Not a problem, sir. I phoned Mom to let her know I was stopping here first. I thought maybe you could tell me better than her what's going on."

A man followed Keller. She didn't have to be told he was the detective in charge; he might as well have COP tattooed on his forehead. Some longtime officers, John Winters for example, could pass for a civilian, if you didn't take into account the cautious, always-watching eyes. Many, like this guy, wore their job like they wore their skin.

She held out her hand. "Constable Molly Smith, Trafalgar City Police."

He took it, his handshake surprisingly limp. "Detective Sergeant Ed Blechta. Are you a detective, Constable?"

"Uniform."

"Then I don't imagine we have any use for you."

*Screw you right back, buddy.* He could have at least pretended to be polite. She hadn't come here expecting to be asked to help with the investigation, nor did she intend to. She wanted only to support her mom. Some of these old-time RCMP guys had a real problem working with women—as numerous lawsuits from female officers testified. She kept her smile in place. "I'm here to see if my chief needs any help, thanks anyway, Sarge."

"Smith?" Blechta said.

"Not an uncommon name," she replied.

"No." He turned to Keller. "Is this…officer…any relation to your companion, Lucky Smith?"

"She's my mom. We like to keep it in the family." That had been a mistake. The chief's face tightened and the look of dismissal on Blechta's face deepened.

They were still standing in the foyer. Smith had not been invited to the offices, to lean back, put up her feet, toss around ideas. Highly unlikely she would be.

The uniform, a stocky woman about Smith's age, watched the exchange with great interest.

"Any sign of Matt?" Smith asked Keller.

"No."

"Paul, why don't you let this young lady take you back to your hotel? You need a rest, have something to eat."

Oh yeah, Molly Smith definitely did not like Sergeant Ed Blechta.

Keller rubbed his hand over his chin. He hadn't shaved, probably not since yesterday morning, and the stubble was coming in thick and gray. Blechta and Smith watched him, struggling to make up his mind. He wanted to stay, to be on the spot if news came in, but he was exhausted, probably ravenous, and in need of a shave and a shower. His phone rang, making up his mind for him.

A quick glance at Smith let her know the caller was her mom. He let out a long sigh and said, "I'll be right there."

"Problem?" Smith asked.

"My ex-wife, Karen, is here, wanting to talk to me. She's at the hotel."

"I'll call you soon as I have anything new," Blechta said.

"Thanks. Anytime, day or night."

"You got it." The Mountie went into the offices. Paul Keller grimaced at Smith. "I have to talk to Karen. Where are you staying, Molly?"

"At the Banff Springs, I think. Mom said she'd find me a room. Me and Sylvester."

"You brought the dog?"

"Why does everyone keep saying that? I brought the dog because I didn't have anything else to do with him."

"There are no kennels in Banff," the uniformed officer said. "You'll have to go to Canmore."

"Not necessary yet. He's good in the car for several hours, even overnight. He enjoyed the drive, chasing other cars away if they got too close, so he'll sleep well. Thanks anyway."

They stood under the overhang above the front door while rain splashed their feet. The police station was located on a pleasant residential street. Two people rode past on bikes, hunched over the handlebars, buried under rain ponchos, and a patrol car turned into the station lot, kicking up a spray of water. "You should take your mom home, Molly," Keller said. "Our vacation is obviously ruined, but I want…I need to be here. For a while yet, anyway."

"I'll suggest it, but I don't see that happening. She'll want to stay, to be supportive."

Keller gave her a long look. "Molly, your mother…"

The door opened behind them and the uniformed woman came out. "Excuse me," she said, sliding past them and heading down the sidewalk. They followed, and Smith was very glad indeed she didn't have to hear the rest of the chief's sentence.

# Chapter Twenty-eight

**BANFF SPRINGS HOTEL. BANFF, ALBERTA. SUNDAY EVENING.**

When Smith tried to check in at the hotel she found they didn't have a reservation for her. Fortunately they weren't full and she was able to get a room. She choked when the smiling clerk told her the price, but handed over her credit card, hoping Lucky would remember that she said she'd get the bill. Lucky appeared to be a scatterbrain sometimes, but she was normally pretty well organized. Not like her to forget to do something she'd promised to do, like book the room.

Smith had parked the car at the far end of the lot next to a patch of grass under a generous canopy of spruce. She left Sylvester with a bowl of food and another of water. The temperatures weren't hot and they weren't cold; if she popped out now and again to give him a stretch he should be okay for one night. Hopefully, it wouldn't be more than that. Either this case wrapped up soon and Matt Keller, whether he'd killed someone or not, was found, or it would drag on for weeks, maybe months. Maybe forever. Come what may, she had to be back at work on Thursday, four days from now.

She vaguely remembered Matt from their school days. He was older and hadn't been in any of her classes, but he'd been on the ski team. She seemed to remember he'd been a good kayaker as well. Other than that, nothing but a teenage boy she'd paid no attention to.

She'd been to the Banff Springs before, checking the place out, admiring the stately grandeur, wishing she could afford to stay here. But she'd never been on the upstairs floors or inside the rooms. The hall was dark and quiet when she got off the elevator, made her way to her room, and slipped open the door. It was just a hotel room, like so many others: neatly made wide bed, wooden desk, industrial carpet, mass-produced prints, TV mounted on the wall opposite the bed, clean bathroom. But when she bounced on the mattress, dried her hands on the towels, and stood at the window admiring the view, she knew why she was paying so much.

She flipped through the hotel directory, checking out the restaurants and amenities, regretting that Adam wasn't with her.

She forced herself to come back to earth and remember why she'd come. This was no vacation.

She called her mom's room, and the phone was answered immediately. "I'm here, all checked in. Room 576. Do you want me to come to you? The chief should be back, is he?"

"He's cleaning up. We're meeting Karen downstairs in fifteen minutes."

"Want me in on that?"

"Probably better not. It'll be all blame and insinuations. Nothing at all helpful."

"Call me when you're done. I need something to eat. Maybe we can go out to dinner and talk over what we're going to do next."

"Oh, dear. Dinner."

"What about it?"

"I forgot to cancel our reservation."

"Talk to you later, Mom."

She hung up the hotel phone, and pulled her own out of her pocket. "I've arrived," she said to Adam. "I'm staying at the Banff Springs."

"Nice."

"Very nice. Wish I could enjoy it. Did you learn anything?"

"Sergeant in charge is named Ed Blechta. Twenty-five-year career, mostly in rural or small-town Alberta. Nothing stands out."

"He ever have an internal complaint against him, say from a woman?"

"Why do you ask?"

"Just a feeling."

"Nothing on his record that I can see. I can look into it. Call some friends on the QT."

"If it's not too much trouble. I don't think that has the slightest thing to do with this case, but I like to know what I'm dealing with."

"Any sign of Keller's son?"

"No. I haven't been filled in yet. Mom and the chief are meeting with Matt's mom right now. I'm going to have a bath, and then meet them for dinner."

"Molly?"

"Yeah?"

"What do you hope to accomplish there? You won't be allowed into the investigation and you're not a detective in any case, you know that."

"I'm not sure, Adam. I want to be here for my mom and if I can be of some help to the chief, then I will."

"Wouldn't you be more help to Lucky by bringing her home?"

"Probably, but she won't see it that way. Worst-case scenario, this drags on and on. Matt Keller has taken a runner. He might have hitched a ride with a passing truck and could be just about anywhere right now."

"Running usually means guilt, Molly."

"Yeah. I know. The chief's gotta know that, too. I'll call in the morning, let you know if we're coming back. Sorry about the turkey dinner thing."

He laughed. "Kitchen looks like the turkey tried to escape and had to be wrestled into submission. I'll cook it myself. We can eat turkey sandwiches for the rest of the week."

"I don't know if the pecan pie filling is salvageable. The pastry's in the fridge. Uncooked."

"Take care, Molly."

"I will."

She ran hot water into the large, luxurious tub and her body tingled with the joy of being loved.

# Chapter Twenty-nine

**WALDHAUS PUB. BANFF SPRINGS HOTEL. BANFF, ALBERTA. SUNDAY EVENING.**

Molly Smith didn't have to be a detective to know that the meeting with Karen Keller had not gone well. Lucky's face was pinched in disapproval and the chief's scowl was a sight to frighten small children.

They met in the pub. No one wanted to go to the restaurant for a fancy Thanksgiving dinner. The pub was crowded and noisy and they wouldn't have to worry about being overheard.

Lucky, Smith thought, looked strained. New lines had appeared overnight on the delicate skin under her eyes and around her mouth. When Lucky greeted her daughter with an enthusiastic hug, Smith felt the soft, comfortable, familiar body tremble with tears being held under control.

The chief, frankly, looked like hell. Bags the color of fresh bruises lay under his eyes and the eyes themselves were flat and empty of light. Dressed in black slacks and a brown sweater rather than his neat tailored uniform, he appeared smaller than she remembered, insignificant almost. The scent of fresh tobacco smoke hung around him like an aura. Everyone at the station knew he was trying to quit. He'd obviously fallen off the wagon.

She didn't bother to try to be cheerful, just let Lucky know that Sylvester was safely snoozing in the car and Adam was cooking their turkey. Other than that, they didn't have much to say while the waitress—Maura, Scotland—greeted them in a deep Highland burr and brought drinks. A German beer for the chief, the local Kokanee brew for Smith, water for Lucky.

They placed their food orders and then Smith turned to Keller. "What have you learned?"

"Not a lot. Matt's description has been circulated to the park wardens and a BOLO put out on him all over the West and down to the U.S. border. No sign of him. I don't have to tell you that a heck of a lot of transport trucks pass by on the highway, heading to points all across North America. He might have hitched a ride, could be on his way to practically anywhere by now."

"Did he take his wallet with him?"

"Probably, as it isn't in the apartment or in his car. Meaning cash, if any, and credit cards. Driver's license. If he tries to use his cards, he'll be spotted."

"Was he likely to have much money on him?"

The chief took a long swallow of his beer. "Don't know. His roommate said he paid cash mostly, but they have no idea if he had any last night. His job said he was paid about a week ago, but he makes good tips and apparently the bar was busy last night."

"Last night," Smith said. "You want to tell me what happened?"

She listened while Keller told her about the phone call and what they found at Matt's apartment. Lucky didn't interrupt, but her face was pale and grim.

"How'd Matt know you were here?"

Lucky and Keller exchanged glances. Then the chief sighed and told her the story. Smith winced. At first telling, she'd pretty much assumed that the chief's son, a guy she'd known in her own youth, had happened upon a killing and, frightened, had run for his life. The story of the bullying of Lucky, first at the coffee shop, which didn't matter all that much, but then the deliberate escalation at the restaurant, put a new sheen on things. If Matt Keller was the sort to threaten a middle-aged woman like Lucky Smith, who the hell knew what else he could be capable of? Or what sort of crowd he ran with?

"We," Lucky said, "left that part out when we spoke to Karen."

"She wouldn't believe it in any case," Keller said. "Nothing Matt ever did was his fault. Not in Karen's eyes."

"Bratwurst?" The waitress arrived, bearing plates piled high. Keller leaned back. Smith accepted her burger, and Lucky had the Caesar salad. At the next table two couples were digging into a pot bubbling with cheese fondue.

Lucky lifted her water glass. "I suppose I should say happy Thanksgiving."

They clinked glasses.

"Maybe it will be, Mom. Thanksgiving Day isn't until tomorrow."

Lucky gave her daughter a world-weary smile.

"What's forensics come up with?" Smith asked as she wrestled her burger, two-handed, trying to keep the juices from dripping down her chin.

"Going through that apartment's like searching for fingerprints on the Walmart sale counter at the end of Black Friday. At least ten individual patterns have been found. So far. Four men lived there. They had friends, girlfriends, and let's say dusting wasn't one of their main priorities. The neighbors reported parties, musical jam sessions, fairly constant changeover of residents. The place probably hasn't been properly cleaned for years." Keller lowered his voice, although the noise level in the crowded pub was high enough to ensure their privacy. "The only blood in the living room was Caseman's, the dead guy. He showed no defensive wounds. The knife, an ordinary kitchen knife with a four-inch blade, quite sharp, found at the scene, got him first in the lower back. A strong enough blow to drop him, and then they finished the job with a slice across the throat. The body was not moved after the attack. It was about two feet into the apartment. Possibly he'd opened the door, admitted his attacker, then turned and was knifed in the back as he walked away." Keller's voice had turned firm, no-nonsense. He was talking like a cop, relating facts without emotion or speculation. Molly Smith's chief was back.

"A friend or acquaintance, then."

"Looks that way. Someone he was expecting, at any rate."

"You think he answered the door? Means it wouldn't likely have been someone who lived there. They'd have a key."

"Good point. But easy enough to argue that the roommate had lost his key, or had his hands full. Plenty of reasons Caseman would open the door. This is a low crime town. People don't have multiple locks on their doors. Plenty of people, young men anyway, aren't likely to bother to check who's there before opening up. It's also possible he was walking the other way, showing his guest out the door, then forgot something, turned his back for a moment, maybe."

"Did the knife come from the kitchen?"

"Hard to tell. Everything in that place is a mishmash of cheap stuff left behind over the years. The guys who live there seem to have no idea what implements belonged in the kitchen or if anything was missing. Unlikely the kitchen's ever been used to cook anything more substantial than the odd piece of toast or reheat pizza in the microwave. They couldn't say if they recognized the knife or not."

"Prints on the knife?"

"Several, all still unidentified. Not Matt's."

"That's one good thing." Smith did not say that he could have been wearing gloves. "The prints might not be significant. That sort of place, girlfriends come and go. At first they want to clean up, cook their new guy a nice dinner. Then they give up, and usually move on. Has the autopsy been done yet?"

"It found a moderately high level of alcohol consumption, not enough to incapacitate him, but sufficient to make his reactions slow and instincts stupid. Caseman was a healthy, well-fed individual with no substantial health problems, other than a prodigious consumption of both alcohol and all sorts of drugs over many years. His teeth were in poor condition, probably had some niggling pain from a broken filling, indicating either no money for a dentist or content to self-medicate. He'd smoked a joint within an hour or so of his death, but had not engaged in sexual intercourse recently." Keller stopped talking abruptly. He turned to Lucky, and concern crossed his face. "Are you okay with this, Lucky? Molly and I can talk about it after dinner, if you'd prefer. For a while there I forgot where we are."

She held up her fork, speared with a chunk of dressing-covered romaine. "You're not ruining my appetite, if that's what you're thinking. I saw that man. I have that image in my head, and nothing you can say can be harder than that."

Molly put down her burger and touched her mom's empty hand. Lucky gave her a sad smile.

"Okay," Keller said. "The end of his most recent joint was found in an ashtray in the apartment. It was the only end there. Quantities of marijuana, enough to indicate regular consumption, although not dealing, were found in Caseman's room. And, I must add, in Matt's."

"One joint only, means he didn't entertain his guest."

"Or the guest didn't indulge. There were so many used beer bottles in that apartment it's hard to tell how much was drunk last night. But forensics think they have three that had probably been consumed within the previous couple of hours. Caseman's prints on them all."

"Three beers isn't much, not for a regular drinker."

"Right. So far we can't trace his movements since he left work at around six the evening previous."

"Where's he work?"

"He's a licensed mechanic. Works at a garage not far from town."

"Regular employment?"

"He's only been there a couple of months. Blechta tells me that that's the way it is here, lots of transients, seasonal jobs, young people drifting through."

"Sounds like Trafalgar."

"Yes, except that they have a much higher percentage of foreign students coming to work for a season or two. Makes it hard to conduct an investigation when your witness might have gone back to Australia or Austria."

"Cry me a river."

Keller laughed and Smith was pleased to hear it.

"John dug up some info on Caseman. Small-time troublemaker by the sounds of it. Certainly the sort to have enemies."

Otherwise, Keller had little of significance to report. No one knew, or was saying, what Barry Caseman had done between leaving the garage shortly after six and being found by Matt Keller just before three in the morning. Matt had worked at Reds Wine Bar until it closed at two, helped clean up, and left around two-thirty. He phoned his father from the apartment at quarter to three. He had not been seen since. The two men who shared the apartment with Matt and Caseman had not been home since the previous morning until the police escorted them in. When asked if anything was missing from Matt's room, they said they thought he kept camping equipment but couldn't remember when they'd seen it last. They knew nothing about Matt or Caseman's movements or activities. "We weren't, like, buddies, man, we just shared this shit-hole," was how the musician Alistair put it.

Matt's phone had been left behind in the apartment and it showed that all his recent calls were to and from his girlfriend, Tracey McMillan, his roommates, Reds Wine Bar, and the offices at Sunshine where he was scheduled to begin work as a ski instructor as soon as the hills opened for the season.

"Why would he leave his phone?" Smith asked. "Most people these days, it's like an extension of their arm."

"It was found under a dresser next to the door. We can only speculate he had it in his hand. He dropped it, and it bounced. Shock, perhaps, on seeing the body." Keller looked away. He cleared his throat. "Or dropped it when he went for the knife."

"Tell me about the girlfriend," Smith asked, running her last sweet potato fry through a smear of garlic aioli. The burger had been fabulous, the fries even better. "What's her name?"

"Tracey. She says she last saw Matt when she popped into the wine bar that evening. She didn't stay long and he was working when she left. She heard about the killing when she got to her own work at seven, tried phoning Matt but he didn't answer."

"What sort of a relationship do they have? Close, casual, romantic, or simply for sex?"

Keller looked confused. "I've no idea. Why?"

"If they were close, in love, say, he'd be more likely to confide in her than if she were a casual lay."

"My impression," Lucky said, "is that she's in love with him, or at least thinks she is, but is highly insecure in the relationship. That could be because he doesn't return the feelings, or because she's simply an insecure person. Which I suspect she is."

"Insecure in what way?"

"She's young and could be pretty, but her makeup's cheap and her hair's limp and badly cut. I suspect she trims her bangs herself. She's of normal weight, as far as I'm concerned, with a bit of a round tummy, but not skinny or fashionably fit and toned. Not much money, I'd guess, and probably not educated. She told me she's jealous of the women Matt meets at the wine bar. What are you thinking, dear?"

"I'm thinking I'd like to talk to her. With your permission, chief. She might confide better in me than in Sergeant Blechta. I assume he interviewed her?"

"He did. He didn't learn anything. If you think you can help, go ahead. As long as you remember you're here as a friend, not as a police officer."

"No worries. Sergeant Blechta made sure I know exactly where I stand on that point." Smith glanced at her watch. "It's almost eight. I'll give her a call, ask if she wants to go out for a drink or something."

"She works at a car rental company in the evening," Lucky said. "Don't they usually close around nine or so?"

"Good timing then. What's her number, Mom?"

Lucky pushed her empty plate aside and scrambled in her bag for the scrap of paper. She handed it to her daughter.

"Can I get you anything else?" Maura, Scotland, asked.

Smith would have loved another beer. She reluctantly passed, thinking she'd better not if she had to take this Tracey out drinking.

# Chapter Thirty

**GLOBAL CAR RENTAL. BANFF, ALBERTA. SUNDAY EVENING.**

The print on the computer screen shifted and wavered as Tracey blinked away tears. She wiped her eyes with a tissue, torn and damp from overuse. She'd managed to get through most of the day without thinking about Matt too much. She had to do her job, first at the restaurant, and later here at the car rental agency. Sure, Kevin had told her she could go home early if she needed to, but he didn't mean he'd *pay* her if she took time off. The boss of the car place was a right prick at the best of times so she wasn't about to ask him for any breaks.

The bell over the door tinkled to announce new arrivals. Tracey gave her eyes another wipe with the back of her hand, and tried to force her face into a smile. The couple leaned against the counter. "We're here to turn the car in. Glad we made it before you closed. There's a bear sitting at the side of the road up by Lake Louise and the traffic's stopped for miles as everyone tries to get a look."

"Did you see it?" Tracey asked.

"Yup. A big black bear. Just beautiful."

"Nice." Tracey completed their paperwork. She could see Tom outside, checking over the car, before getting into it and driving it to the back of the lot. This car was booked out again tomorrow.

The couple left and Tom sauntered in. He went into the cramped back office and came out with a mug of coffee. He hadn't offered to get her one. Not that he ever did.

"Heard anything more?" he said, sipping his drink.

She didn't need to ask what he was talking about. She shook her head and felt the tears gathering once again. "I'm so worried."

Tom shrugged. "You think Matt did it? Whacked old Barry?"

"Of course not. How can you say that?"

"I didn't say it, just asked what you think."

Tom had been edgy all evening, edgier than usual. He tried to hide it, but Tracey could tell he was spooked. Whether by the death of one of his roommates and the disappearance of another, or by the police attention, she didn't know. When she asked, he'd told her the cops had been around earlier, asking questions about Matt and Barry. He tried to play it casual, as if he'd brushed them off, but she recognized the bluster for what it was. A good deal of her childhood had been spent around men who got edgy at police attention.

Sometimes they had no reason to be, but often they did.

Tracey hadn't worked here for long before she started to wonder if Tom was up to something. Something not quite aboveboard. That business yesterday with the Japanese couple and the chip in the windshield and the way Tom occasionally hustled a car to a space at the back of the lot, against the fence, even when there were plenty of spots closer. When she was alone in the office and things were slow, she spent her time poking around on the computer. She was pretty sure the boss was involved; he wasn't a total fool. At best he turned a blind eye to Tom's activities, skimmed some off the top. Not that she intended to do anything with what she learned. She wasn't going to jeopardize her job by letting anyone know her suspicions.

"What you lookin' at?" Tom snapped.

"Nothing."

"Make sure you aren't. Fuck, but I need a drink."

Her phone rang, and she had it instantly in her hand. She checked the display—number withheld—and punched the button to answer, her heart racing. "Matt!"

"Uh, no. Sorry," a woman said. "This isn't Matt. Are you Tracey?"

Her heart dropped back into place. "Yeah."

"My name's Molly Smith. I know Matt's dad, Paul Keller, and I was hoping you and I could meet for a chat."

"Why?" Tom was listening, his face curious. He'd never paid any attention to Tracey before, except to sneer if he thought she was watching him. She turned her back.

"I'd like to help with the search for Matt. You met my mom earlier."

"I don't know."

"Are you at work?"

"Yes."

"It's eight now. When do you get off?"

"Nine."

"Why don't we meet for a drink? I'm new to town. Do you know a nice place?"

"I don't…"

"My treat."

"Reds Wine Bar. I can be there by nine-fifteen."

"Sounds good. I'll grab us a table."

"I like to sit at the bar."

"I guess that's okay. I'm wearing black jeans, a turquoise sweater, and a pale blue scarf. Thanks Tracey. See you soon."

Tracey put her phone away, wondering why she'd agreed to meet the unknown caller. If the woman had been a cop she would have said so, wouldn't she? She didn't have to go. Easy enough to phone back and say she'd changed her mind. And why on earth had she suggested Reds, where every corner would be full of the memory of Matt?

Stupid. Stupid. She wasn't dressed for Reds, and didn't have time to go home and change. Better to just not show up. Let the woman drink on her own.

"Who was that?" Tom asked.

"No one."

"Right. You're going to Reds with no one? Matt's not been gone a day and you're already meeting some other guy? Naughty, naughty, Tracey."

"It's a girl, if you must know. I like Reds, so there. Oh, and Tom. Do me a favor, will you, and fuck off."

# Chapter Thirty-one

**REDS WINE BAR. BANFF, ALBERTA. SUNDAY NIGHT.**

Molly Smith arrived at Reds Wine Bar shortly before nine. The place wasn't full, and a table for two beside the roaring gas fireplace looked highly appealing, but Tracey had said she wanted to sit at the bar, so the bar it would be.

She didn't have to look at the menu to know this place was going to be expensive. The lines were sleek and modern, the furniture black with red accents, the walls covered in smoky glass. The staff, both male and female, wore black pants and matching shirts with buttons and collars, accented by bright red bow ties, and the women sported red glass earrings. A small candle flickered at each table.

Smith pulled herself onto a bar stool, told the handsome waiter with a South African accent she was meeting someone and would have a glass of water while she waited. He brought her drink, full of ice and a slice of lemon, and gave her a wide smile that stopped a fraction short of being flirtatious. Charming and professional.

She considered asking him about Matt, but remembered that she wasn't here as a police officer. She might, later, but would hear what Tracey had to say first.

She'd been surprised Tracey suggested this place for their meeting. Lucky had said the girl was highly upset about Matt's disappearance, so you wouldn't have thought she'd want to come to the bar where he worked. Then again, maybe she wasn't as concerned as she pretended. Or maybe she just liked it here, and wanted to be in familiar surroundings.

The waiter brought her a menu. Small, wrapped in black leather. "Thought you might want to have a look while you're waiting. Where you from?"

"B.C."

"On holiday?"

"Sorta."

He had a deep, permanent tan, a shock of blond hair artificially highlighted, and blue eyes in a strong-featured face. "Let me know when you want to order." He gave her a smile full of teeth, and went to serve customers at the far end of the bar.

Smith flipped through the drinks menu. Boy, this little jaunt was going to cost her. Maybe she'd be lucky and Tracey would be a teetotaler.

The door opened, bringing in a gust of wet wind and a well-groomed couple in their thirties, looking very much as if they belonged in this sort of place. She shouldn't have trouble recognizing Tracey. Reds Wine Bar probably didn't get a lot of women on their own, and it wasn't busy tonight.

She glanced at her watch. Ten past nine. She'd give Tracey until ten o'clock to show. She'd sounded hesitant on the phone, might well change her mind.

If she did, Smith would then have to track her down.

At nine-twenty the bartender slid up to her. "Friend late? Why not have something in the meantime?" His blue eyes twinkled as they studied her face. Nice. He was flirting with her. "I can make some suggestions."

"South Africa?" she said.

"Yaw! You recognized the accent? Not many Canadians do."

She'd arrested a South African woman for drunk driving over the summer. She'd been over the limit by a substantial margin, and the Trafalgar police learned several new words that night. "I've met a few. I live in a tourist town, too."

Another gust of wind announced the opening of the door. The bartender's lips compressed into a tight line. The sparkle disappeared from his eyes, and the smile from his lips. Smith turned.

The girl was wrapped in a black nylon jacket, with a missing button, a tear in the right sleeve, and splotches of mud, new and dried, around the hem. Her cheeks were pudgy, her face pale, her lips cracked, and an acne spot was healing on the side of her nose. Her hair was plastered to her head and rainwater dripped onto the black tiled floor around her running shoes.

"Tracey," the bartender said, not a touch of warmth in his voice. "What are you doing here?"

"She's meeting me," Smith said.

He gave her a look, one that indicated she'd dropped a considerable amount in his opinion. Then he shrugged and said, "Call me when you're ready to order."

Smith gestured to the empty stool beside her. Tracey hopped up. She didn't take off her jacket. Smith held out her hand. The girl hesitated, and then accepted it. Her shake was wet and limp.

"Thanks for meeting me. Do you want to go to the washroom and dry off?"

"I'm fine."

"You're really wet."

"I *said* I'm fine."

"Okay. Would you like a drink?"

The wine list was on the counter in front of her, but Tracey didn't pick it up. "I'll have a glass of the Okanagan Chardonnay."

Smith bravely refrained from swallowing audibly. "Okay." She waved to the bartender and placed the order for two glasses. She'd come in a cab—more expense—expecting she might have to have a drink along with her "guest."

Tracey glanced around the room. She shifted uncomfortably on the stool. Water dripped from her hair and her jacket. "Why don't we take a table?" Smith said.

"No. I like sitting here."

"Okay."

Their drinks arrived, a splash of golden liquid in long-stemmed glasses. The bartender rolled his eyes at Smith and gave Tracey a barely concealed sneer.

"Prick," Tracey said to his retreating back.

"You know him?"

"I know everyone here. I come in sometimes when Matt's working. So we can be together. I buy my drinks, don't cause any trouble. He," she nodded down the bar, "his name's Andre, says he's having a gap year, whatever the hell that is. I suspect Andre's been having a gap year for the last ten years."

A gap year is a British term for a year off between high school and university. Andre had to be pushing thirty, if not past it. "Never mind him. My mom's Paul Keller's friend. She called to tell me what happened, so I came to see if I could help."

Tracey swallowed a good-sized mouthful of her wine. She didn't ask why this woman would think she could help with a police matter, and Smith didn't enlighten her. She took a sip of her own wine, and almost groaned with pleasure as the wealth of flavors released themselves in her mouth. She feared she was being ruined for any drink she might actually be able to afford. "This is good."

"It should be for what it costs," Tracey said. "Look, I don't know much of anything. If I did…if I did I'd do something. I called Alistair earlier. He said the cops are asking about Matt's camping stuff. He thinks it's gone. That means Matt's gone into the woods."

"You're friends with the guys he shares the apartment with?"

Tracey shook her head. About a teaspoonful of liquid remained in the bottom of her glass. Smith waved Andre over. Two more. It would have been cheaper to have bought a bottle.

"Not friends, no. Alistair's okay, I guess. Just looking for his big break. Aren't we all?" She glanced, probably unwittingly, down the bar. "All of us who don't have a rich daddy keeping us on a permanent *gap year*. Tom works at the car rental place where I do. He's a prick, but Barry was the worst of the lot. I know you're not supposed to speak badly about the dead, but

I don't care. He was a mean bastard, and he made Matt mean. Matt followed him around, did what Barry told him to. Things'll be a lot better, now Barry's gone."

For a moment, Smith considered asking Tracey what *she* was doing in the wee hours of this morning. She looked at the wet eyes, the quivering chin. Tracey might have killed Barry in a moment of anger, but she wouldn't leave Matt twisting in the wind. And it was highly unlikely she was that good an actress. Besides, Smith reminded herself, she wasn't here to solve the murder of Barry Caseman. She just wanted to find Matt Keller. To make her mom happy again. And then go home.

The bar began filling up with the after-dinner crowd. The air was full of the scent of expensive perfume and good food; the fireplaces glowed with light and warmth, and Smith was hot in her sweater and scarf. Tracey's face was flushed with the wine, the heat, and the strength of her emotions, but she didn't so much as unbutton her jacket. Smith was about to point Tracey toward the coat rack in the corner and then thought better of it. The girl's pants were black, faded from too many washes, spattered with mud, her running-shoes' laces torn. She was probably still wearing her uniform shirt. All the other patrons were well-dressed, well-groomed, fresh from dining in expensive hotels. Even Smith herself, never exactly a fashion plate, had combed her hair into a sleek ponytail, dressed in crisp dark jeans, a pure-wool sweater and silk scarf, and put gold hoops into her ears. She picked up her glass, and light from the candles on the bar sparkled off the diamond on her finger. Tracey eyed it, then looked away, and finished her drink.

"Have you had dinner, Tracey?" Smith asked. She certainly wasn't hungry, not after that huge burger and mountain of fries, but she didn't want Tracey having any more to drink on an empty stomach. Smith was not a detective; she didn't know much about conducting an interview. Not that this was an interview, but she figured she'd have to stay as long as Tracey did. Maybe the girl had something to say, something she didn't even know she knew, which had to be worked out of her slowly and carefully.

Then again, maybe Smith was just wasting a heck of a lot of money. Tracey shook her head, and Smith asked for a plate of spring rolls and another of bruschetta.

Tracey ate all the food, and threw back four drinks. Smith had three, more than she should but they were so good, increasingly regretting not only the waste of money but of time. Tracey's conversation was mostly a litany of complaints, about where she lived, where she worked, the people—other than Matt—she knew. She had nothing to say tonight she hadn't told Lucky earlier. She hadn't heard from Matt; she didn't know where he might have gone; she had no idea why he'd run. She was adamant, although Smith hadn't asked, that Matt would never have killed Barry. When asked to speculate as to why Matt hadn't phoned the police, or waited until his father arrived, Tracey shrugged and said Matt hated anything to do with the cops.

Smith asked if Tracey had ever met Matt's family.

"His mom came to visit about a month ago. His parents are divorced, I guess you know that, and his mom lives in Calgary. She's got a new boyfriend, some old rich dude." Tracey sighed, a trace of envy in her voice. "They stayed at the Banff Springs, and Matt and I went for lunch one day. It's so nice there. Matt… well, I don't think Matt had told his mom I was coming. She looked surprised to see me with him. Her boyfriend said we could have anything we wanted for lunch, even drinks. I thought he was nice. Matt didn't like him. I guess a guy wouldn't, eh?"

"Wouldn't what?"

"Like the new man who's screwing your mom. Makes you think about things you'd rather not think about. Easy to pretend your parents don't sleep together, isn't it? But not when she's with a guy and they hold hands and smile at each other and kiss each other and stuff."

Smith squirmed in her seat. Her parents had held hands and smiled at each other and kissed up until the day Andy died. But she understood what Tracey meant. She wondered about Tracey's family, if her parents didn't even kiss each other.

She wasn't here to learn about Tracey's home life.

They'd been in the bar about an hour and a half when Tracey slipped off her stool, saying, "Be right back." Smith watched her walk, somewhat unsteadily, toward the back. Andre gestured to Smith's empty glass. "Another?"

"Just the bill, thanks."

"Get what you came for?"

"What do you mean?"

"You're not friends with that *slet*. All you've done is get her liquored up and ask questions about Matt."

Smith didn't know what a *slet* was, but she figured she didn't want to know. She shrugged.

"You don't look like a copper, but I've been wrong before."

*I'm sure you have.* "Why don't you like her? She seems harmless enough."

He shrugged. "She's a right whinger. Follows Matt around with her tongue practically hanging out. He's happy enough to go along with it, so she must be giving him something he likes, 'cause it sure can't be her fashion sense."

"Maybe she's just a nice person. Ever thought of that?"

"That must be it… 'cause Matt's such a nice guy."

"What do you know about him?"

"You a cop?"

"My mother's good friends with Matt's dad. We're trying to find him."

Andre glanced down the length of the bar. No one needed his attention. A table of six was getting to their feet, shrugging into coats, searching for umbrellas. "I don't have much to do with him. He does his job, I do mine. Rarely at the same time."

"Have you heard from him since last night?"

"No, and I wouldn't expect him to come to me asking for anything."

"Would you tell the police if you did hear?"

He gave her a look. "I wouldn't keep any secrets for him, if that's what you're asking. I'm here on a work visa, and I must keep my nose clean. Get it?"

Smith got it. "I'll have the bill now."

"Hey, watch it!" Tracey had tripped and fallen into a chair. The woman seated in it did not look pleased and her companion was getting to his feet. A waitress hurried over.

"Can you call me a cab?" Smith asked Andre.

# Chapter Thirty-two

**GRIZZLY RESORT, OUTSIDE OF TRAFALGAR, BRITISH COLUMBIA. MONDAY MORNING.**

First thing Monday morning, John Winters drove out of town toward the location of the proposed Grizzly Resort. He hadn't been there for a couple of years, and wanted to see how far the new development had progressed before tomorrow's meeting with the RCMP to discuss strategy should opposition to the resort continue.

Which everyone knew it would.

It was Thanksgiving Day, a holiday for most people. Winters didn't expect anyone to be at work, just wanted to have a quick look around. Almost everything in town was closed, including Big Eddie's Coffee Emporium, and thus Winters was forced to do with a mug of Jim Denton's execrable coffee.

Trafalgar was situated in a bowl, a valley surrounded by mountains on all sides. As soon as he drove past the car dealership and the kennels, the road began to climb and all signs of habitation dropped away. Five minutes from the office and he might as well be in the middle of the wilderness. The trees, pine, spruce, fir mostly, were tall and dark. On the few aspens and cottonwoods only a handful of yellow leaves remained. Ten minutes further and he was at the top of the first pass, where the road branched off to the Blue Sky ski hills and fresh snow was sprinkled on the branches. But the sun was rising and the snow would soon be gone. For now. Winter was on its way.

Then he was descending again, so fast his ears popped, and in twenty minutes he'd met up with another highway and the entrance to the resort.

No one was around, but signs with pictures of grizzly bears and environmental slogans were propped up against trees. A barrier that wouldn't stop an elderly lady in a walker guarded the access road. Winters parked his car and climbed out. He had scarcely reached the No Admittance sign before a man came out of the woods.

Not as casually undefended as it appeared.

The man wore the uniform of a private security company. He held a radio in one hand and lifted the other in the universal halt gesture. "Private property."

Winters flashed his badge. "Heard you had some trouble yesterday."

"Wasn't my shift, but yeah, a bunch of tree huggers showed up. They kept off the property, marched up and down, yelling and looking stupid. Mounties were here, looking bored."

"Let's hope it stays that way. Mind if I have a look around?"

"Should be okay. The boss is in."

"I didn't think he would be, with the holiday."

"Boss don't seem to care much about time off. Guess that's why he's the boss. I'll tell him you're coming. Office is around that bend, about a hundred yards."

"I know where it is."

The guard lifted his radio, pushed a button, and spoke over a burst of static.

Winters did know where the office was. He'd been here before, first escorting Eliza to a fancy al fresco party and later on a police action, back when Reg Montgomery and Frank Clemmins, and then Clemmins alone, had plans for a luxury fractional-ownership resort.

The signs had changed, new logo, new look to the depiction of the proposed buildings and grounds. The land along the highway was thickly forested, but as soon as Winters rounded the bend, all he could see was mud and holes in the ground. The door of a double-wide trailer opened, and a man came out to greet him—smile broad, arm outstretched. Winters climbed the steps.

"Sergeant Winters. Pleased to meet you at last. I'm Darren Fernhaugh. Chief Keller speaks highly of you." Winters knew the chief was in contact with Fernhaugh. He didn't need the blatant reminder. "What brings you out here today? Not that it isn't a pleasure." Fernhaugh stepped back, waved Winters into his domain.

The office hadn't changed much. A receptionist's desk, now unoccupied, inside the door, a large center room, two small rooms, one an office, the other a cramped meeting space. The walls were covered with site plans and blueprints. This was the headquarters of the construction site itself, the sales department and business offices were in Trafalgar.

"I'm meeting with the RCMP tomorrow," Winters explained, "to talk about security."

"Good. I fear we're going to need it. Damn tree huggers. We don't have much time left until we have to shut work down for the winter. I don't want any more delays. Do you want a look around?"

"I've been here before, but I'd like to see what's new. You bought the place from Frank Clemmins. Are you using his plans?"

"Take a seat. Can you I get you a coffee? I've nothing ready, but it won't take a minute."

"No thanks."

Fernhaugh swept blueprints aside and Winters pulled a chair up to the table in the center of the room. Fernhaugh went to a filing cabinet and brought out a brochure. Multi-page, thick glossy paper, colored photographs. He handed it to Winters who flipped through it while Fernhaugh said, "Clemmins was building fractional-ownership properties. I'm putting in single-family vacation homes." Obviously a sales tool, the pamphlet showed drawings of neat buildings with wide front porches nestled amongst giant trees. Other drawings were of swimming pools and golf courses, a few photographs of smiling silver-haired men and women drinking wine around a table scattered with glowing candles or enjoying a few beers on a spacious deck. There appeared to be five floor plans available. Winters whistled at the price.

"Two hundred thousand? For Southern B.C. wilderness property? Surely that's only for the land?"

Fernhaugh beamed. "We're aiming at the lower-middle of the market. Folks in Vancouver or Calgary who want, who *deserve*, a piece of our country's vast riches. A place they can bring their children, and then their children's children. Something to pass on, down through the generations. Memories most of all. Because at Fernhaugh Resorts we believe, truly believe, that everyone should have equal opportunity, we've done all we can to bring our vacation homes within the budget of the average consumer."

"Isn't that fractional ownership then, like Clemmins had planned? Where people don't fully own their places themselves but share?"

"Fractional ownership. A nice idea, but it didn't work out. No one wants to *share* their homes. They don't want to plan their vacation time around people they don't even know. A week here, a week there, scrambling for Christmas, summer long weekends, the best bits of time. Clean up every time you leave and take all your belongings with you. No, we offer full ownership. Of the cottages."

*Nice speech.* Winters peered at one of the floor plans. It looked attractive: kitchen, living room, two bedrooms, even a loft space. He looked at the tiny scale at the bottom of the page, blinked and looked again. "How big are these *homes*?"

"Between seven and nine hundred square feet. Designed for maximum use of every inch of space." Seven hundred square feet. Eliza's condo in Vancouver, which Winters thought pokey, was eight hundred. Not a lot of room for all the children and grandchildren who were supposedly going to flock to vacation here. "How many of these cottages are you planning on building?"

"Two hundred and fifty."

So much for anything resembling privacy. Or peace and quiet.

"All our residents will have full access to the common areas. Swimming pools, party rooms, children's play area, shuttles to the ski hills in winter, the lake in summer. A restaurant and coffee shop. Spectacular mountain views, many overlooking the river."

"For an extra cost."

Fernhaugh grinned. "Five hundred thousand for the cliffside cottages. None of the worry or expense of maintenance. All that will be covered by a small monthly fee. Exactly like a condo building. Interested, Sergeant?"

Winters put down the brochure. "I don't think so."

"Don't mock it." Fernhaugh's voice deepened as he dropped the sales pitch. "Why shouldn't the ordinary working folk, blue-collar workers with two jobs, three kids, be able to own a place in the mountains? If I told you I was building twenty multimillion-dollar chalets on the same property you wouldn't turn your nose up."

"Regardless of the size of the cottage, two-hundred and fifty families will take up more resources, have more of an environmental impact, than twenty who probably won't even use their place all that much."

"Because they have other places to go, other lands to despoil, if that's the way you look at it."

"I'm not looking at it any way, Mr. Fernhaugh, I assure you. I'm trying to estimate what sort of opposition you're going to get."

"Opposition. Aye, there's the rub. Tree huggers to the left of me, corporate raiders to the right."

"What do you mean?"

"To the right? This is prime land, Sergeant Winters. I got it at an exceptionally good price. Frank Clemmins wanted to be rid of it. We're friends and he gave me first refusal. I worked darn hard to put a consortium together so I could buy it. You think my project is going to be environmentally unfriendly? Believe it or not, I do intend to make the least impact we can, and I intend to put my money where my mouth is. Others, maybe not so much. I've received some offers to buy. Not ones I'm interested in." He got to his feet with a sigh. "We've cleared the ground for the first bunch of cottages, hope to get the foundations laid while the weather holds. Come on, I'll show you the layout."

# Chapter Thirty-three

**BANFF SPRINGS HOTEL. BANFF, ALBERTA. MONDAY MORNING.**

Smith groaned and pounded the button on the alarm clock. If this was being a detective, she'd stay in uniform, thank you very much.

She wasn't used to drinking so heavily. She might have a beer now and again when she and Adam went to a bar to hear live music, or a glass of wine at a rare nice dinner out. Sometimes she'd go with the boys and girls from work if they were celebrating a promotion or a retirement but now she wasn't living in town, a stagger away from most bars, she had to keep herself sober if Adam wasn't there to drive them home. Three glasses of wine with Tracey wasn't so much, but then after…

She downed the remainder of the water she'd had the foresight to leave on the bedside table and climbed out of the big, luxurious, welcoming, warm, comfortable bed.

She was due to meet her mom and the chief for breakfast when the grill opened at six-thirty to fill them in on what she'd learned last night. After dinner the chief had gone back to the RCMP detachment to find out what was happening. If Matt had been found, he'd have phoned to tell her, no matter what the time.

She shook a couple of aspirin into her palm, swallowed them with water, and headed for the shower. She let the steamy water caress her face and pound her back for a long time. The evening with Tracey had been a total waste of time. She'd learned nothing, other than a listing of Matt Keller's virtues, numerous as they were.

Smith did feel somewhat sorry for Tracey. She seemed so *needy*, so desperate for approval, well aware that she didn't belong where she wanted to be. She hadn't said much about her family or where she was from, and Smith didn't care. She'd heard it all before. Some people had bad childhoods and got over it; some had great childhoods and turned out to be miserable adults determined to make everyone around them equally miserable.

Still it was tough to be young sometimes, as Smith well remembered. Tracey was vulnerable, brittle, wanting approval of people like the charming, handsome, vacuous Andre. Tracey held on stubbornly to her pride, as in refusing to remove her jacket, and was fiercely loyal to Matt. Whether Matthew Keller deserved that loyalty was another matter entirely.

Andre had ordered them a cab and they'd left the wine bar, Smith leaving the miserly tip she figured he deserved. Tracey said she'd walk, but Smith didn't think that was a good idea. The girl could barely stand upright. At least she didn't have a drinking problem. Not if a few glasses of a really good wine could just about knock her out.

Besides, Smith wanted to check out where Tracey lived. The cab ride through the dark, wet streets was short, and it pulled up in front of a nondescript two-story apartment building. Smith instructed the cabbie to wait, and helped Tracey inside.

"I don't feel too good," Tracey said, fumbling in her pockets for her key.

She got the door open, and they walked up one flight of stairs. The building was nothing fancy, but it was clean and well lit. They went down the corridor to the apartment at the end. Tracey found another key and, after some difficulty, got the door open.

Typical transient female accommodations, moderately tidy with movie-star and cute animal posters on the walls, candle stubs in glass holders on the tables, colorful throws over the back of the sofa, cardboard boxes piled in the corners.

"Which is your room?" Smith said, helping Tracey take off the wet-again jacket. A hallway went past the kitchen with three doors leading off. One of which was probably the bathroom.

Tracey dropped onto the couch. "Here."

"What?"

"This is my room. All I can afford. This sofa. Matt and me are going to get a place together once ski season starts." She lay down and tucked a cushion under her head. "Thanks for the drinks, Molly. Let's do it again sometime." And, fully dressed and still in her damp running shoes, she fell asleep.

Smith let herself out of the apartment. The taxi was waiting.

"Do you know where the Mandrake Root is?" she asked the driver.

"Sure."

"Let's go then."

The Mandrake Root, Tracey had told her, was the bar where Matt's roommate Alistair played. The cab pulled onto a side street, and light and sound spilled from the building at the center of the block. Smith paid and got out of the taxi. A small crowd, under thirty-five mostly, milled around outside, trying to find some shelter from the rain in the awning above the front door. The usual crowd of smokers, out to get their fix.

Smith walked into the bar and stood in the entrance, looking around. It was like countless others: a collection of battered wooden tables, big-screen TVs mounted on the walls, a bar along one side, bottles on shelves behind, a man and a woman busy pouring drinks and taking money. A raised floor at the far end of the room served as the stage. Musical equipment was stacked on the stage, but no one was there now. Break time.

The place wasn't overly crowded and Smith made her way to the bar. A young woman, dressed all in black with black makeup and nail polish, black jewelry, and short black hair, leaned over. "What can I get you?"

"I'm looking for Alistair Campbell."

"You probably passed him. He's outside taking a smoke break."

"Thanks. How will I recognize him?"

The woman shrugged. "Short, thin."

Smith made her way back outside. The description was so vague as to be almost useless, but not entirely, and there weren't a lot of men to choose from.

"Alistair?"

"Yeah." He turned to her with a smile, expecting an eager fan. He was cute, with a youthful face, a mass of curly black hair, long lashes above warm brown eyes, and good skin. He was very short, at about five feet five, and must weigh a hundred pounds soaking wet. Which he wasn't now because he kept himself under the shelter of the awning.

Smith spoke in a low voice. "Can I buy you a beer? I'd like to ask a couple of questions about Matt Keller."

His attractive eyes narrowed. "Why? I've told the cops all I'm going to."

She repeated her line about being a friend of the family, while taking note of his words. *All I'm going to say,* not *all I know.*

"I doubt I can help, but it's your dime. Break's over in a minute, time to get back at it. Have a drink. I'll join you at the end of this set."

He ground his cigarette beneath his foot and went back into the bar. Most of the smokers followed, as did Smith.

She found a table in a far corner, and sat with her back to the wall. A waitress sauntered up and put a beer mat in front of her. "What can I getcha?"

"I'm waiting for Alistair to finish."

The woman's grin wasn't friendly. "Cover charge if you don't order a drink is thirty bucks."

"Thirty?" Smith would bet good money the waitress made that up on the spot. "Okay, I'll have a Kokanee."

"Be right up."

Smith drank her beer and listened to the music. It was better than she'd expected. The band consisted of four men: two guitar players, a drummer, and a singer. Alistair played guitar and sang backup vocals. They mostly played classic rock, the old stuff

Lucky liked, but alternated that with some heavy metal and even a couple of what they said were their own compositions.

Smith finished her beer easily and ordered another. No one bothered her, and she was glad of it.

When the set broke, Alistair pulled up a chair at her table. "I'll have a Kilkenny draft." She ordered that, and then one more for herself to keep him company.

A couple of his bandmates had been approached by women, smiling, simpering, flirting, but Alistair had been left alone. Alistair was small man, not only short but with bones as substantial as those of a sparrow, and not a spare inch of either flesh or muscle. She thought of Adam, at six feet four and two hundred solid pounds, and of women who'd be happy to see him single again.

Life could be as tough, she suspected, for a small man as for an overweight woman.

Their drinks arrived. Alistair took a long pull at his beer, and came up with a foam mustache.

"Last time I saw Matt," he wiped the foam off with the back of his hand, "was Saturday afternoon, at the apartment. He was getting ready for work. I didn't go home Saturday night after we finished. Some of us went jamming, work off some steam, drink, maybe have a joint or two."

Smith, the police officer, let that one slide.

"I got home around six to find my place crawling with cops."

"You haven't heard from him?"

"No."

"What can you tell me about Matt? He ever been in any trouble you know of?"

"Nah. Look, Molly, we weren't friends, we didn't hang out. Didn't have much in common, other than where we lived."

"How about Barry?"

"Barry. Now he was a nasty piece of work."

"In what way?"

Alistair shrugged. He finished his beer. Eyed it pointedly. Smith got the hint, and lifted her hand to attract the waitress' attention. She held up two fingers. She needed to keep drinking so this would look more like a chat than an interrogation, but this would be her fourth beer. On top of three glasses of wine.

Better slow down.

"He just was," Alistair said. "Barry argued all the time. About his share of the rent money, about who ate the last of the three-day-old pizza, or who'd drunk his beer."

"Not the sort of thing you kill a man over."

Alistair grinned. "I don't know. I might kill a man took the last of my beer. But seriously, I did wonder sometimes if he was on the take."

"What do you mean?"

"He seemed to have more money than he should, wasn't shy about flashing it around, either. More than he got from the garage, I mean. Yeah, he did some odd jobs, fixed friends' cars, that sort of thing. But nothing that would bring in big money."

"And he had big money?"

"Sometimes. I'm not talking tens of thousands, you know. But an extra couple of hundred, maybe a thou, here and there. It seemed to come and go. When he was flush, he liked to spend it."

"How do you think he got this money? Dealing?"

"Unlikely. If he was selling drugs, he'd have tried to push it on his buddies, wouldn't he? It's possible he was smart enough not to want to shit on his own doorstep, but smart isn't a word I'd use to describe Barry. He was a mechanic at a garage, right? I figure he was gaming the system. Charging for repairs that weren't needed, or buying used parts and saying they were new."

"Did you tell the police this?"

Alistair's lip curled. In another time or place he might have spat on the floor. "What do you take me for? I have as little to do with the cops as I can. That sergeant who spoke to me? I felt like leaping to my feet and shouting *Seig Heil*. Get him out the door as fast as possible, that's all I wanted. Pigs."

"Why are you telling me then?"

"You bought me a beer. Two beers. My loyalty comes cheap. And maybe because you're one gorgeous chick and I want to get to know you better. Stick around, we finish at two. There's a party at Suzie's place after. Some good B.C. bud I've been told. Not that I indulge, of course."

She wiggled the fingers of her left hand. The diamond flashed.

"I was hoping that was just for decoration."

"'Fraid not."

The tone of conversation around them changed as the band members pushed themselves away from their tables and got to their feet. Alistair finished his drink. "See you around, maybe."

"Maybe. Thanks for this."

She listened to the first song of the set, and then phoned for a cab and went outside to wait. The rain had stopped and the cold, moist air hit her like a slap in the face. Her head spun and her stomach rolled over. She waited for her ride under the awning.

A police car pulled up and an officer got out. He studied her, his eyes narrow with suspicion. "What are you doing standing here?"

She suppressed a beery burp. "Waiting for a cab."

"You by yourself?"

She burped. "Yes."

He didn't look impressed. "Where are you staying?"

"Banff Springs."

One eyebrow rose. He was an older guy, waiting impatiently for retirement. She did not smile. The last thing she wanted was for him to think she was standing alone in front of a bar because she was soliciting.

Lights flashed on the street as her taxi had pulled up. She'd run for it gratefully, knew the Mountie was watching her.

Now, as the shower ran and some life came back to her body, as well as her head, she tried to estimate how much she'd spent last night. Way more than she should have, that was for sure.

She turned off the hot water, and let a blast of icy spray finish waking her up.

While she dressed she admired her room. Such a waste. That huge, lovely, soft bed, and no one to share it with. Wondering if Adam had managed to successfully cook the turkey, she headed out the door.

For breakfast she ordered tomato juice, which she hated; bacon, which she never ate; fried eggs; fried potatoes; and white toast with lots of butter. And tea, gallons of tea. For once, she wished she drank coffee.

Her mother eyed her suspiciously. "Not feeling too good this morning, dear?"

"Give me a break, Mom. I was working. Tracey was pretty much a waste of time. She had nothing new to say. But I did learn some interesting things from Matt's roommate, Alistair, about Barry."

"What sort of things?" Paul Keller asked. He looked like hell. He'd missed a couple of spots shaving, his cheeks were hollow shadows, his eyes red and tired, his face grim, and he emitted the faint sour smell of extreme stress along with tobacco from his morning cigarette.

"Alistair figures he was getting money from somewhere. The sort of money that came in suddenly, not as part of a regular paycheck."

"Drugs?"

"Probably not. Alistair never saw him dealing. Alistair thinks maybe something dodgy at the garage."

"That would tie in with what we know about Barry Caseman. Can't keep his nose clean."

"He runs with the sort of people who might take action, if they think they've been cheated or insulted. Or for not much of a reason at all."

"Exactly."

His roommate, Matt Keller, might well know those people too. And, if he came home in time to see who'd killed Barry, decide it would be a good time to leave town with no forwarding address. "Are the police looking at anyone in particular?"

"They're still interviewing Caseman's acquaintances. Some of whom are known to the police. Most have alibis. No one stands out as having been in the right place for the right reasons. Caseman was out drinking with some buddies Saturday night. Apparently he left early, before the bars closed, which was unusual for him."

"They say why he left early?"

Keller shook his head.

"Anyone seen to leave with him?"

"No."

"Anything else new with the investigation?"

"Not much. Blechta's going through the motions, interviewing friends, people Caseman came into contact with. His family's been notified. They're coming from Nova Scotia, arriving this afternoon. Blechta's circulated a photo of Matt. Asking anyone who saw him to come forward."

"Nothing yet?"

"No. He seems to have dropped off the face of the Earth." Keller wiped his hand over his eyes. Lucky reached out and touched his arm. "When they find him," the chief swallowed, "they're going to charge him. I have to say, I'd do the same. They have no other suspects. There's no doubt he was at the scene at the time, and now he's run.

"Matt left the place where he works around two-thirty, according to all witnesses, give or take five minutes. It's a ten-minute or so walk from there to his apartment." Keller had ordered eggs Benedict. He pushed the food around on his plate, scarcely touching it, making a mess of yellow yolk and hollandaise sauce.

"He called me at two forty-five. The autopsy estimates the time of death as very shortly before the police arrived." Keller rubbed his face. "Matt is definitely in the frame, timewise, and right now he's the only one who is. It's considered unlikely Caseman was entertaining visitors prior to being killed. Only one joint in the ashtray, no evidence of anyone else having a drink, although Caseman himself drank three beers shortly before he died."

"Anyone see Matt—leaving, I mean?"

"They've interviewed the neighbors. No one saw anything. It was late, and dark that night."

"Not too late," Smith said. "The bars close at two. Partyers would still be around."

"True, but once you get off Banff Avenue and away from the hotels, people have to get up in the morning for work. A woman who lives in an apartment down the hall was awake at the time in question with her baby. She thinks she heard knocking on a door. But she can't be positive where it was coming from. She didn't have anything favorable to say about the residents of that unit. Coming and going at all hours, parties, loud music. The police have had noise complaints there."

"Did she know them at all? Barry and Matt, in particular?"

"She says she's never so much as exchanged a word with them. The residents of that apartment come and go, one day one of them's gone and a new one's moved in."

"Barry worked at a car repair shop. Alistair thinks he was doing fake repairs or charging new prices for used parts. Maybe the other mechanics or the shop owner figured he was getting greedy or they had a falling out."

"We're not here to investigate the murder," Lucky said, stirring her yogurt. "We're here to find Matt. If we can."

"The police might not know about Barry's other income. Alistair didn't have nice things to say about Blechta. I suspect he wouldn't have told me if he knew I'm an officer. He was, if I may say, trying to make nice 'cause he wanted to get into my pants."

Lucky snorted, and a smile appeared on Keller's face. It wasn't much of a smile, but it went a long way toward lightening the mood around the table.

"I've an idea. Do you need your car today, Chief?"

"I can take a cab into town, get a ride with the horsemen if I need one. Why?"

"Because mine's being used as a kennel at the moment. And yours is newer and in better shape."

"Have you been out to check on Sylvester?" Lucky asked.

"Yes. He's fine. I'm thinking the chief's car is having mechanical problems. It needs to be checked out."

"Good thinking," Keller said. "Doesn't hurt to follow up on what small lead we have."

"You're a pleasant, middle-aged lady, Mom, with no idea whatsoever of how a car works."

"That's certainly true," Lucky said. "You want me to take the car to the garage where Barry worked?"

"Yup. Tell them you heard a noise. It's stopped now, but it keeps starting up again. They'll check it out. If they're honest, they'll find nothing wrong."

"If not, I'll need a very expensive brake job."

"Right. Even if Barry was on the take, it doesn't mean the other guys there are, but it's difficult to run a scam in a place like that on your own. Inventory control, billing, all that stuff isn't done by one mechanic. I took the liberty of checking out the garage on the Internet before coming down. It's independently owned, but looks like a good-sized place. You might be able to get a feel for things there, Mom."

"Did you notice when they open?"

"Eight."

"I'll call them then. If this wasn't so serious, and we weren't all so worried, I'd be rather excited at going undercover."

"Spare us," Smith said.

# Chapter Thirty-four

**TRACEY'S APARTMENT. BANFF, ALBERTA. MONDAY MORNING.**

"Hey, wake up. What the hell's the matter with you? Wake up."

Tracey swam toward the surface. She'd been dreaming about Matt, dreaming they were in the desert, searching for water. Water, she needed water. Her stomach lurched, and she tried to roll over, tried to bury her face into her pillow. But the pillow was snatched away from underneath her.

"She's drunk," a voice said.

"Stupid bitch. Wake up," said another.

Tracey rolled over, shielding her eyes from the sun streaming through the windows. "What time is it?"

"Eight."

"Shit." She was supposed to be at work at seven. She'd forgotten to set her alarm when she went to bed last night. Went to bed. Did she even go to bed? She was on the couch, and it hadn't been opened up to make her bed. Instead of sheets and her quilt and a proper pillow, she'd pulled the red throw over her and dropped her head on Crystal's fancy pillow with the embroidered kittens and tassels.

"Ugh," Crystal said. "Look at this. You've drooled all over it."

They were standing over her, Amanda and Crystal. Crystal shook the pillow in reproach. Amanda's mouth was a tight line of disapproval. "You're drunk."

"Am not." Tracey struggled to get up. She was fully dressed, still had her shoes on. What the hell had happened? Traces of memory drifted through her head. She'd been to Reds. Matt? No, not with Matt. With a woman. The night began to come into focus. They'd drunk wine and talked. The woman was nice, friendly, had plenty of money to spend. Andre had tried flirting with her, but she'd brushed him off. Good for her. She'd asked questions, lots of questions. Tracey's stomach rolled over, she was going to be…

"Don't you dare be sick," Amanda shrieked.

Tracey ran for the bathroom. She was in there for a long time. Her stomach wanted to throw up, but there wasn't much to come up. She washed her face and drank a lot of water.

She was late for work. Kevin would have a fit. She needed a shower, but she'd have to call Kevin first. She opened the door and came out. Amanda and Crystal had tidied up the couch and were sitting on it, faces stern with matching looks of disapproval.

"This isn't working out, Tracey," Amanda said. "We've been talking it over, and it's time for you to leave."

"Leave?"

"Yes leave. Move out."

"But…"

"We don't mean like today," Crystal said. Amanda threw her a sour look. "How about the end of the month? That should give you time to find someplace else, won't it? You can't be happy here, anyway, not sleeping on the couch."

"Weren't you and your boyfriend going to move in together next month anyway?" Amanda said, malice glittering behind her excessively made-up eyes.

"We won't have the money until December," Tracey said.

"I guess another month…" Crystal began.

Amanda cut her off. "Another month will run into two months. And before you know it, it'll be summer and she'll still be here, stinking the place up. Besides, who knows where the boyfriend will be next month? In prison probably."

Tears gathered behind Tracey's eyes, but she refused to let them fall. Not in front of these two. Matt was not going to prison. Matt hadn't hurt anyone. He was scared and he ran, that was all. He'd be back, maybe he was back now. Maybe he'd tried to call her and she hadn't heard because she was asleep. She patted her pockets. No phone. The jacket she'd been wearing last night was tossed over a chair. She crossed the room in two strides, grabbed it, thrust her hands into one pocket and then the other. Nothing. Throwing the jacket aside, she pushed between Amanda and Crystal, dug her hands into the back of the couch, felt among the crumbs and lost coins. The girls jumped to their feet with squeals of protest.

"Give me your phone," Tracey said to Crystal.

"What?"

"I said give me your phone!"

"Okay, don't have kittens." She handed it over. Tracey dialed her own number, her hands shaking so much she had to keep correcting herself.

Then, from beneath the coffee table, music sounded.

She threw Crystal her phone and dived under the table. Tracey came up with her own phone and checked the display.

Disappointment washed over her. She dropped onto the couch. Two calls—the one she'd just made and the restaurant.

"I coulda told you you'd gotten a call," Amanda said. "Without so much fucking drama. I heard the damn thing earlier."

"It's my work, wondering where I am, I guess."

"Better tell them then, hadn't you? Look, I have to go. Unlike some of us, I don't like to be late for work." Amanda was a clerk at a store, a place that sold low-end, made-in-China souvenirs: plastic carvings of bears and moose, sweatshirts with panoramic pictures of high mountain ranges, fake "native-Canadian" jewelry, mass-produced prints of famous paintings. "End of the month, Tracey. Be outta here." She picked up her bag and left, slamming the door behind her for emphasis.

Crystal gave Tracey an embarrassed shrug. No point in arguing with Crystal. She'd agree to anything Tracey asked and then say she hadn't meant it when Amanda got through talking to her. Amanda's name was the one on the lease. "It's probably for the better," Crystal said. "You don't want to hang around here. I saw Matt's picture on the news. The police are looking for him. He killed that guy, Tracey. Forget about him. Go back to Ontario. See you later. Maybe we can catch a movie or something before you go." Crystal left.

For a moment, Tracey considered doing just that. Packing her stuff and going home. She didn't have much, nothing more than would fit into her two suitcases. She could be on a Greyhound bus headed east by noon. Her mom would take her in. Say what you liked about Tracey's mom, she always took her daughter in.

If Matt cared, really cared about her, he'd know how worried she was. He'd call, wouldn't he? Get a message to her somehow. No matter what, he'd let her know he was okay. Let her know he was innocent of whatever they said he'd done. Tell her he'd be back for her.

She called the Lighthouse Keeper. "Sorry, Kev," she said, when he answered. "But I slept in. I was up all night, trying to find Matt."

He grunted. "I told you, you could have gone home early yesterday, but you didn't want to. You can't just not come in with no notice. I'm not running a charity here, Tracey. I had to call Ellen to come down and fill in. I'll be paying for that for a long time."

Ellen was Kevin's wife. She worked at the restaurant only when she had to and made sure everyone, customers as well as staff, knew she was doing them an enormous favor.

"I can be there in half an hour."

"Forget it," he snapped. "It's quiet today, holiday people gone home, and Ellen can manage." His voice dropped and a touch of warmth crept into it. "I'm sorry about Matt, Tracey. I know you're worried. But, take my advice, you're better off without him."

"He didn't kill Barry."

"That remains to be seen. The cops think he did, and take it from me, once they get someone in their sights they don't let him go, innocent or not. Regardless of how this ends, Matt's bad news, Tracey. Cut him loose. Be here tomorrow morning." He hung up.

She went into the cramped, overcrowded bathroom. The countertops were covered with bottles and pots of makeup, hand creams, perfume, brushes, a hairdryer, used tissues. Amanda's mess. The mirror was spotted with dried drops of water and sprayed toothpaste. Tracey eyed herself, checking out every flaw.

Matt. All she had in this world was Matt. She knew he was innocent, but was Kevin right? Would the cops convict him anyway? She'd wait for him to get out of jail, no matter how long that might be. But how would she live? She needed to get out of this town; she needed a decent job with good money and regular hours.

All that could wait. The important thing was to be here for Matt. Matt had brought something good into her life. Love. Friendship. And, for the first time she could remember, hope. Hope that they'd have a future together.

He'd be calling her soon. He'd want to clear his name, get on with life. She'd be here, waiting.

# Chapter Thirty-five

**BANFF SPRINGS HOTEL. BANFF, ALBERTA. MONDAY MORNING.**

Smith crossed the hotel lobby. A long line snaked in front of the reception desk, as people waited to check out. Leaving the fairy-tale castle, heading back to their real lives.

She was probably the only one in the entire place who wanted to get back to her real life. Tension was carved into Paul Keller's face like time into granite. No matter what happened, this was not going to end well. Best-case scenario—Matt would be found unharmed, cleared of the murder, and go back to his own life, still estranged from his father.

Worst-case scenario—no point in going there. Not yet.

Paul Keller was her boss. He was a nice enough guy, a hands-off sort of boss. He'd been a good cop in his day, was now a competent administrator. Smith had been dragged into his personal life—where she did not want to go—by her mother's involvement with the chief.

Of all the people for the widowed Lucky to take up with.

Still, Smith reminded herself, it could have been a lot worse. There was a case in town about a year ago when a widow married a younger man and invested most of her savings in his business venture. Her son, who lived far away and never paid any attention to his mother in any event, only found out his mom was now penniless when she phoned asking if he'd heard from her husband who hadn't come back from a business trip to South America.

The husband was now living in Brazil. The woman had turned out to have had—past tense—far more money than anyone, except for the man in question, had realized. And then there was a high school friend, whose lonely widowed father had married a woman whose bitter tongue and constant fault-finding drove all his friends, as well as his children, away.

Paul Keller was a good match for Lucky. We don't choose our families and Paul hadn't chosen for his son to turn out bad.

Today, Smith wanted to find Tom Dunning, the other roommate, see if he could tell her more than Alistair had. Tracey said Dunning worked at the same car rental place she did.

Other than that, she had no idea of what do to next. If Matt had disappeared into the wilderness, and if he had good equipment and knowledge of survival, he could stay there as long as his supplies lasted. Longer, if someone was helping him hide. Or until snow fell. She hadn't thought to ask Alistair if Matt's tent and sleeping bag were good for the winter.

If anyone was helping Matt, or keeping him hidden, it wasn't Tracey. She was beside herself with worry about him. Smith would pop around to the Lighthouse Keeper this morning and ask if Tracey had heard from Matt overnight. If Matt told her not to tell the police, she'd do precisely as instructed.

But first, Smith needed to take Sylvester for a walk.

A man and a woman were coming out of the elevator. Karen Keller, the chief's ex-wife. She started when she saw Smith, and then put on a smile. "Molly, how nice to see you. Are you vacationing with your mother?"

As if Lucky would bring her adult daughter along on a romantic weekend.

Mrs. Keller didn't look as if her recent divorce had done her any harm. She wore red ankle boots, gray slacks, and a red leather jacket over a white blouse. She'd lost weight since Smith had seen her last and her hair and complexion glowed, but fresh worry lines were appearing in the delicate skin around her eyes and mouth.

"I'm here to help Chief Keller."

"That's nice of you."

A man hovered at Mrs. Keller's shoulder. He was attractive, for an older guy, and had a highly prosperous air about him. He and Karen looked like they belonged here in the lobby of the Banff Springs Hotel.

He gave Smith a wide smile and said to Karen Keller, "Are you going to introduce us, darling?"

"Where are my manners? This is Molly Smith, dear, one of… one of Paul's fine officers. My friend, Jonathan Burgess."

He held out his hand and they shook. Smith waited for him to say something patronizing like, "they didn't make cops so pretty in my day. Ha Ha." But he didn't, just said, "Pleased to meet you, Molly. Smith did you say?"

"Lucky's my mom."

"I see the resemblance. You're much taller, and the coloring is very different, but it's there."

"So I've been told. My dad was tall and fair."

His eyes focused on her face. No wandering to her chest, which would have been creepy, no looking behind her searching for someone more interesting, which would have been rude. Instead his smile was wide, his eyes focused, his look as professional as that of Andre the bartender. "It was nice of you to come. I don't know what you and Paul can do that the Mounties can't, but I figure all the help Matt can get, he needs, right?"

"Right. Did you hear anything new last night, Mrs. Keller?"

"You think I'd keep it to myself if I did?"

"I didn't mean…"

"Nothing." Burgess put a calming hand on Karen's shoulder. "Not a word. We have an interview with the detective in charge this morning."

Karen's face tightened, and her eyes narrowed. Her gaze shifted and she was looking across the room. Smith moved slightly, trying to see what had attracted the woman's attention.

Lucky Smith and Paul Keller were crossing the lobby.

They formed an awkward group. The men exchanged good mornings, Karen glared at Lucky, Lucky pretended to admire a vase of flowers.

"I've gotta go and give Sylvester a run," Smith said. "Call me when you have an appointment time, will you, Mom?" She dashed off.

Sylvester, as could be expected, was delighted to see her. She'd been out earlier to let him have a quick pee and to refill his water bowl, which he'd spilled all over the floor. Now, she took him into the woods for some exercise. He was used to being off-leash, but this close to the hotel she kept him on the lead. After he had a good long sniff of the underbrush, she set off at a light jog, the happy dog bounding along beside her. She'd spent all day yesterday in the car, and last night drinking far too much. She needed a good long run. But Sylvester was getting too old for that, and they'd both have to settle for five minutes or so.

The path was well-marked and well-maintained, the air crisp and full of the scent of the forest closing down for the winter. The undergrowth rustled. Sylvester's ears twitched and his head swung in search, but they encountered no one else. Smith felt her head clearing as she sucked in cool crisp air and took strength, as she always did, from the woods around her. She'd spent her teenage years and her early twenties working as a wilderness guide for her parents' adventure vacation business. She'd led multiday camping and kayaking trips in the summer, backcountry skiers in the winter. She missed it sometimes, now that she spent her days in a city--where the predators were far more dangerous and unpredictable than anything she'd ever encountered in the woods, where the exhaust from cars filled her lungs and there was no getting away from the smell and noise and light of humans. She'd enjoyed the two years she spent living in a small apartment above Alphonse's bakery, overlooking Front Street, although light would always be stealing through the windows no matter the time of night, cars driving up and down the street, or people talking too loudly on the sidewalk below. It had been nice, for a while. But now she was living in the woods again, this time with Adam, and that was where she belonged.

She'd considered, many times, looking for a job in a major city. As far away as Toronto even, to get big-city policing experience. The sort of experience she'd need if she was to get anywhere in her career.

At first, she couldn't bear to leave her mom, particularly not after her dad's sudden, unexpected death. Then she decided to commit herself fully to Adam Tocek. But most of all, Smith now understood, she couldn't bury herself in the city. Even a city like Vancouver, which was close, but not close enough, to the wilderness.

She held the car door open and Sylvester jumped happily into the backseat. She gave him a rub on his back and a scratch behind the ears, and he rewarded her with a shake of his head and a spray of spittle. Telling him to, once again, guard the car, she set off at a trot back to the hotel.

# Chapter Thirty-six

**GLOBAL CAR RENTAL. BANFF, ALBERTA. MONDAY AFTERNOON.**

Dumb, stupid, arrogant Barry. In one final screw up, he'd chosen this week to get himself killed.

Tom Dunning heaved himself off the bench in the office as a Lexus pulled into the lot, and he went outside to meet them. He'd checked out their papers earlier, a German couple who'd had the car for three days. No doubt they'd taken it off the highway. Some of these rough mountain roads could cause a lot of damage to a car, particularly to the front window.

It was the German couple's lucky day. Without Barry to make, or rather not make, the repairs to the windshield, no point in telling them they'd have to pay up.

Tom fingered the knife in his pocket. A little nick and scratch, could be expensive to repair on a valuable new car. Maybe a quick jab to the tire.

Nah. All he could do now was wait and see what the bosses decided. They were not happy. Tom had heard Simpson on the phone earlier: easy to guess he was talking to the manager of Kramp's Auto Repair, where Barry had worked. They had a nice scam going in fake repairs. It wasn't big business, a few hundred here and there, maybe a thousand or so, but it provided a welcome extra income for Tom and Barry—once the bosses had taken their cut, of course, and tossed scraps to the guys who'd done the real work.

Not good if they were going to shut the operation down while the cops poked around. Who knew how long that might be? Tom made fuck all checking rental cars in and out; he needed that extra cash.

Tom knew better than to rely on any one job or any one person. A man had to look after himself, always be ready for the main chance.

Good thing he had another line of income.

Even hearing only one end of the phone conversation, Tom could guess that McIntosh at the garage was nervous. The cops had been nosing around, asking questions about Barry. Questions like did he have any enemies they knew of? Was he ever in any trouble? Who might have had it in for him?

Simpson reminded McIntosh that Barry never met with the customers. If anyone was out for revenge at being ripped off, they'd be after the folks at the car rental company. Tom blinked. The boss meant him. Simpson would never dirty his manicured hands telling some tourist whose English wasn't good enough to order a burger and large fries at McDonald's that they'd be out hundreds of bucks for car repairs.

Not likely to be a problem. If anyone did get home after their vacation and bother trying to find out if those repairs really were done, or if the car was damaged by the check-in assistant himself, they'd be on the phone to their lawyer. Not creeping around apartment stairwells after dark armed with a knife.

No, Barry's death had nothing to do with the business. He'd gone too far for once and paid the price. An angry boyfriend probably, maybe an aggrieved father. Hell, these days he might well have been done by some girl he'd gotten drunk and stupid. And then found out she wasn't quite as drunk or as stupid as he'd hoped.

What the hell any of that had to do with Matt Keller, Tom didn't know. Or care. Unlikely Matt had stabbed Barry himself. Matt didn't do anything without Barry's approval. Tom snorted to himself. Matt was as weak a man as he'd ever met. The guy had a real beef with his father, a cop. Get over it, Tom thought but never said.

From the day he'd walked out of his house, turned his back on Mad Mike, Tom had made his way through life on his own terms. He needed nothing from no one. Unlike Matt, who hung around Barry like a lapdog, doing what he was told, seeking the other man's approval as if Barry was some sort of father-substitute.

Pathetic. No, Matt hadn't killed Barry. Tom doubted he had the guts to kill anyone who threatened Barry either. Or if he did, he'd have dropped to the floor, curled up into a ball, and waited to be arrested.

The rent on the apartment was paid up until the end of the month. He shouldn't have any trouble finding new roommates: cheap accommodations around here were as rare as a well-paid job.

Tom had no idea why Matt had run, and didn't much care except that it threw yet another complication into the business. Matt's girlfriend Tracey worked here. And the cops had their eye on her, hoping he'd contact her.

Still, they had no reason to connect Matt with the car rental company itself. Tom could only hope they'd give up on Tracey. And soon.

This was definitely not a good time to have the cops watching them.

He found himself glancing to the back corner of the lot, where the beige Corolla was tucked in behind a couple of vans.

That car was supposed to be picked up tomorrow.

*Just get it the hell out of here.*

Tom checked the Germans in, told them to have a nice day, and thanked them for renting from Global Car Rental. It paid to be friendly when the boss was on the lot.

He glanced at his watch. Long time till lunch break. Inside the office, Simpson was leaning over Jody's shoulder, reading her computer screen. The look on her face would curdle milk. She wiggled off her stool and stood against the wall, arms folded over her chest.

Simpson had been known to accidently brush up against her almost non-existent breasts now and again.

She'd threatened to quit once, after his hands had wandered, but Tom told her to stay on. It would be hard, he said sensibly, to get another job. He'd keep an eye on the boss, make sure he didn't get out of line.

Jody hadn't liked it, mentioned that Tom wasn't always there. Frankly, Tom couldn't care less where Jody worked, except that he liked having her here, knowing she wouldn't question why he showed particular interest in one vehicle over another. She wasn't in on the scam, didn't concern herself with what happened with cars that needed repairing. Tom and Simpson handled that part of the business.

Time to cut Jody loose anyway. She was getting clingy, wanting to go out to restaurants for dinner, or to bars at night. Wanting to do stuff that cost money.

If she wanted money she should tell the boss she'd agree to an extension of her job description, if he paid enough.

Still, it had been mighty handy having Jody as an alibi for the time of Barry's murder. Tom knew the cops weren't sure whether or not to believe her. They'd questioned her again, when he wasn't around. They'd tried to get tough with him, too.

Screw them. About that, he really did know nothing.

A car pulled up as the office door shut behind him. He turned and glanced out the window. A Neon, one that had driven a lot of miles on bad roads. A woman was driving and a large shaggy dog smiled out the back window.

Tom watched her. The woman was definitely hot. Young, blond, tall and slim, casually dressed in jeans and a denim jacket. Normally he would have leapt forward, eager to help, but something about her made him wary, the way she looked around before coming inside, the way her eyes moved, checking everything out. She didn't look like a cop, and that was no police car. But these days, cops might look like anyone, and it wouldn't be wise to make assumptions. He crossed the room, went behind the counter, and waited to see what the woman wanted.

# Chapter Thirty-seven

**GLOBAL CAR RENTAL. BANFF, ALBERTA. MONDAY AFTERNOON.**

"Help you?" the Asian woman said as Smith walked in.

"I'm looking for Tom Dunning?"

"That'd be me." Dunning was about Smith's age and height. Overweight, flabby. He had an unkempt brown goatee beneath round cheeks and small black eyes full of suspicion.

She held out her hand, and he leaned across the counter to take it. "Pleased to meet you. My name's Molly Smith and I'm a friend of Paul Keller, Matt's dad."

Dunning snatched his hand back. "Don't know anything about Matt. Sorry."

An older man, dressed in a shirt and tie, probably the boss, was also in the office, pecking at a computer. "What's this about?"

She turned to him. "I'm helping with the search for Matt."

"The cops have been here," Dunning said. "I told them what I know. Which is nothing. I shared an apartment with Matt and Barry, but we weren't friends. We didn't hang around, do things together, you know."

And that, Smith had come to realize, was the problem. None of these people actually seemed to like each other. They shared space, more than lived together, in order to save money. They went their own way, lived their own lives. "Can I ask you a few questions anyway?"

"Tom's working right now," the man in the suit interrupted. "We have a large number of vehicles scheduled to be handed in today."

She tried to get her question in before she was shown the door. "What about Saturday night? The early hours of Sunday morning?"

"I told the cops I wasn't home," Tom said. "And I wasn't."

"Now, if that will be all. Tom, what's the status of the Lexus that just arrived? We have customers who've booked it this evening for three days. Have you checked it over?"

"Not yet, Mr. Simpson."

"Then you'd better do so, hadn't you? Immediately." He spoke to Tom but was looking pointedly at Smith.

"Thank you for your time," she said, thoroughly humiliated. She'd gotten used to—too used to perhaps—the power that came with being in uniform.

She stood in the yard, glancing around, wondering what to do next. Late-model cars, in neat rows, sparkled in the sun. Neither Tom Dunning nor his boss had wanted her here, but that didn't mean they had anything to hide. They were probably sick of answering questions, having their business disrupted.

She headed for her own car and climbed in to be greeted by an enthusiastic Sylvester. Sylvester was always enthusiastic, whether she'd been gone overnight or five minutes.

Her phone rang. Adam.

"Hey, babe. How's it going?"

"Not well. No sign of the chief's son. No other suspects."

"That's gotta be tough."

"I miss you."

"I miss you too, Molly. I think Norman misses Sylvester. He doesn't say anything, but mopes around sniffing in corners."

She smiled at the image.

"I can't talk for long. I'm about to head out, but I got a call from an old friend I thought you'd be interested in."

"Shoot."

"Sergeant Edward Blechta. Eddie to his friends."

"What about him?"

"This is all internal gossip mind, but it seems that a couple of years ago Eddie was rapidly transferred way up north to some hole-in-the-wall detachment. He'd been working in Red Deer. An officer made a complaint about him. A female officer, brand new shiny young constable straight out of college."

"Do tell."

"She claims he propositioned her. She wasn't interested. He wouldn't take no for an answer. She wasn't intimidated as much as he'd thought, and she made a complaint. Of course, he was all, 'it's a misunderstanding, just trying to be friendly, overreaction.'"

"I'm surprised he's the one who had to move."

"She probably'd have been transferred posthaste, with a note on her record saying she was unstable, if not for the fact that there'd been whispers about Blechta before. Nothing they could charge him with, just rumors, innuendo. You know."

"Yeah, I know." It had never happened to Smith; it didn't happen as much as it used to, but all the women knew there were still male officers who thought women needed to be put in their place. One way or the other.

"Anyway, he was, so my contact says, about to be made a staff sergeant. That never happened and he was sent to the back of beyond. He seems to have learned his lesson, no more talk anyway, so he came to Banff recently. Never did get to staff, though."

"He probably blames that woman for the loss of the promotion."

"You watch yourself, eh?"

"Forewarned is forearmed. It shouldn't matter. I won't have anything to do with him. He managed to make that perfectly clear."

They said their good-byes, and Smith ended the call.

Before turning the key in the ignition, she looked back at the office. Tom Dunning stood at the window, watching her. He was not smiling.

# Chapter Thirty-eight

**TRAFALGAR CITY POLICE STATION. TRAFALGAR, BRITISH COLUMBIA. MONDAY AFTERNOON.**

John Winters settled into his desk chair with a cup of coffee in hand.

First, he opened his e-mail and sent a note to Rose Benoit in Vancouver. They'd been partners for a number of years, as well as good friends. Rose was an inspector now, working major fraud cases. He wouldn't expect her to be working on Thanksgiving Monday, and decided against giving her a call. She'd be relaxing at home with her husband Claude. The finances of the Grizzly Resort could wait.

Then, armed with only a name, he went onto Google.

Several pages of hits popped up. But it wasn't difficult to find the person he was interested in. He clicked on images, and up she came, Robyn Winfield, the woman he'd seen yesterday. Grainy newspaper photographs, snaps from homemade YouTube videos, press releases.

She was with an organization called Free the Wild. Winfield seemed to make a habit of attending protests at sensitive environmental areas and writing strongly worded letters to newspapers. She kept a blog, which got a substantial number of comments and links, detailing her latest indignation. Of Free the Wild, he couldn't find much, and nothing without her name attached, so he suspected Winfield was pretty much the whole thing.

Her blog posts were articulate, sensible, and highly literate, illustrated with photographs that concentrated on the beauty of nature, not the ugliness of its destruction. Her passions for the environment and the animals that live there were expressed in every word. He found the beginning of the blog and started to skim. As the afternoon passed, along with the years she'd been doing the blog, her frustration increased, her language got sharper, verging on threatening at times.

The latest posting, dated last week, discussed the situation in Trafalgar. She said she was heading there, intending to help coalesce opposition into an effective movement, and calling for others to join her. The blog ended: "This *must* stop. This *will* stop!"

Now that he was sure of her real name, he ran a records search. Not an unusual name, but at least he had a rough idea of her age.

She'd been arrested twice, both times for engaging in civil disobedience, once for a demonstration on Parliament Hill against development of the Alberta tar sands, and again for attempting to close a highway in Alberta taking construction equipment north. The latest occurrence had been three months ago. In both cases she got no jail time.

Recently she'd been photographed in the company of a man on whom the RCMP was keeping a close eye—an individual suspected of carrying out a bombing campaign with the intent of intimidating tar sands workers. A couple of minor explosions had occurred. Fortunately, no one was hurt and property damage was minimal. No arrests were made.

John Winters leaned back in his chair and ran his thumb across his watch as he studied the grainy photograph of the man, one Steve McNally.

The man in the photo was clean-shaven, bare-headed, glowering at the camera.

The guy at the demonstration yesterday sported a heavy growth of beard and had been wearing a ball cap. Hard to be sure, but the resemblance was there.

Whether it was the same person or not, Winters reminded himself that just because Robyn Winfield might have been seen in McNally's company it was a mighty hefty leap to assume she was now involved in eco-terrorism. Similar interests didn't mean similar tactics.

He thought about the Grizzly Resort. In his mind he saw the remains of tree stumps, the massive holes dug into the ground. If he had his way, he'd prefer the resort not go ahead. It was a stunningly beautiful piece of land. Trees that hadn't been logged for a long time, steep cliffs overlooking the fast-moving river below, the forest thick enough, wild enough, that bears were known to live there, along with cougars, elk, and coyotes. What would happen, he thought, the first time one of the vacationers came face to face with a bear or a cougar, the animal not inside a cage, the human not confined to a car?

Regardless of who survived the encounter, the call would go up for the animal to be destroyed.

Yes, Winfield and Free the Wild had a point.

Then again, Winters' own house was located in what had not so long ago been pure wilderness. Trees cut down, birds' nests destroyed, road put in, house built, grass and shrubs and flowers planted. The original inhabitants driven further and further up the mountain. What would happen, when nowhere remained for them to go?

He had to have someplace to live. He and Eliza owned twenty acres, of which the house and garden occupied a small portion. The remainder of the property was left wild, and they shared it with the animals. He often came across bear or elk tracks in the mud or snow, and some dark cold nights they could hear coyotes calling to each other across the hills.

The Grizzly Resort, on the other hand, with two hundred small buildings, sidewalks joining them all, road access and parking spaces, outbuildings, swimming pools, restaurants, and all the maintenance that went with it, would be far too crowded to live comfortably alongside nature.

A thought niggled uncomfortably at the back of his mind. Should only people such as Eliza and him, because they had sufficient money, be allowed to own a place in the wilderness?

They loved living here, so did plenty of people. But what about the people who wanted to escape from the city, to bring their children on vacation, but couldn't afford the indulgence of twenty exclusive acres.

He shoved his chair back and got to his feet with a grunt. Time for another cup of coffee. Not his job to decide who'd be allowed a place in the wilds and who would not. Thank heavens for that. The Grizzly Resort consortium owned the land, and they had permission to build their vacation homes on it. The Mounties would see that construction was allowed to go ahead and the Trafalgar City Police would see that business in town continued unimpeded.

He glanced back over his shoulder at the computer screen. A photo of Robyn Winfield, standing beneath an enormous tree. A shaft of sunlight broke through the branches and lit her short red hair as if it were on fire. Her arms were lifted in the air and her smile was radiant.

# Chapter Thirty-nine

**KRAMP'S AUTO REPAIR. BANFF, ALBERTA. MONDAY AFTERNOON.**

Lucky Smith shifted on the uncomfortable seat and brushed at the dust on a pile of magazines. Kramp's Auto Repair shop didn't waste money on furnishings, nor on cleaning services. The seats had been removed from cars and unceremoniously plunked in the waiting room. Most of the magazines pre-dated the century and were covered with a thick layer of dust. Which, she thought, probably also pre-dated the century.

She'd called Kramp's as soon as it opened. She was, she said, due to drive back over the mountains tomorrow and was very nervous about taking the trip—alone—in her car. What with the strange sound she heard when she put her foot on the brake. They said if she came right away, they'd try to fit her in.

The waiting room had a dirty glass wall overlooking the shop floor, and she was able to watch the men working. When the fellow behind the counter, a small black-eyed man with skin the color of creamy coffee, took her keys, he explained, again, that it might be a while before they could see to her car. The sudden death of one of their employees had put them seriously behind.

Lucky repeated that she absolutely *had* to be heading home tomorrow, and he said they'd get to it as soon as they could.

She wasn't lying, she told herself, she was acting. Not that the part required a whole lot of theatrical chops. A woman who didn't know anything about cars, worried about a strange noise. She flipped through a fashion magazine wondering if anything in the world was more useless than an out-of-date fashion magazine.

She'd wanted to be an actor once, a long time ago. She studied drama at the University of Washington and performed minor parts in several plays. She hadn't been all that good, and had known it, deep inside where it mattered.

She had one great success on the stage. It hadn't led to a stellar career of greasepaint and floodlights, but it had led to her name. She'd been an understudy for *The Glass Menagerie*. On opening night, the actress playing Amanda Wingfield came down with a severe cold, and young Lucy Casey went on to star. Andy Smith had been in the audience, clapping and cheering enthusiastically. Lucy had, to no one's surprise more than hers, been a triumph. At the cast party later, the actor playing the Gentleman Caller commented that she'd been very lucky, and others took up the chant. Lucky Lucy, they called her.

Later, as they walked home from the party and stopped to admire the lights of the city, Andy Smith told her he was leaving for Canada. He'd received his draft notice and was not planning to report. Would she, he asked, come with him and be his Lucky Smith?

She'd been Lucky since that day. Lucky, she always reminded herself, in so many ways. They'd had a good life together, Andy and Lucky, and she'd never regretted tying her star to his. Although she did occasionally think, while enjoying a good movie with a strong female lead or watching the Oscars, about what might have been.

She'd wondered, when Moonlight was young, if the girl had some acting talent she should encourage. Instead, Moonlight found her place not on the stage but on lakes and ski trails almost before she could walk.

Lucky was on her third magazine when a man in overalls, wiping greasy hands on an equally greasy rag, came into the room. She'd watched him earlier, taking Paul's car out onto the road for a test drive. "I can't find anything wrong, Mrs. Smith," he said. "I took it for a spin, didn't hear anything out of the ordinary. I checked the brakes over anyway, but don't see a problem. Your car's in good shape, I'd say. You might have gotten a rock or a piece of ice trapped in the brakes, and all it needed was to be kicked out or melt."

"I hope that's it. Thank you."

She paid a minimal amount for the mechanic's time and that was the end of that. Her undercover operation, like her acting career, had come to naught.

# Chapter Forty

**BEARTRACK TRAIL. BANFF, ALBERTA. MONDAY AFTERNOON.**

Tracey spent the day checking her phone and moving house.

She'd gone to Matt's apartment earlier, mainly because she could think of nothing else to do, but wanted, needed, to be doing *something*. The police had finished with it and told Alistair and Tom they could move back in. At ten o'clock, only Alistair was home, packing his bags. Black powder smudged the surface of almost everything . A patch of carpet close to the door looked clean. Noticeably clean amongst the ground-in dirt and years of muck covering the rest of the floor. Tracey swallowed, realizing what that meant.

"I'm done," Alistair said in answer to her question. "Outta here. I can't stay where a guy, a guy I knew, died."

"Where will you go?"

"Jamail's gonna put me up for a while. I'll decide what I'm gonna do then. I'm thinking of heading to Vancouver. Friend of mine's talking about putting together a new band."

"What about the rent on this place?"

"It's paid up 'til the end of the month. Matt's name's on the lease. I guess if he doesn't come back, they'll rent it out again." He shrugged thin shoulders. "Give me a hand will you, Trace? My car's outside, can you carry that guitar down?"

She helped Alistair take his belongings, more music equipment than anything else, to his battered van. He wrestled two keys off the chain and handed them to her.

"What's this?"

"One for the front door, one for the apartment. Lock up, will you? You can leave my keys on the hall table."

Without a wave or a backward glance he drove away.

Tracey studied the keys in her hand. She didn't know if the police had found Matt's keys or if he'd taken them with him. If he didn't have them, if…when…he got back, he'd need to get in.

She needed a place to stay. Amanda told her she had until the end of the month. Amanda could go screw herself. Tracey didn't need her charity, didn't need Crystal's pitying looks either.

Matt would be happy to find her waiting at home for him.

She stopped at a liquor store on her way back to her apartment and picked up a couple of empty boxes. Amanda and Crystal were at work, and Tracey quickly threw her things into her suitcases and the boxes. It wasn't, she thought, very much. But that didn't bother her; she'd never had much.

Amanda would try to screw her on the rent, but Matt's place was paid for so she'd come out all right. At Matt's she'd have her own room, Matt's room. She'd have to share the apartment with miserable Tom, but Tom wasn't around much, and she could shut the door to her room whenever she wanted. No longer put up with Amanda and Crystal and their drunken slutty friends hanging around, sitting on *her* damn bed watching sappy movies or reality TV, sneering at her. Or worse, their druggy boyfriends, trying to cop a feel when Amanda or Crystal were in the kitchen getting drinks or making popcorn.

Tracey treated herself to a taxi to get her stuff to her new home. It would have been nice if the cab driver had offered to help her carry it all in, but he just dumped everything on the curb and stuck out his hand for his money. She paid and lugged suitcases and boxes up the stairs and through the front door. The apartment, she had to admit, wasn't exactly welcoming. If she could fix it up a bit, maybe they could keep it after Matt got back. Get new people to share with, young couples like themselves, or single women, not the usual bunch of layabouts. She'd be more than happy to see the back of Tom.

She made room in the small cupboard and hung up her clothes. The closet was tiny, but it didn't matter. Matt didn't have much and Tracey had less. She hung up her work clothes, jeans and sweaters, and the single nice dress she rarely got the chance to wear. She made space in the bottom drawer for her underwear and her few scraps of jewelry.

That done, hands on hips she studied the room. The double bed filled most of the space, and it was unmade. Towels, dirty socks and underwear were tossed haphazardly on the floor, dresser drawers open, t-shirts and clean underwear spilling out. She began gathering up the stray items, placing them in a pile on the floor of the closet. Tomorrow she'd take the sheets and towels to the Laundromat. She made the bed, tucking the sheets in at the corners, straightening the duvet, puffing the pillows before placing them carefully against the headboard.

As a finishing touch, she laid out the one precious, unnecessary thing she'd brought with her from Ontario. A pink and purple My Little Pony. Somewhat tattered now, the ribbons fading, the mane ragged. She'd had it since she was very small. It probably hadn't even been new when she found it under the Christmas tree one morning, but she'd loved it all these years.

Time to tackle the kitchen.

Under the sink she found a couple of dirty rags, an almost empty bottle of bleach, and an empty container of dishwashing liquid. She made a mental note to shop for cleaning cloths, furniture polish, glass cleaner, and all the other things she'd need to turn this transient dump into a pleasant home.

The kitchen looked to be more of a storage room for empty beer bottles than a place to cook, or even eat. The small table against one wall was buried under beer cases and empty pizza cartons. What dishes there were, as well as pots and pans, were piled in the sink, encrusted with days' old food. Probably the guys just wiped off a frying pan and plate when they wanted to use it again, and ate in front of the TV with their food balanced on their laps.

She cleared empty pizza cartons off the counter, and took everything out of the sink. Then she ran hot water and by taking the top off the dishwashing liquid container was able to get enough soap to make a cheerful mountain of suds. Leaving the dishes to soak, she stacked the beer cases into a reasonably orderly pile on the floor so she could sweep around them. She used the one available rag and the soapy dishwater to wipe up what she could of lumps of dried food, beer spills, mud, and who knows what else off the floor. A good cleaning would have to wait until she could get the necessary supplies.

All that, she realized, was going to cost a heck of a lot. She'd ask Tom to pay. He just might, if she was the one doing the grunt work.

She plunged her hands into the hot water, soon realizing that steel wool would have to be added to her shopping list. Still, she did what she could and with a lot of elbow grease and good intentions she soon had a pile of clean dishes stacked beside the sink. It wasn't hard to find a place to put the plates and glasses and cutlery, once she'd dried them with one of Matt's face cloths, as nothing was in the cupboards aside from the odd unused bowl, a couple of jars of jam, sticky around the lid, a nearly empty jar of peanut butter, a few boxes of Kraft Dinner, and one enormous box of corn flakes.

She peeked into the fridge. Bottles of beer, a tub of margarine, an opened packet of bacon, turning gray around the edges. Something red and viscous coated the bottom of the meat compartment. At one time someone must have intended to eat something healthy as a pile of rotting, nearly liquid lettuce leaves were in the vegetable cooler. She lifted a carton of milk to her nose and sniffed. She recoiled in disgust. The whole fridge smelled so bad something might have died in there.

And then, it all came rushing back. Two chairs, with torn vinyl padding, were pulled up to the Formica table, which might be older than Tracey herself. She dropped into a seat. Someone *had* died in here. Not in the fridge, of course, but in this apartment. She'd been so happy cleaning, making a home for Matt to return to, she'd almost forgotten *why* he wasn't home. *Why* there was space for her to move in.

She hadn't liked Barry but he didn't deserve to die, and then to be forgotten. She'd barely given Barry a thought, all of her fears and worries were concentrated on Matt. Tracey's mother believed in the power of positive thinking. She believed if you wanted something, wanted it hard enough, and for all the right reasons, it would come to you.

She'd learned that on Oprah or some other afternoon TV show.

Tracey had thought it was a pile of bunk. If it worked, why couldn't her mom conjure up a lottery win, or make her right knee better? Or even find herself a decent job. About the only thing positive thinking had done was give Mom a win at bingo one night. She collected a thousand dollars and as far as she was concerned, that was proof enough that Oprah's guest was right. Tracey hadn't bothered to mention that after spending several thousand bucks over the years at the Bingo Palace, she was due for a win.

The thousand hadn't lasted long. Most of it went to lottery tickets, which Mom concentrated so intently on thinking positively about she might have been praying to the little scraps of paper. What she didn't spend on the lottery went toward fixing the brakes in the car before they failed totally and killed someone, and a new outfit to wear to bingo. Not entirely a selfish woman, she bought Tracey some glittering earrings and a sexy top that fell apart after the first wash.

Tracey's mom still believed, despite all the proof to the contrary, and if she were here she'd tell Tracey to think positive thoughts about Matt.

She tried, she really tried. But at the back of her mind, a tiny voice kept saying, what if… What if Matt had murdered Barry? What if he hadn't, but the killer had killed Matt and dumped his body? What if he decided he was better off without Tracey and never came back?

Nothing she could do about that now, except be ready for Matt if…when…he came home.

She pushed herself to her feet, threw the rotting food into the trash and dumped the lumpy milk down the sink. She took the garbage to the chute in the hallway, and then wandered through the quiet apartment back to Matt's room. Their room now. The police had taken Matt's iPhone and his MacBook Pro that used to sit on a small table with a wobbly leg, wedged in a corner under the window. His car was still parked on the street. The top shelf in the closet had been disturbed. That, Tracey knew, was where he kept his camping equipment. His tent and sleeping bag, good to minus-forty degrees. Camp stove, propane lamp, small axe, sharp knife, a handful of freeze-dried food packages.

All of that was gone, and she was pleased to know that if he was in the wilderness, waiting until he was cleared and could come back, he'd at least be warm and dry and fed.

Almost five o'clock. Time to get ready for work. She'd finish cleaning tomorrow.

Positive thinking might not help Matt, but right now it was the only thing that could help Tracey.

She pulled on her work clothes and went to the bathroom to tidy her hair and wash her hands. The bathroom was, as could be expected for something shared by four men, disgusting. Toilet bowl cleaner and new brush, more cloths, shower spray and squeegee, not to mention fresh bars of soap, went onto her mental shopping list.

She left the apartment, locking the door behind her.

Tom would think he'd walked into the wrong unit.

# Chapter Forty-one

**TRAFALGAR CITY POLICE STATION. TRAFALGAR, BRITISH COLUMBIA. MONDAY AFTERNOON.**

John Winters checked the display on his phone.

Rose Benoit.

He should have known she'd be checking e-mail, holiday or not.

"Happy Thanksgiving," he said in greeting. "Why are you working?"

"Claude's going to Paris tomorrow. Something about a sculptor he's been wanting to meet for a long time. He'll spend all of today rushing about and panicking that he'll have forgotten something. I prefer to stay out of the way. You're one to talk, as usual."

They chatted for a few minutes, catching up on each other's news, and then Rose said, "Grizzly Resort and Darren Fernhaugh. They look totally aboveboard to me. Never a whiff of scandal around Fernhaugh. He bought that land near Trafalgar for a ridiculously low price because Clemmins was desperate to sell. He and Darren Fernhaugh go way back. I think they're cousins-in-law or something. So he let Fernhaugh have it with no competition."

"Clemmins could have gotten a better price?"

"Almost certainly. The place was tainted somewhat after the Reg Montgomery killing, and then that other case. But business is business and prime mountain territory doesn't come up every day."

"Thanks, Rose. This whole thing is about to blow up in our faces again, and I wanted to have all my facts lined up."

"I'll keep my ears open, but right now I'd say the company's legit. Makes a nice change in my line of work to be able to say that."

He laughed. "Take care, eh?"

"Will do. Speaking of blowing things up, the Grizzly might be the least of your problems environmentally wise."

"What do you mean?"

"There's talk of good shale deposits around your lovely town."

"Meaning?"

"Fracking, my friend. Some exploratory stuff's going on, all on the QT for now. But word is that the Mid-Kootenays might be the next big place for fracking."

Winters groaned. Of all the controversial things, fracking—extracting natural gas from shale by a complicated process of forcing water and chemicals into the ground—ran a close second only to the tar sands.

"No need to panic yet," Benoit said. "Nothing may come of it. Much is explored, but few are developed. Or something like that. You and I might be comfortably retired long before it becomes an issue."

"Retirement. I don't know if I'm looking forward to it or dreading it."

"Love to Eliza."

"Will do."

# Chapter Forty-two

**GRAPES WINE BAR. BANFF SPRINGS HOTEL, BANFF, ALBERTA. MONDAY EVENING.**

The red light on the hotel phone was blinking when Smith got back to her room. She grabbed it, thinking it might be her mom, someone, anyone with news.

Instead it was the deep voice of Jonathan Burgess, inviting her to have a drink with him in the hotel bar.

She went into the bathroom, stripping off her soaked running clothes as she walked. A shower first.

A long, exhilarating run had worked the cobwebs out of her head, but hadn't helped her to reach any clarity as to what was going on. The area around the town and hotel was a maze of hiking paths and mountain biking trails. Smith had found a promising route on a map the concierge gave her, and set off at a trot. As soon as she passed into the trees and the hotel fell behind her, the crowds of camera-toting tourists dropped away and she had the forest largely to herself. Not wanting to get lost, she simply ran in one direction for half an hour, then turned and ran back, leaping over fallen logs, rounding animal hideaways, splashing through streams fed by yesterday's rain, occasionally running along the banks of the swift-moving river. She emerged from the trail onto the manicured lawns where she spent ten minutes stretching and cooling down. The hotel loomed over her, gabled windows and turrets imposing in the sun.

The run and time in the wilderness had made her feel a good deal better, but all too soon the euphoria began to wear off. What was she doing here? She was accomplishing precisely nothing. It was all so damned frustrating. At least the chief was allowed to follow the detectives around. Not that he was accomplishing much either. She'd phoned him earlier for an update and all he said was that Blechta had re-interviewed Matt's roommates and his co-workers at Reds but learned nothing new. Officers had called everyone on his phone's contact list, but no one had heard from Matt lately. Or, if they had, they weren't admitting it. Forensic reports were starting to come in, and the results of tests run by the pathologist, all of which were telling them nothing they didn't already know. Plenty of sightings of Matt were being logged at the detachment. The obvious cranks were ruled out, and the possible genuine ones followed up. Again, nothing.

Even over the spotty cell connection, Smith could hear the strain in the chief's voice.

"What about the dead guy, Caseman?" she'd asked. "Any idea what he was up to that night?"

"Blechta tracked him down to a bar in town where he was well-known. He drank a fair amount, the waiter says, which was normal for him for a Saturday night. He talked to a few of the regulars, also normal behavior. He left alone, at one, early for him. He was not seen by anyone after that. According to his fellow drinkers, he'd been unusually quiet, had said nothing of any significance."

Toweling herself off, she returned Jonathan Burgess' call. He answered immediately and repeated the invitation to join him for a drink. "Give me twenty minutes," she said. It was coming up to the top of the hour, and she wanted to catch the local news on TV.

The death of Barry Caseman and the disappearance of Matt Keller was, as could have been expected, the top story. Smith sat on the bed to watch. Blechta came on first, giving rough details of what little they knew so far, trying to make it sound as if an arrest was imminent. A few shots, taken from a distance, of the police walking in and out of an apartment building and cruisers parked on the street with lights flashing. Then a photo of Caseman appeared on the screen. He was an ugly son-of-a-gun, with greasy blond hair and thin lips. Then Matt's picture, with a plea for anyone who knew his whereabouts to contact the police. They didn't say that Matt was wanted for murder. They didn't have to.

Smith leaned forward. It had been a lot of years since she'd seen Matt Keller, and she never paid him much attention even then, but he hadn't changed much. The resemblance to Paul Keller was strong.

The piece ended, and she switched off the TV. She dressed, brushed out her hair, and applied a touch of makeup. At the last minute she added a silver necklace and replaced gold studs in her ears with giant silver hoops.

Burgess was waiting for her in the lobby. Wearing sharply-ironed khaki trousers and a hand-woven sweater, he stood as she approached, smiling in welcome. "Where's Mrs. Keller?" Smith asked, after initial greetings.

"Resting. I thought it best if you and I have a private chat."

Smith eyed him warily. "Why?"

"You don't beat about the bush, do you? For a moment there I forgot you're a police officer. It's been an emotionally draining day, as you can imagine. Let's have that drink."

He led the way up the stairs to the Grapes Wine Bar. This early, the small bar was almost empty and they took seats in an alcove beneath enormous windows set into wood-paneled walls, looking out over the Bow Valley.

The French doors were open to a closed-off balcony. "If you're chilly, I can close the windows." The waiter arranged menus and place mats.

Burgess lifted an eyebrow in question. Smith said, "It's fine, thanks. The fresh air's nice."

"I'm going to have a beer. Molly?" Burgess said.

"Kokanee, please."

"A true B.C. girl."

She shrugged.

"Karen told me your name's Moonlight, but you call yourself Molly?"

"Moonlight's the name I was given when I was born, but it's hardly a cop name. I prefer Molly, although Mom refuses to change. I'm okay with that," she added quickly. Although she wasn't. Anyone who met her under the name Moonlight automatically assumed she was some modern-day hippie chick. She remembered the first time she'd gone to court. Her first time as the charging officer. She'd been so nervous, awake half the night. The judge read out her name and the defendant, up on a drunk driving charge, laughed out loud. Ever since then she'd made sure all police and court records said Constable M. L. Smith. Moonlight was bad enough. God help her if people found out the L stood for Legolas, the *Lord of the Rings* elf with the long shiny blond hair.

Gracing her with an unfortunate name was the about the worst thing her parents had done to her, and she knew she was lucky indeed.

"I thought it best if we get to know each other without Karen around," Burgess said. "She still has a, shall we say, sensitive spot about your mother."

"She shouldn't. She left the chief, as far as I and everyone else knows. What did she expect him to do after that? Take his vows?"

"I'm only telling you the situation, Molly. How well do you know Matt?"

"I haven't seen nor heard of him since I was in high school. He's older than me, and he dropped out of school early."

Burgess' face fell. "For some reason I thought you'd kept in touch."

"Not at all. Who told you that?"

"Just an impression, I guess. In that case, it was nice of you to come and try to help find him."

"I'm doing it for my mom. And my boss."

They stopped talking while the waiter served their drinks and asked if they'd like something to eat. They both passed. "This is a beautiful room, isn't it?" Burgess said. "It was originally the writing room. In the days when ladies and gentlemen would spend an entire afternoon writing letters before going in for afternoon tea. Hard to imagine, sometimes, all we've lost in the rush to the modern world." He glanced around, taking in the paneled walls, the tall glass windows inset with lead panes and crests of stained glass, the paintings and framed maps.

"I scarcely know the boy myself. Not that he's a boy anymore. We've only met once, about two months ago. Karen wanted a visit, so we came here for one night, and met Matt for lunch. He asked his mother for money. I understand that wasn't the first time, either. Kids these days." He forced a smile to take some of the sting out of his words, but to Smith the smile was all teeth, no sincerity.

Still, she'd cut Burgess some slack. It couldn't be easy, trying to start a new relationship when you didn't approve of the woman's adult child. And, from what little she'd been able to gather, Matt sounded like a slacker.

"He was a good skier," she said, for some reason feeling she had to come to Matt Keller's defense. "I remember that."

Burgess sipped his beer. "Karen told me he was looking for a loan. A loan to tide him over until ski season began and he got more work. I would have liked to believe her, but I got the impression she's given him many loans. Which were never repaid. But that's neither here nor there. I was hoping, Molly, you'd be able to give me some insight as to what's happening with the search for Matt."

"Why?" she asked bluntly.

"What business is it of mine, you mean? I'm about to ask Karen to marry me. I've booked a Christmas vacation in Turks and Caicos and intend to pop the question while we're there. If this business is hanging over her, I'd like to know as much as I can." He cleared his throat. "I am, Molly, not without means. I intend to make Karen a happy woman. I do not intend to have her son scrounging off me."

"Fair enough. Everything I know, you understand, is strictly informal. No one but the chief has told me anything and I doubt he's been kept fully in the loop. The working theory is that Matt has taken off into the backcountry. He's good in the wilderness, and he's probably equipped."

"Is he a suspect in this killing?"

"My impression is that he's the only suspect."

Burgess leaned back in his chair. "What's your opinion, as a police officer?"

"I'm not a detective, and I don't have enough facts to have an opinion. But I do know Matt ran from the scene and isn't coming forward as a witness. That's highly incriminatory. Provided, of course, he's able to come forward. Look, Mr. Burgess..."

"Jonathan, please."

"Jonathan. You asked for my opinion, so I'll give it. For what it's worth. I'd recommend you not put any more money down on your Christmas vacation, okay. Matt Keller was at the scene around the time a murder took place, and then he fled. This isn't Mexico or Columbia where he might conceivably be on the run from crooked cops. Even if Matt bolted into the night after calling his dad because he thought he'd been seen by the killer, he has absolutely no reason to stay hidden."

"I appreciate your honesty. It's why I wanted to talk to you. Without Karen."

She finished her beer. "Thanks for the drink."

He pulled out his wallet, threw a twenty-dollar bill on the table, and got to his feet without waiting for change. They walked out of the bar together. The elevators were directly across the hall. "I'd better go up to check on Karen," he said.

"I'd better go out and check on my dog."

He pushed the up button. "You brought a dog?"

"Yes, I brought a dog. My mom's mutt. I couldn't think of anything else to do with him on the spur of the moment."

A soft ping announced the impending arrival of the elevator. It was going up and it was empty. Burgess got in and turned to face the front. "I won't tell Karen about our conversation, and

I'd prefer it if you don't, Molly. She's worried enough." The doors shut with a silent whoosh.

Smith took the stairs down to the lobby. She hadn't cared for Jonathan Burgess on first meeting, but she was warming up to him. His concern for Karen Keller did seem genuine. Nothing wrong with worrying that he was about to be stuck with gigantic legal bills for a young man he didn't know well or even like.

# Chapter Forty-three

**GLOBAL CAR RENTAL. BANFF, ALBERTA. MONDAY EVENING.**

Jody looked up as Tracey entered the car rental office. "Anything?"

Tracey shook her head.

"No news is probably good news," Jody said. "It's better Matt stays out of the cops' way."

Tracey didn't quite see it that way, and she doubted Jody did either. But she was trying to be supportive, and that's what mattered.

Jody got up from her seat and followed Tracey into the back room. Tracey hung up her jacket, and Jody took her raincoat off the hook.

"Stay strong, eh?" she said. "Matt'll be back and they'll catch the guy who attacked Barry and everything will be back to normal."

*Normal.* Only two days ago, the last thing on earth Tracey wanted would have been for life to be normal. Now, it sounded like the best thing possible.

Jody wrapped Tracey in a hug. It was a good hug, from the heart, and Tracey clung to the other girl as the tears she'd fought all day began to rise. Jody broke away and said, "See you tomorrow."

"Right. Tomorrow."

Tom was coming into the office as the women walked out. There were no customers, and Mr. Simpson was nowhere to be seen, so Tom grabbed Jody around the waist, pulled her close, and gave her a long kiss, noticeably grinding his hips against hers. Then he released her, slapped her on her rump, and said he'd be around when he got off work.

He glanced at Tracey and the edges of his mouth turned up in a smirk.

Jody was a nice girl. What on earth she saw in Tom, Tracey couldn't imagine.

She took her seat at the counter and logged onto the computer to check what was scheduled to happen this evening.

Soon a couple came in to pick up the Lexus SUV they'd reserved. At Global Car Rental they didn't get a lot of high-end cars. The Lexus had only been booked this morning, for four days. The people were from Ontario.

Tom leaned up against the counter. The woman talked to Tracey while her husband studied maps on display.

"You'll enjoy driving that car," Tom said to the man. "Where you off to?"

"We drove in from Vancouver, spent a couple of days at the Banff Springs. Fabulous place. Some folks at the hotel were telling us Waterton and Glacier are pretty special. Figured we'd try them out."

"You're planning to cross the border?"

"Yup."

"Look," Tom said, dropping his voice. "I don't usually ask favors of the customers but if you're going to Glacier, I wonder if you can take something down for me?"

The man's eyes narrowed with suspicion. "Certainly not."

Tom laughed. Perhaps only Tracey heard the tension behind that laugh. "It's a book. Not wrapped or anything, nothing inside it but paper and words. My sister wrote it. An aunt of ours wants to read it, and my sister insists she has to have a signed copy. I was about to mail it, but you're going down there anyway. Won't even be out of your way. My aunt owns a café in the park. She'll treat you to the best coffee and peanut butter squares in Montana."

"I..." the man said.

"Here, let me get the book. I'll show you." Tom dashed into the office, and was back before the customer could gather his wits. He held up a glossy trade paperback and flicked through the pages. "No hidden compartments, no secret partitions. Just paper and ink. A book. What do you say? You'd be doing me a favor. Tell you the truth, I was supposed to mail this weeks ago and my sister's been on my case." Tom snatched a piece of paper off the counter and jotted down an address and phone number. "It's not much of a book. My sister's sorta, well, mentally challenged is the phrase they use, and the book's self-published. But it means a heck of a lot to her." He thrust the object in question out with an embarrassed smile.

The man had little choice but to take it.

"Hey, thanks. Here's the address of the café. Like I said, best coffee and squares in the West. I'll fetch the car now. I'll give it a special going over 'cause you're doing me a big favor."

And Tom was gone.

"What," the woman asked her husband, "was all that about?"

He shrugged. "I guess it can't hurt."

Paperwork completed, they took chairs in the waiting area. Before long, Tom delivered the gleaming Lexus. They walked outside to meet him, and he handed them the keys. They drove off and Tom came inside.

"You don't have a sister," Tracey said.

"Sure I do."

"That's the first I've heard of any book."

"You mind your own business, Trace, and I'll mind mine. Okay?"

"Mr. Simpson will not be happy if he finds out you've asked paying customers to run personal errands."

Tom walked up to her, standing very close. Before Tracey could back away, he took her chin in his right hand. His muscles clenched and his fingers constricted. She shook her head, trying to get free. His grip tightened. "I said, bitch, mind your own business. Think Simpson wants to hear how you've been mooning around worrying about Matt so much I've had to correct all your mistakes?"

"You haven't."

"I have if I say I have."

He looked into her eyes for a long time. Her skin crawled. Her jaw ached, her teeth forced so tightly together they hurt. For the first time, Tracey wondered if Tom knew something about Matt's disappearance he wasn't telling. Telling her or the police. Would Jody lie for Tom if he asked her to?

Yes. If Jody thought she was in love with the prick.

"There are things about Matt the cops would like to know," he said. "If I decide to tell them. Do we understand each other, Trace?"

What things about Matt? Everyone had secrets, at least everyone Tracey knew, things they'd just as soon the police not know about. Was that all Tom meant? Or did he mean something about the death of Barry?

She forced out a nod.

Whatever that business about the book, and she'd seen that it was only a book, it had nothing to do with Matt. Therefore, nothing to do with her. She kept a lot of things that went on around here to herself.

"Good." Tom gave Tracey's face one last hard squeeze, twisted her neck, and then abruptly released her. He grinned. "Very good."

A cube van drove into the lot and Tom went out to check it in.

# Chapter Forty-four

**BANFF SPRINGS HOTEL. BANFF, ALBERTA. MONDAY EVENING.**

Lucky Smith had to decide if there was any point in staying here much longer. She was due to be at the store on Wednesday morning, and Paul was due to be behind his desk. She'd be able to call on the staff to fill in for her, and Paul was, after all, the boss. But this hotel wasn't cheap, and certainly not with meals in restaurants and a separate room for Moonlight. The hotel wasn't full, so there should be no problem extending their stay. Paul would be sure to want to do so.

How long could Paul remain here? They might not find Matt for weeks, months even. She would never say so out loud, but he might never be found. The Canadian wilderness was an enormous, empty place, even in this busy national park. An accident, a fall down a cliff, a broken leg. Plenty of animals to drag a body away or bury the bones.

She wiped at her eyes. She couldn't imagine how Paul could bear it. The simple *not knowing* of it.

If she asked him what he wanted her to do, he'd tell her to go home. She doubted that was what was in his heart. No, she'd stay as long as he did. If they didn't find Matt, perhaps even more if they did, he would need her support.

She tried to read, but the minutes until dinnertime ticked by so slowly. She had the spare keys to Moonlight's car, and decided to pop out and take Sylvester for a quick walk. Sylvester would like that, and so would Lucky.

As could be expected, his greeting was enthusiastic and effusive. After many scratches and much oohing and cooing, she refreshed his water bowl and let him run in the woods for a couple of minutes. Then she held the back door open and gestured for him to get in. Tail sweeping, ears up, he made the leap. His back left leg crumbled and he collapsed onto the ground. He recovered quickly and jumped into the car. No harm done. This time.

Sylvester was getting old, although he was still in good health and spirits. It wouldn't be too many more years before…

Lucky burst into tears.

She was getting old. Paul was getting old. Andy had already gone.

She reached into the car and wrapped the dog in a tight hug. She buried her face in his soft fur and wept. At first, Sylvester snuggled into her embrace, but soon he tried to wiggle free. She held him tighter and wept all the more. She didn't know why she was crying. For herself, perhaps, for her lost youth and for the unstoppable passage of time. For Paul, who was aging before her very eyes as each hour passed with no news of his son, and for Moonlight, who had come to help and now chafed at her own helplessness because she loved an old dog whose ears smelled bad and who suffered from arthritis in his hips.

Sylvester whined and at last Lucky released him. She gave him a pat with one hand and wiped her eyes with the other. He gave her face a lick, and then he glanced at the driver's seat. Telling her to get in and take him home. He had rabbits to chase and a fireplace to stretch out in front of.

"Soon," she said. "Soon. We'll all be going home soon."

Back in the room, she splashed cold water on her face and got ready for dinner.

Moonlight was waiting in the restaurant, but she was alone.

"The chief's tied up. They've got a lead from someone who called to say he saw a man of Matt's description heading out of town on a hiking trail in the early hours Sunday morning.

He and Blectha are at the trailhead waiting for the police dog to join them."

"That's good news, right? The dog will find him?"

"Don't get your hopes up, Mom," Moonlight said, studying the menu. "That's what we thought had happened. It'll be dark soon, and they can't do much without daylight."

"But it's something, dear, it's something."

After dinner, Molly went to the wine bar where Matt worked to talk informally to his coworkers in the hopes that they'd know something they hadn't told the police.

Lucky was unlocking the door to her room when she heard the phone ringing. She almost flew across the room to get it.

Karen Keller wanted a meeting. Right now. Nothing more than curious, Lucky agreed. Karen said she'd be in the lobby, and Lucky spent some time tidying her hair and washing her face.

Karen remained seated as Lucky approached. Karen hadn't bothered to try to hide physical signs of her distress and Lucky's heart reached out to the other woman. A mother, just like her.

Two armchairs sat beneath a tall window overlooking the gardens, separated by a tall, lush fern planted in a substantial stone urn. Lucky took the other chair. It was not a comfortable place to talk. She had to lean forward and crane her neck to see Karen. Neither of the women bothered with empty greetings.

"Paul tells me you met Matt's girlfriend," Karen said.

"Yes. Her name's Tracey."

"I know. We had lunch, here at the hotel, a month or two ago. I was not impressed. White trash, was the phrase Jonathan used. I hoped Matt would be rid of her by now. Apparently not. Paul said you have her phone number. I want to talk to her."

"Why?"

"Because she's my son's girlfriend, that's why. She might know something about where he's gone. Plus she's a potential daughter-in-law, perhaps the mother of my grandchildren some day, perish the thought."

"You're getting ahead of things, Karen. I didn't get the impression their relationship has progressed that far."

"I have no interest in hearing about your impressions of anything to do with my family."

"I suggest you keep your grievances toward me to yourself for now. I met the girl, and I liked her. She's obviously very fond of Matt and worried about him. Isn't that what counts right now?"

All the anger fled from Karen like air from a popped balloon. She almost visibly shrank into the buttery leather of her seat. Lucky remembered Karen Keller as a plump, cheerful woman, comfortable in her role of small-town police chief's wife, as casual in dress and manner as everyone else in Trafalgar. This well-dressed, expensively groomed, *brittle* woman could be the evil twin of the Karen Lucky had known.

"Perhaps," Karen said in a small voice, "she's heard from Matt since you last spoke to her."

"That could be. He might have told her not to contact the police."

"Can you call her, Lucky? Please. Ask her to meet with me… with us. I am his mother. She can confide in me."

Lucky pulled her phone out of the depths of her sweater pocket. "I believe she works at a car rental place until nine. I'll ask if she's able to meet us after work."

Karen watched eagerly, almost hungrily, as Lucky made the call. Tracey sounded hesitant when she realized it was Lucky calling, but that soon turned to enthusiasm when Lucky explained that Matt's mother wanted to talk to her. "Can we pick you up at work when you get off?"

"No. Come around to our place. Matt's and mine, I mean. We have a roommate but he won't be in so we can talk. Tell Mrs. Keller I'm looking forward to seeing her again." She rattled off the address, and hung up. Lucky clutched her phone thinking. The address Tracey had given was Matt's apartment. She hadn't been living there yesterday.

"Is something wrong?"

"No. She said to drop in around nine-thirty." Lucky glanced at her watch. Eight-fifteen.

"I don't know about you," Karen said, "but I need a drink. And, as I can't walk into a bar on my own, I guess you'll have to do. Come on."

"Where's Jonathan?"

"On the phone. He'll be there for a long time yet. Business doesn't stop because of family emergencies. He has a very important deal about to close and negotiations are getting tricky. Some property in the Kootenays, I think he said."

# Chapter Forty-five

**BEARTRACK TRAIL. BANFF, ALBERTA. MONDAY NIGHT.**

She was a popular girl today. First, Lucky Smith called saying Matt's mom wanted to meet with her, and then it was Lucky's daughter checking in.

Tracey told Lucky Smith she'd meet them at the apartment. She wanted to make sure Matt's mom knew they were living together. Good thing she'd gone to all that trouble to clean up before going to work.

"What you smiling at?" Tom said as the clock dragged itself reluctantly toward nine.

"Nothing." Tracey involuntarily stretched her aching jaw. Tom smirked.

Matt's bedroom door had a lock on it. Good thing, Tracey thought, if Tom was going to be hanging around before Matt got back.

She was starving, and realized she hadn't eaten a thing all day. A pot of coffee was kept on the go in the back room, but it was no substitute for food. No point in asking Tom to go out and get her something. In the unlikely event he did as she asked, she'd be afraid he'd spit in it. She remembered boxes of Kraft Dinner in the apartment. No milk to cook it with, but a sizable chunk of margarine would make it edible. She could hardly invite Matt's mom and Lucky Smith to join in her a pot of Kraft Dinner, and she couldn't eat in front of them.

Tracey had told Molly Smith she could meet up for a late dinner. Let her pay. She looked like she could afford it, and she was after information, wasn't she? Tracey said she was working late. She wasn't sure why she lied. Afraid, probably, that if she said she was meeting Molly's mom, then Molly would have no reason to want to talk to her.

The hands on the clock over the counter turned very slowly indeed. A few cars came in. No more were scheduled to go out. Tom watched her with his perpetual sneer, and she did her best to ignore him. The Corolla he was so interested in, and trying to look as though he wasn't, squatted in the far corner all day, untouched.

She locked up the office promptly at nine. Tom had disappeared fifteen minutes earlier.

She arrived at the apartment to find Matt's mom and Lucky Smith standing on the doorstep. She wanted to give Matt's mom a hug, but the woman's stiff posture and stony face sent the message loud and clear: *Stay back.*

"Hi, Mrs. Keller. Nice to see you again. Come on in." Tracey led the way upstairs and opened the apartment door. Karen's nose twitched and she visibly recoiled. Lingering traces of pot, stale beer, rotting food, unwashed clothes, and damp towels, all overlaid with the scent of the inadequate cleaning products Tracey had on hand for her task.

She'd been so proud. Proud of the job she'd done cleaning up, proud to be doing what she could to help Matt. Now, she looked at the apartment through the women's eyes.

It was a dump.

Karen was wearing a camel trench coat with a dark red scarf and brown leather gloves. She made no move to take the gloves off. "Is this where," she swallowed heavily, "it happened?"

"Yes," Tracey said. "But you can't tell. It's all tidied up now." She kept her eyes off the clean patch of carpet.

"Perhaps," Lucky said, "we shouldn't have come." She looked long and hard at Tracey's face, as if seeing something there.

"Boys will be boys, I guess," Karen said. "I wasn't aware you were living here, Tracey. I believe when I spoke to my son last, he said he shared with three other men."

"It's a new development."

"I see." Karen walked into the living room. She looked around the apartment, not liking what she saw. Lucky gave Tracey an encouraging smile.

"The police called me," Karen said. "Sunday morning. Looking for my son. They'd found my name in his contact list on his phone. I had to say I didn't know where he was, I hadn't spoken to him in some weeks. Things have been difficult between us lately. Jonathan thinks I spoil the boy. I only wish I'd spoiled him more." Tears filled her eyes.

"I'm sure he's fine," Tracey said. "He might not even know we're all so worried. I bet that's it. He's done that before, gone off into the backcountry when he needed to get his head on straight without a word to anyone. Yes, that's what's happened. He doesn't take his phone or computer or anything with him, says he wants to be away from the world. He won't know there's a search on for him."

"He's always been like that. When he was a boy, he'd want to get away by himself. You must remember, Lucky. Matt was one of your regular customers, wasn't he? Even before he got a job and made proper money, he'd be saving his allowance for a new sleeping bag or a Coleman stove."

Tracey McMillan and Karen Keller smiled at each other, pleased with their logic. "There's going to be such a to-do when he comes back to town and realizes the effort the police have put into searching for him. Paul will have a fit."

"Paul?"

"Matt's father. He never did have any time for Matt's daydreaming, as he called it. I've always said, if Paul would have let Matt be himself, he would have turned out…"

"All of which is beside the point," Lucky interrupted, her color rising. "Tracey, have you heard from Matt since we last spoke?"

"No."

"If you do hear from him," Karen said, "will you tell him to call me?"

"Sure."

"I'd appreciate it, dear, if you could let me know immediately when you hear. Before calling his father or the police, I mean."

Lucky chewed her lip, but said nothing.

Karen looked around the apartment. She went to the window and pulled back the dusty white sheet that served as a curtain. Passing cars threw light from their headlamps into the room, illuminating the lines of stress and worry on the women's faces. "I'm sure this is a lovely view during the day."

"It is," Tracey said, pleased Karen was trying to find something good to say about their home. She should offer her guests a drink. But she didn't have tea, and the coffee in the cupboard was instant, and there wasn't milk or cream to go with it anyway. Unlikely either Lucky or Karen were the sort to quaff domestic beer straight from the bottle.

"You and Matt don't live here alone, do you?" Karen asked.

"We need help with the rent so we have roommates. One of them left this morning, and I'm hoping the other will be gone soon. He's not very nice."

Karen dug in her Coach bag and placed several new twenty-dollar bills on the coffee table.

"I don't need…" Tracey began.

"You'll have expenses until Matt gets back. I want to help. It's not much."

Tracey felt tears behind her eyes. Mrs. Keller looked at her for a long time. "Thank you," she said at last. "Thank you for caring about my son."

Tracey sniffled.

Karen placed a card on top of the money. "This is my number. Call me any time, day or night, and tell Matt to call as soon as you hear from him. Tell him to phone me before he speaks to his father."

Lucky cleared her throat. "The police…"

"The police," Karen said, "can wait. His mother comes first." She headed for the door, put her hand on the knob. "I'm glad we had this talk, Tracey. I'm sure all will be resolved soon."

She left. Lucky followed.

Tracey shut the door, and leaned up against it. Wow, Karen Keller wasn't such a snooty bitch after all. Her stomach grumbled. She eyed the money on the table. Better save that in case she needed it to help Matt. Let Smith buy her dinner.

# Chapter Forty-six

**CHINA WOK RESTAURANT. BANFF, ALBERTA. MONDAY NIGHT.**

More expense. Smith sighed and put away her phone. Tracey wanted to meet for dinner. No doubt she'd expect Smith to pay. Wouldn't be so bad if she actually wanted to eat, but she'd indulged in a huge ribs and fries dinner and about the last thing she needed now was more food.

Hopefully Tracey would choose some place more down-market this time.

It was shortly after ten o'clock. Tracey said she'd be at the China Wok on Banff Avenue in fifteen minutes. This time Smith drove herself into town. Sylvester bounded happily in the back. She didn't intend to have much to drink, not after last night. She'd been to Reds, trying to find out what she could about Matt. The place was quiet so the staff had time to talk. Unfortunately, they had nothing to say. They didn't socialize with Matt after work, didn't know much about his life or where he lived. Didn't know and didn't care. One of the waitresses, a tall icy blonde, mentioned that Tracey came in sometimes, sat by herself and nursed a drink for hours, watching Matt through adoring eyes.

Smith finally ran out of questions to ask and people to ask them of. She killed time waiting for Tracey to call by taking Sylvester for a walk down Banff Avenue, the town's main drag.

Cascade Mountain, its outline visible in traces of moonlight, framed the end of the street. Along with the usual array of tourist shops both cutesy and junk-filled, galleries featuring local art, and high-end women's fashions, the town sported some pretty good wilderness equipment stores. She peeked in windows, drooling at the array of supplies, while Sylvester sniffed under lampposts and left messages telling any dog who might follow that he'd been here.

She was debating coming back tomorrow when one particular store was open and trying on the ski jacket in the window when Tracey called.

By the time Smith got Sylvester back to the car and arrived at the meeting place, Tracey was seated, with a bottle of beer in front of her while she studied the menu. The restaurant was decorated the same as every Chinese restaurant Smith had ever been in. Walls colored red and gold. Small tables, unadorned by tablecloths or candles. Paper-wrapped chopsticks and a couple of small bottles of sauce. This time of night, on a holiday Monday, the place was empty other than Tracey and the waitress who bustled over, smiling, to greet Smith as she entered.

"Just green tea for me, please."

"You're not eating," Tracey said, disappointment in her voice.

"I had dinner earlier. You go ahead. I'll get it."

"Thanks."

"What happened to you?"

"What do you mean?"

"Your face. Did someone hit you?"

Tracey flushed, and dipped her head into her menu. "Of course not, don't be silly."

"Hardly silly. What happened?" The girl's jaw was bruised, looking as if she'd fallen and it had struck the pavement. Or someone had held it, hard. "It's fresh, must have happened within the last couple of hours."

"Nothing happened. I bumped into a door. Wasn't watching where I was going."

"Never heard that one before. Have you seen Matt?"

"No! Not since Saturday, as I keep telling people. And even if I had, Matt never hit me. He wouldn't."

"Someone did."

"Drop it, will you? Why are you so sure, anyway? Are you a nurse or something?"

"Not a nurse. No."

"Okay then."

"Ready to order?" The waitress' smile was stiff, her eyes wary. She'd heard the raised voices.

Tracey requested egg rolls, General Tao chicken, green beans in spicy sauce, and steamed rice. Smith repeated that she'd have green tea.

Tracey had nothing new to tell her, and Smith realized the girl had only agreed to meet hoping for another free meal. She should have been annoyed, but something about Tracey's vulnerability touched Smith deep inside.

She hoped Matt Keller was worthy of this intense, loyal young woman.

She doubted it.

She remembered Matt as a strutting high-school athlete, popular among his peers and the girls, center of attention, cocky in school, minor troublemaker out of it. The young Matt wouldn't have given this timid, insecure girl a second glance. She was young, very young, compared to Matt's early thirties. Not hard to see what Tracey saw in Matt, but the other way? It wasn't even as though Tracey had some money behind her. No accounting for taste, Smith reminded herself, and it had been a lot of years since she'd known Matt Keller.

People could change. *Couldn't they?*

Smith sipped tea while Tracey ate.

"You gonna tell me what happened to your face?" Smith said as Tracey scooped up the last of her rice and sauce.

"A guy at work. His name's Tom. He shares the apartment with Matt. It's nothing. He's on edge. We all are."

"You're on edge, as you say. Have you hit this Tom?"

"Of course not."

"My point exactly. I don't care what's eating him, he can't go around hitting you."

"He didn't hit me."

"If you say so. Causing bruising to your face, however done, is not acceptable behavior among colleagues."

Tracey mumbled into her food.

"Do you want me to go with you to the police?"

"No! I was asking him questions. Butting into stuff that's none of my business."

"Always an excuse. Next time, call the police."

"There won't be a next time."

"Sure there will. There always is. You're making a mistake, Tracey, but if that's what you want, fine, let it go. You have to promise me if you learn anything about Matt, hear anything, hear from him, you will not keep it to yourself. Absolutely no good will come of that."

Tracey studied Smith's face for a long time. The waitress slipped the bill onto the table, and it lay there between them, untouched.

"I'm afraid," Tracey said at last. "So afraid."

Smith's hand reached across the table. She laid it on the back of Tracey's. "I understand. But anything Matt's trying to do on his own, whether hide from the authorities, track down the killer himself, or just run away, will come to grief. Believe me on this, Tracey."

"I do." Tracey's voice was very low. In the kitchen, a man said something in Chinese and the waitress laughed.

Smith picked up the bill. "I'll give you a lift home. You look like you haven't slept for days."

"I haven't."

# Chapter Forty-seven

**BEARTRACK TRAIL. BANFF, ALBERTA. MONDAY NIGHT.**

Lucky Smith and Karen Keller walked the half-block to Paul's car in silence. Lights were on in many of the apartment units and music blared from more than one open window. Cars drove past, and people walked dogs. The night air was crisp, but not cold, clean with the scent of snow on the mountains and coniferous trees in the forest.

Lucky touched the key fob and the car blinked at them in greeting. They climbed in, and Lucky put the key in the ignition. Before she could turn it, Karen said, "Did Paul tell you I wanted to stop the divorce?"

Shocked, Lucky half-turned in her seat. They were parked beneath a streetlight, and long shadows filled the crevices in Karen's face. "It's true. I soon regretted leaving him. We hadn't been getting on for a while. I wasn't happy at my job. They had new owners who were making what they called efficiencies, and I called mean-spirited. I was missing my friends and my sister in Calgary. The kids didn't need me anymore. I was tired, depressed. So I told Paul I was leaving him, and I packed my bags and moved to Calgary. It didn't take long to realize I was no happier in my new job, living by myself in a small apartment, with my sister constantly introducing me to her singe male friends. Most of whom were well into their seventies, and hadn't washed their underwear since their wives died. That was precisely what they were looking for in a woman. An underwear-washer.

"I foolishly insisted we sell the house. I wanted an apartment of my own, and I needed my share of the money. I wasn't prepared for how fast it sold."

Neither, thought Lucky, was Paul. He'd been lost, cast adrift when his wife left him, his house sold pretty much out from under him. He'd wanted to move in with Lucky and she'd decided things were happening far too fast and she wouldn't see him anymore.

"I'd always known he loved you, Lucky. I bet you didn't know that either. When we first lived in Trafalgar, when Paul was a detective, it was Lucky Smith this and Lucky Smith that. I was so pleased when Paul got the job in Calgary and we finally got the hell out of Trafalgar."

"I never…"

"I know. It was obvious to everyone that you and Andy adored each other. Despite all his faults, and they are many, Paul is no philanderer. The years passed and I'd forgotten about you, so it didn't raise any red flags when Paul was offered the position of chief constable in Trafalgar. And then we were back and not only was it once again all the outrageous things Lucky Smith was doing, but now Moonlight Smith came into his life."

"My daughter has no relationship with Paul aside…"

"Aside from being one of his officers, yes. I doubt she even knows he's prouder of her than he is of his own children. Cheryl's doing fine. She and her husband own and manage a couple of Subway sandwich shops. Not a career Paul wanted for his daughter. As for Matt…well you know all about Matt."

Lucky's head spun. She'd fallen into her relationship with Paul Keller without much thought. She hadn't given any more thought to where it was going. Was Karen going to ask Paul to come back to her? What would Paul say if she did?

"I don't know why I'm telling you all this, Lucky. That drink at the bar loosened my tongue, maybe." Karen had downed two large glasses of wine in quick succession. It left a glaze across her eyes that made Lucky think she wasn't used to drinking much. The abrupt attitude change toward Tracey, now true confessions to Lucky. She'd be sorry tomorrow. "I swallowed my pride, and told Paul I was sorry. I wanted to stop the divorce proceedings, come back home. I wanted us to try again."

"What did he say to that?"

"It was too late. He'd bought a condo down by the riverfront. A condo suitable for a bachelor. He was in a relationship. I wasn't at all surprised when I heard from a Trafalgar friend that everyone in town was talking about you and Paul. The odd couple, they call you. Perhaps I should have fought for my marriage, for my husband. But I had too much pride, so I didn't speak to my lawyer and the proceedings went ahead. It's surprisingly easy to get a divorce when there are no areas of contention, I found."

Yes, Lucky thought, Karen should have tried harder. Paul and Lucky had stopped seeing each other for several months. Around the time he bought the condo. He was lonely, if nothing else, and he probably would have taken Karen back if she'd pushed. A movement beside the car, and someone came down the sidewalk. Tracey, hands stuffed in her pockets, shoelaces trailing on the ground, walking rapidly in the direction of town.

Tracey was not Lucky's concern right now. "You seem happy with Jonathan, Karen."

"He's a lovely man, yes. I don't know why I'm telling you all this. Perhaps seeing that sad, unhappy girl, and realizing that she does seem to love my son has put me in the mood for facing the truth. I hope Matt's strong enough to look past her sloppy appearance and social awkwardness and see that she has a good heart. But I doubt it. I doubt my son has much more disregard for superficial appearances than I do.

"We'd better get back. Jonathan will be wondering where I am. I can't complain. I shouldn't complain. I've been rewarded for my foolishness by finding a lovely new man. Not many women can say that." Karen touched the ring on her right finger. "I thought being married to a police officer was lonely. That's nothing compared to a businessman. He's always on the phone, always wheeling and dealing. Still," she sighed, "the side benefits are attractive. Sometimes. This isn't me, you know."

"What isn't?"

"What you see here. The expensive hair, the equally expensive clothes." She twisted her hand. The emerald flashed in the glow from the street lights. "The manicure, the weekly spa visits. Jonathan pays for it all. It's what he expects of me. We met at, of all things, a police retirement function, some old colleague of Paul's. I'd wanted to show everyone how well I was doing since leaving Paul. How prosperous and independent I was. I'd lost a good deal of weight—depression and worry mostly. I spent far more than I could afford on a new dress and shoes, matching jewelry, had my hair and makeup professionally done. I met Jonathan that night, and I could tell he liked a woman who appreciated the finer things. From then on, I could hardly go out to dinner in jeans and a t-shirt, could I? Or let my roots and wrinkles show." She sighed and leaned back into the headrest.

Lucky put the car into gear and drove to the hotel. Neither woman said another word.

# Chapter Forty-eight

**RCMP DETACHMENT OFFICE. BANFF, ALBERTA. MONDAY NIGHT.**

As Molly Smith and Tracey McMillan left the China Wok, the waitress flipped the sign on the door to closed. The street was quiet, a few restaurants still open but not much activity. The mountains loomed over them, dark bulk against a dark sky. Only the flashing red lights warning aircraft to keep away marked their place.

"My car's over there." Smith pointed across the street. A RCMP patrol car was parked behind her. As they crossed the street, she flicked her key fob to unlock the Neon.

A uniformed officer got out of his vehicle. "Molly Smith?"

"Yes."

"I'd like you to come with me, please." He did not smile at her.

"What?"

"Matt," Tracey shouted. "You've found Matt. Where is he? Take me to him."

"If you mean Matthew Keller, I don't know anything about that. It's Ms. Smith here the Sergeant wants to talk to."

"I've promised my friend a ride home. I'll drop by the station after that," Smith said.

"Afraid not, miss. I was told to bring you in soon as you appeared. Let's go."

"My dog's in my car."

"Your dog will be fine."

Smith didn't care for the look in his eye or the tone of his voice. This was not one cop exchanging professional courtesies with another. She felt a small frisson of fear touch her spine.

"I can walk," Tracey said, as if she had the choice. "I'll call you, Molly if...you know."

The cop opened the back door of his patrol car.

"I'll sit in the front," Smith said.

"You'll sit where I tell you to."

"Are you aware that I'm a police officer?"

His eyes widened slightly.

"Constable Smith. Trafalgar City Police. Do you want to see my ID?"

"No need. Get in."

She walked around the car and sat in the front passenger seat. She snapped her seat belt closed. "Who wants to see me?"

"Sergeant Blechta."

"Does he have news about Matt Keller?"

"Not that I know. He sent out your tag numbers, said to bring you in. That's all."

"What's your name?"

"Andy Jones."

She couldn't help but laugh. "My dad was named Andy Smith."

He turned his head slightly and grinned at her. Then Jones activated his radio to contact dispatch and told them to tell Blechta he was bringing Smith in.

The laugh died in her throat. She did not like the sound of that. If Blechta wanted to talk to her, all he had to do was ask Paul Keller for her phone number and she would have come down to the station without wasting Jones' time.

At least Jones didn't drive her around the back, to the secure bay. He pulled up to a side door, and she got out. She didn't thank him for the ride. He muttered something like, "See you around," and pulled away.

Blechta was waiting for her at the door. Paul Keller was not with him.

"My office, Ms. Smith," the sergeant said.

"Constable Smith."

He gave her a look, but said nothing more until he was seated behind his desk and she was shifting from one foot to the other, like a naughty schoolboy called up in front of the principal.

"You have no jurisdiction here."

"I know that."

"You've been asking questions, poking around where you're not wanted."

"I have at no time represented myself as a police officer, or implied that I'm involved in the investigation. I'm doing what I can to help out a friend of a friend. Like anyone would."

"Anyone," he said, "would let the police handle it."

She debated asking how well the police were handling it, considering that Matt Keller had now been missing for two days. She held her tongue. She hadn't done any better. "Where's Chief Keller?"

"Back at his hotel, I assume. Where you should be. Look, Ms. Smith."

"Constable Smith."

He studied her for a long time. She kept her face impassive, but her heart was pounding. The heat in the office was turned up too high, and she was sweltering in her coat and scarf. She forced herself not to wipe her palms against the leg of her jeans. What had Adam told her, whispers said Blechta had trouble with women? She could believe it. But she couldn't believe he was going to try anything now. Here. She wasn't under his command; she wasn't dependent on him for a good job assessment or plum assignments. She'd done nothing that so much as skirted the law since she'd been in Banff. He'd had her pulled off the street like a common criminal in a blatant act of intimidation. He'd overplayed his hand. She would not be intimidated.

She tried to believe herself.

He broke the stare first. "There's nothing you or your chief can accomplish here. Go home and take Keller and your mother with you."

She didn't bother to mention that she'd decided to do that very thing while she watched Tracey gulp down chicken and rice. She could meet Tracey every day, feed her and ply her with drinks, and never learn a darn thing. Because Tracey didn't know a darn thing. Matt had run out on her, as much as he'd run from his father and from the police. It would be a long time before Tracey came to accept that, and Smith had better things to do.

Besides, Sylvester was getting restless in the car. He'd found a loose piece of fabric on the back of the front passenger seat and pretty much tore it to shreds. Smith decided she could afford to concede, just an inch, to Blechta. "I'll talk to Chief Keller."

"Good. I'm glad we understand each other. Constable Jones will take you back to your car. Good-bye, Ms. Smith."

# Chapter Forty-nine

**TRAFALGAR CITY POLICE STATION & GRIZZLY RESORT. TRAFALGAR, BRITISH COLUMBIA. TUESDAY MORNING.**

John Winters was settling himself behind his desk on Tuesday morning, a cup of steaming coffee in hand, when his phone rang.

"Morning, Ron."

"We've had a call from the security guard at the Grizzly Resort. He's found something he says we'll want to see. I thought you might like to be in on it."

"What sort of something?" He glanced out the window. Clouds were thick with the promise of more rain.

"Didn't say."

"I'll meet you there." Winters carried his mug out to the GIS van.

By the time he arrived at the construction site, the road was lined with RCMP vehicles, including Ron Gavin's forensic van. The private security guard was gone; a uniformed officer stood at the gate. It had rained since Winters' visit yesterday, leaving the dirt track thick with mud. Winters pulled off to the side of the road and climbed out of his own van as Adam Tocek's truck pulled up. Adam jumped out, followed by Norman. The dog's tail wagged and his ears were up. He almost looked as though he were smiling at the prospect of going to work.

"Where are they?" Winters asked the uniform.

"About a hundred yards down the path. Can't miss 'em."

"Thanks."

As Winters, Adam, and Norman rounded the bend, they could see a group of police up ahead. Darren Fernhaugh was with them, waving his arms, yelling at the private security guard. Two men stood beside them, hard hats tucked under their arms, faces set into dark lines. The men clustered around a bulldozer. Another machine was parked close by.

"Take a look at this, John," Ron Gavin called. "Adam, keep that dog well back."

Winters and Adam exchanged glances. Winters approached while Adam ordered Norman to sit. At the base of the bulldozer, right about where the driver would step to climb up, lay one of the most vicious pieces of equipment John Winters had ever seen. Metal plates and chains formed a loop, with a row of sharp teeth in the center. The whole thing was about the size of his forearm.

"Nasty." He crouched down to have a closer look, taking great care to keep his hands away.

Leghold traps were legal in B.C. But not this type. Not the ones with teeth.

The ground around the trap was compacted earth; the path had been cleared a long time ago. This hadn't been here yesterday.

Winters got to his feet. He looked at Fernhaugh. A vein pulsed in the man's forehead.

"Any idea who would do this?"

One of the workers spat. "Goddamned tree huggers, that's who. Coulda taken off my fuckin' foot." The men wore steel-toed work boots and thick overalls. If they had stepped into the trap, they would have felt it. But it would have been unlikely to do any serious damage.

Whoever set the trap would have known that.

One of the Mounties was holding a large, thick branch. At a nod from Ron Gavin, he plunged it into the center of the trap. The teeth clamped shut with a sickening crunch. The branch snapped in two and the watchers shuddered. Norman barked.

Winters let out a long breath.

"Adam," Gavin said, "see if Norman can get a scent. And for God's sake, people, watch your footing."

Every one of the men looked down.

Adam showed Norman the trap. The dog sniffed at it, and then the surrounding ground. Adam relaxed the leash, letting the dog have his head. They watched as Norman cast about, searching for a scent. He set off back the way they'd come, head down, ears up. One of the uniformed Mounties went with them, to watch Adam's back while his attention was focused on his dog.

"What happened?" Winters asked the workers. "What's your name?"

"I'm Morris Jennings. This here's Danny. We got here at seven-thirty, regular time, ready to start work. Gotta clear some of those woods. We went into the office, put on the coffee, like always, checked the day's orders. Came out fifteen or so minutes later, heading for the dozers."

"I arrived," Fernhaugh said, "as Morris and Donny were coming out of the office. A minute later, I heard them shouting and ran to see what was happening."

Morris pointed. "That's right where I woulda put my foot, to climb into the cab. If I hadn't happened to look down, I woulda."

"Did you touch anything?"

"Are you fuckin' kidding? We ran back inside, told Darren to call the cops."

Winters studied the ground. The trap lay out in the open. No attempt had been made to bury it or to cover it with earth or leaves and twigs. It was intended as a threat, nothing more.

"Did you check the other bulldozer?"

"Yeah," Donnie said. "Nothing. We looked around the yard but didn't find anything more."

"This is an outrage," Fernhaugh said. "Intimidation, pure and simple. Intended to stop work. We're going to have to search the entire property before I can let anyone step foot onto the ground. What about tomorrow? And the day after that? Do I have to search everything, every day? We'll never get any work done. We're behind schedule as it is."

Which, Winters reflected, was precisely the point.

"We're taking this very seriously, sir," Gavin said. "We'll find out who's responsible."

"You had better," Fernhaugh muttered. "You two get to work. At least you'll be safe in your machines." His face paled. "You don't think..."

"No," Winters said. "I don't think you're in any more danger. This was clearly intended as a warning, nothing more."

"Warning! Couldna taken off my fuckin' foot," Morris said. Donnie nodded. "What's next? A snake in the cab?"

"I want protection," Fernhaugh said. "For my men as well as my property."

"I'll see that you get it," Gavin said.

"Obviously," Fernhaugh said, "this private bunch I *thought* were guarding my property aren't exactly up to the task."

"Look, I told you," the security guard said, "if they came in through the woods, didn't make a noise, kept out of sight, what was I supposed to do about it? I'm just one guy."

"If I get one of those hippie bastards alone in a dark alley," Morris said. "He's the one who'll need protection."

"Threats," Winters said, "are not helping."

The men muttered some more. But eventually, with much theatrical checking of every place they put their feet or hands, they got into their machines. They lumbered down the path, heading into the woods.

"I'll join you in a couple of minutes, Mr. Fernhaugh," Ron Gavin said once the bulldozers were out of sight.

Fernhaugh grunted and went back to his office.

Gavin rummaged in his forensics kit and came out with a bag. He pulled on his gloves, picked up the trap and dropped it into the bag. The look on his face would curdle milk. "Disgusting thing." He wrote the date and location onto the bag. "You think this was a deliberate warning to the Grizzly Resort, John?"

"Can't see that it would have been anything else. No trapper's going to be working around here. Most of the animals are long gone. That trap's illegal anyway. If it had gone off, it wouldn't have done much damage to a man in construction boots, but I suspect that's beside the point. Things are escalating and that worries me."

Gavin grunted. His radio crackled. "Go ahead, Adam."

"Norman picked up a scent right away. It goes into the woods, and it's pretty darn muddy in here. Footprints are easy to see. Looks like two sets to me, both of them coming in, then going out. I remember an old logging road about a kilometer or so further east. They seem to be headed there. Probably where they left their car to avoid the guard at the main entrance."

Gavin hefted his pack. "Hold up and wait for me. I'll be right there."

He turned to Winters. "It rained late yesterday afternoon, so footprints and tire treads should be clear. I'd like to take the casts now, in case it rains again. Do you want to talk to Fernhaugh, John, see if he has anything more to say?"

"Happy to."

Darren Fernhaugh sat behind his secretary's desk. He was on the phone and waved Winters to a seat. When he hung up, he said, "I was letting Nancy know what's going on. So she wouldn't be frightened by all the police activity."

"Good idea."

Darren Fernhaugh could shed no light on who might have been responsible for laying the trap. He simply shook his head. "Whoever it is, though, they don't know how damaging this is. This sort of thing is going to slow us down, all right. If we have to check equipment before we use it. Watch where we're going. Morris is a drama queen. Any sort of nick or cut and he'll be yelling for compensation and sick time. We're supposed to start pouring concrete next week, and I need the foundations cleared for the first lot of cottages." He rubbed his head. "My investors are already getting antsy. They keep wondering why we're not working faster. I don't suppose you can keep this under your hat, Sergeant?"

"Afraid not. But even if we could, I expect your bulldozer operators will be spreading the story far and wide."

"In every bar in the district." Fernhaugh groaned. "Every recitation more lurid than the last."

"I don't have to tell you to stay alert."

"No."

Winters walked through the woods to his car. The scowling security guard was back at the gate, an RCMP car parked prominently on the road. Tree huggers, Fernhaugh and his men had said. They seemed to think that was a good enough description of the vandals.

But John Winters wasn't so sure. What sort of environmentalists would lay an illegal leghold trap? They would have wanted to be in and out under cover of darkness. The trap would have had to have been set at least an hour or two earlier. They might not have minded if a man in a work boot had stepped into it, but would they have taken a chance on an animal passing by? A coyote or a lynx, a deer, or an elk? Even a curious dog, out for its morning walk.

Highly unlikely.

# Chapter Fifty

**BOW VALLEY GRILL. BANFF SPRINGS HOTEL. BANFF, ALBERTA. TUESDAY MORNING.**

"When I came in last night," Paul Keller said, apropos of nothing, "a couple of guys were asking the concierge about the best places to find fish."

"When all this is over," Lucky said, "we'll come back. And you can go fishing."

"When it's all over."

"It's time for me to go home," Smith said. "You should come with me, Mom."

"No."

"Molly's right, Lucky," Keller said. "We're not accomplishing anything here." He popped a slice of bacon into his mouth.

"Are you leaving?" Lucky asked him.

"Not yet."

"Then neither am I."

Keller touched Lucky's hand. They didn't smile, but their eyes exchanged a message.

Smith gulped down a mouthful of tea. Too hot. "Mom…"

"I'll stay with Paul. For a while, anyway."

No point in arguing. No one could argue with Lucky anyway, not once she'd made up her mind. As they'd ordered breakfast, Smith had told Keller about the encounter with Sergeant Blechta the previous evening. He'd sighed and said he wasn't surprised.

Matt had now been missing for more than forty-eight hours. Someone had reported seeing him taking a hiking path out of town before first light on Sunday morning . A police dog had been called out, but too much time, and too many people, had passed and the dog and his handler admitted defeat.

Otherwise, not a peep.

Smith could do nothing more here.

They ate the rest of their breakfast in silence.

"I'll be off then, Mom."

The women stood and hugged. "You take care," Smith mumbled into her mom's hair.

"Tell them at the front desk that I'll take care of the bill."

"Will do." She released her mother. "Sylvester will be glad to be going home."

"Drive carefully," Keller said.

It didn't take long to toss her few belongings into her backpack. She was checking the room for any forgotten items when her cell phone rang.

A bust of words, tumbling all over themselves. Tracey.

"Hey, slow down," Smith said. "I can't understand you."

"He called. Matt called me."

"That's great. Where is he?"

Tracey hesitated. "I can't say. But he wants to meet me, this morning. He says he's leaving Alberta. He wants…he wants me to come with him! I wanted to let you know, that's all. He told me not to tell anyone, but I promised you I would."

"Tracey, wait. Matt can't leave. He's suspected of murder."

"He didn't do it!"

"I know that." Smith didn't know any such thing. The police officer in her figured Matt had done it. Regardless, he had to stop running. Even if he headed off into the wilderness, he'd be found soon enough. This wasn't the wild west. No one could disappear for long in the modern world. "The longer he stays away, the guiltier he looks. You have to make him understand that."

Tracey hesitated.

"Tell me where he is, and I'll go and get him."

"I can't."

"Sure you can. Matt needs to do the right thing. That's the best way for you to help him."

"I can't tell you. I mean you won't be able to find it." Tracey hesitated. "I suppose it would be okay if you came with me."

Not what Smith had in mind. She intended to go for Matt, all right. With backup. "Where is he?"

"A place we know. A nice place. We had a picnic there a couple of times. I'm not much of a wilderness girl, but Matt wanted me to be. He took me hiking and I tried to like it." Her voice trailed off. "I'm not even sure I can find it again. Not without Matt. He said he'd put a signal out for me."

That did not sound promising. But it was all Smith had. "Where are you?"

"It's my day off at the restaurant. I'm at home. At Matt's apartment, I mean."

"I can be there in ten minutes."

"You won't tell anyone, will you? Not your mom. Not Matt's dad. Particularly not the police. I mean it. Promise me you'll come alone, or I won't take you."

"Okay, Tracey. We'll play it your way."

Smith scrambled in her backpack, tossing aside her clothes and toiletries. She put her running shoes on and stuffed a heavy sweater into the pack. She wasn't equipped to venture into the backcountry, but Matt couldn't be too far if he was at a place he'd taken Tracey. She kept a flashlight in the car and emergency supplies, as well as a small knife that fastened onto her belt. It would have to do.

# Chapter Fifty-one

**GLOBAL CAR RENTAL. BANFF, ALBERTA. TUESDAY MORNING.**

Tom Dunning also received a long-awaited phone call.

Someone was coming to get the Corolla.

Tom didn't know what was so special about that car, and he figured he was better off not knowing. Simpson had told him to keep it in the lot, untouched. He told Jody and Tracey it needed some new parts before it could be rented out again. They didn't question him. Vehicle maintenance was Tom's job.

As far as Tom was concerned, he wanted to be rid of the thing. Since Barry's death the cops were showing far too much interest in people who'd known him.

The man who finally came for the Corolla was a tough-looking guy with short black hair and a thick beard. He didn't smile as he showed Jody his Saskatchewan driver's license and a credit card, and filled out the paperwork. Jody asked him if he'd like a free map of the national park and he said yes. She handed him the keys, her fake smile firmly in place. "Enjoy your visit." The car was due to be returned in three days.

Tom took him outside to check over the vehicle.

"Where you heading?" Tom asked.

"B.C."

"Been there before?"

The guy looked at him through dark sunglasses. "Didn't anyone ever tell you not to ask so many questions?"

Tom shrugged. "Just being friendly."

"Don't be." He didn't bother to check out the car for damage. He scribbled a signature on the paper Tom handed him. Then he got into the car and drove away.

Tom stood in the lot watching until the Corolla was out of sight.

Simpson had told him not to bother cleaning the car, and not to open the trunk or check under the seats. He'd assumed it was carrying drugs. Simpson did a good trade sending B.C. Bud, the world's best marijuana, east and south.

No one would be taking pot *to* B.C.

Not his problem. Tom went into the office.

Jody was getting pushy. Last night she'd been whining again that Tom never took her anywhere. Time to dump Jody. Time to dump this town.

Tom was a firm believer that good times don't last. Look at his dad, Mad Mike Dunning—top of the world when his band was the hottest thing in Canada. Five-star hotels, big stadiums, the best booze and drugs and groupies. Talk of a major record deal in the States, even a tour of Europe.

These days Mad Mike was lucky to get a bed in the drunk tank for the night.

Even though that prick Simpson took the majority of it, Tom was making good money here, between the car-repair scam and drug-running. He even did a little freelancing of his own. But he'd had a fright when the cops started nosing around while that Corolla was sitting on the lot. Sure the cops weren't interested in the car-rental business or anything going on there. Their questions were all about who might have killed Barry and where Matt might have gone.

But the last thing he needed was one overeager cop to show an interest in the Corolla.

Or for Jody or Tracey to open their fat mouths and say something really stupid.

Tom didn't much care if Matt had killed Barry or not. He wasn't going to hang around to find out. A high-profile murder case, maybe an expensive lawyer looking for someone else to pin the blame on. That didn't suit Tom at all.

He'd finish this shift. Simpson would be by later to pay him his share of the extra fees for handling the Corolla. Then: time to split.

No one was around and they didn't have another pick up scheduled until noon.

Maybe he could convince Jody to make a quick trip into the washroom with him. Sort of a good-bye gift from him to her.

# Chapter Fifty-two

**BEARTRACK TRAIL & BANFF NATIONAL PARK. BANFF, ALBERTA. TUESDAY MORNING.**

When Smith pulled up in front of the apartment building on Beartrack Trail, Tracey was outside, pacing up and down on the sidewalk. She leapt into the car before Smith had barely come to a stop.

The girl's eyes were radiant and her skin glowed. Joy came off her in waves. "Hey, you've got a dog. Hi there, dog." She put her hand out. Sylvester leaned across the seat and sniffed the offering. Tracey rubbed the top of his head. "What's his name?"

"Sylvester. This isn't a picnic, Tracey."

"I know, I know." She faced forward and snapped on her seat belt. "I'm so happy. Matt called me. He needs help, and he called me."

Smith kept her opinion to herself. Whether Matt had called Tracey because he loved her, or because he knew she would no more betray him than Sylvester would turn on Lucky, only time would tell. "Where to?"

"Turn left at the end of the street."

Smith was pretty sure she was heading for a lot of trouble. She'd been told of the presence of a person of interest to the police yet hadn't called it in. She'd been ordered, more than once, by the local police to butt out. If she were working, if this was Trafalgar, she'd have to report it, come what may.

But here? Tracey had contacted her precisely because she didn't know Smith was a police officer. Matt trusted Tracey, and Tracey had simply brought along a friend.

It was the way it had to be.

Tracey giving directions, they drove out of town onto the Trans-Canada. After only a few kilometers, Tracey said to turn off. They passed an impressive lodge, and soon came to a parking area. The lot was mostly empty, and Smith pulled up beside two women unloading three small children, backpacks, and hiking poles from a mud-spattered SUV.

"How far?"

"About two hours walking. That's with Matt leading the way."

"Let's go then." Smith glanced into the back seat. "Sorry, old guy. You can't come."

She'd briefly considered bringing Sylvester. But this wasn't a casual jaunt into the backwoods, and Sylvester was an old dog. If they did run into trouble, Smith didn't want someone else to worry about.

On her way out of the hotel, she'd dropped into the shop where she picked up bottles of water, granola bars, and bags of nuts and chocolate.

She popped the trunk, pulled out her emergency kit, and began to stuff things into her backpack. Along with the food and water, she took a portable GPS, a high-powered flashlight, a length of rope, her travelling first aid kit, and a box of waterproof matches. She slipped a can of bear spray into her pocket and snapped a small, but good, knife onto the waistband of her jeans. She had not brought her hiking boots, so running shoes would have to do. She had an extra pair of socks, light wool gloves, and a raincoat.

She shifted the pack, checking its weight.

"Wow," Tracey said. "You've got a lot of stuff."

"Ten yards off that path and we're in the wilderness. I do not go into the wilderness unequipped." Smith eyed Tracey. The girl wore her regular running shoes and a jacket. Her bright red plastic purse was slung over her shoulder. "Ditch the bag. You can put anything you need in here."

Tracey took out a packet of tissues and a tube of lip cream. She half-turned, and took a few bills out of her wallet. She stuffed those into her pocket and threw her bag into the car. Smith dug a pen and piece of paper out of her own purse, and slammed the lid of the trunk. She wrote a quick note saying where they'd gone, and why, put it on the dashboard, told Sylvester to guard the car, and locked the doors. She'd left a note for her mom on the desk in her hotel room.

She adjusted the straps of her pack. She felt the comfortable weight of the knife on her hip. She would have preferred to have her Glock, but that wasn't going to happen.

"Did Matt tell you where he was calling from?" Smith said. "He doesn't have his phone with him."

"I didn't think to ask. I was so excited to hear from him. Everything's going to be okay, isn't it, Molly?"

"Lead on," Smith said to Tracey.

The sky was clear and the temperature comfortably cool. The trail began as a paved path. A short walk took them to a spot where the swift-moving river tumbled over a rocky waterfall into a pothole. People milled about, taking photographs, watching the white water churning at the bottom of the falls. Smith breathed in the fresh spray of crisp cold water. She dug her raincoat out of her pack and slipped it on. The trail wound uphill, dense forest on one side, a wooden guardrail on the other. Everything drenched in spray. A handful of people were on the trail, heading, Tracey told her, for the falls further down the path. They passed the second, larger waterfall, the pavement ended and the path became bark and wood mulch, narrowing as it turned away from the water.

"That way goes to the ink pots." Tracey pointed toward a group of people coming up from the valley floor. "We go this way."

The trail got narrower and rougher and began to climb steadily. Talk and laughter fell behind them, and soon they were alone. Signs marked the hiking trails. "We stay on this path for about an hour," Tracey said. "When we come to the end of the trail, we turn left. I think."

"You think?"

"Like I said, Matt always led the way. I just followed. I'm sure I can remember though. It goes to a nice little pond. We'd stop there for our picnic."

If they ever found this nice little pond, Smith suspected Matt would be concealed, wanting to see who Tracey had brought with her. She hoped she'd be unthreatening enough that he'd come out of hiding.

They began to climb. The neatly groomed trail faded away and they jumped over fallen logs and pushed aside struggling saplings. After about half an hour, Tracey began to fall back. Her breathing was labored and her cheeks flushed. "Can't we slow down a bit?" she asked. "Matt doesn't walk so fast."

Smith slowed. "When was the last time you were here, Tracey?"

"About two weeks ago. It looks sorta different."

Smith was glad she hadn't called Sergeant Blechta. If she'd led him and a bunch of his officers on a wild-goose chase, he'd not be happy. As it was she didn't have anything to do anyway. If not for Tracey stumbling along behind, she'd enjoy the hike.

They reached the end of the marked trail. An arrow pointed left, directing them back to the parking lot.

A small path, more a deer track than a hiking trail, rounded an old spruce. Tracey didn't hesitate, but walked on. As the elevation increased, the trees got smaller, the vegetation thinner. Smith thought it was also getting colder.

"Can we rest for a few minutes?" Tracey said after a short while.

Smith shrugged off her pack. "Sure." The women took seats together on a large boulder. The cold of the rock leaked into Smith's rear. She found water bottles and granola bars and handed them to Tracey. She checked her GPS and her watch. "It's almost noon. We've been on the trail for an hour and a half. At three o'clock, regardless of whether we've found Matt or not, we're turning around."

"But…"

"No buts. We can't chance getting caught out here after dark."

"We'll be all right. You've got that thing."

"The GPS helps. It's no substitute for being able to see where you're going." Smith checked her phone. No signal.

Tracey pouted as she ripped open the packaging on her granola bar. *What had Matt been thinking?* Or, most likely, not thinking. Tracey had been all set to rush off into the wilderness, with no equipment, no food, no common sense. One wrong turn and she would have been totally lost.

Smith looked up, through the trees. The sky was still clear. She ate her own bar and took a glug of water. "Let's go."

"So soon?"

"Three o'clock. No longer."

Tracey muttered. She tossed her wrapping behind the rock, into the bush.

"Hey! Pick that up."

"Sorry." Tracey scrambled for it and put the offending object into her pocket.

"That's better." Smith plunged into the woods.

Less than a kilometer further, the deer trail split neatly into two. One arm pointed to the left, the other to the right. Both appeared to have been recently used.

A flash of red caught her eye. On the path leading to the right, the branch of a fir had been snapped off at eye level. The broken wood pierced a scrap of cloth.

"I told you he'd leave signs." Tracey slipped around Smith and touched the fabric. A smile crossed her face.

"So you did." That marker could have been left by anyone, but Smith had no reason to think it hadn't been Matt. The color was bright red, so it hadn't been out in the open for long.

They took the trail to the right.

The scraps of cloth came regularly as the deer trail slipped in and out of groves of trees or disappeared into the bush. Smith wanted to walk quietly, but Tracey's stumbling and crashing behind her put an end to that. They were in the sub-alpine now, thickly covered with small trees of pine, spruce, and larch. At one-thirty, Smith called a halt.

"I thought you said this was two hours in, Tracey? We've been walking for three so far."

"When I'm with Matt time had no meaning."

Smith rolled her eyes. She took out the bag of nuts and passed them over. She wondered if Matt was watching them. It was possible. He had to suspect Tracey would either tell the police she'd heard from him or they were keeping an eye on her.

He'd have to be good in the woods, though, for Smith not to detect his presence.

It was quiet. A few birds flittered among the trees and the brush rustled occasionally as squirrels and other small animals hurried to get out of their way. They hadn't seen a human being since leaving the waterfall. She took a deep breath, pulling fresh air into her lungs. She wished Adam were here.

Even more, she wished Norman were here.

The women both started as a branch snapped. A soft grunt followed. Tracey leapt to her feet. "Matt. Here I am! Matt." She darted down the path, heedless of her footing.

"Wait. Tracey, come back. Stop." Without bothering to pick up her backpack, Smith ran after the girl. She did not like the sound of that grunt. She heard a sharp intake of breath and then a muffled scream. She rounded a bend in the path.

Tracey was frozen to the spot. A bear stood on its hind legs not more than ten feet in front of her. Its mouth opened and its formidable teeth flashed.

"Tracey," Smith said, her voice slow and calm. "Back up. Do not turn around and do not run."

The girl didn't move.

# Chapter Fifty-three

**TRAFALGAR CITY POLICE STATION. TRAFALGAR, BRITISH COLUMBIA. TUESDAY MORNING.**

The moment he got back to the office John Winters looked up the phone number for Paula. He liked Paula. She might dress like something out of a teenage horror movie but she was never anything but polite and friendly toward him. Whenever he saw them in town, her young son, the unfortunately named Beowulf, was clean and neatly dressed, with bright eyes and a wide happy smile. Paula had never been in trouble with the police, but she had been a witness a couple of years ago when one of her friends was killed, and he'd taken down her cell number. It was still filed away on his computer.

She answered on the first ring. In the background children laughed.

"Paula, John Winters here."

"Hi, Mr. Winters."

"I wonder if we could meet. I need to talk to you,"

"What about?"

"The Grizzly Resort."

"I don't know anything about that. I was at the demonstration because Nadine said I should come. We have to protect what's left of the wilderness, you know."

"Yes, yes. I know. How about lunch at George's? Are you free?" He wanted to meet someplace she'd be comfortable. Someplace public so she wouldn't feel she was snitching on her friends.

"I guess," she said after a long pause, "that would be okay. Can I bring Beowulf? It's my day off, so we're at the park."

"I'd love to see Beowulf. Noon?"

"See you then, Mr. Winters."

He spent the rest of the morning doing some further reading on Robyn Winfield. She'd updated her blog the day before. She made an impassioned plea for people to come to Trafalgar to try to stop the Grizzly Resort. The piece was accompanied by pictures of beautiful mountain vistas and happy bears fishing in pristine swift-moving rivers.

He checked on Steve McNally. No information on his whereabouts.

Winters was the first to arrive at George's. The waitress lifted one eyebrow when he asked her to bring a highchair. Soon Paula arrived with Beowulf in his push chair. Winters stood while she unloaded the little boy and settled him at the table.

"This is a real treat for us, thanks. Wolfie doesn't often get to eat in a restaurant. Do you, buddy?" She ruffled his hair. Beowulf stuffed the tail of a toy dog into his mouth and eyed John Winters over a much-chewed ear.

Winters gave what he hoped was a friendly smile. The waitress brought a cup of crayons and a page torn out of a coloring book. The boy dropped the dog onto the floor and grabbed for red. Paula scooped up the toy and opened her menu.

"Something to drink to start?" the waitress said.

"I'll have a Coke, thanks." Paula dug in her cavernous bag and brought out a plastic sippy cup. "And a glass of milk."

Winters asked for coffee.

"There was trouble up at the Grizzly Resort site this morning," Winters said. "I don't want this situation to escalate into violence. No one wants that."

Paula stopped fussing. "What sort of trouble?"

"A leghold trap. Deliberately set where one of the workers might step into it."

"Yuk," she said. She turned her attention back to the menu.

"Might as easily have trapped an animal. A coyote or a wolf. There are a few houses up the road. Be a nice place to walk a dog in the morning."

Her black-rimmed eyes opened wide. "Oh, gosh. That's awful. Who would do something like that?"

"Dog," Beowulf said.

"I'm hoping you can tell me about the outsiders who were at the demonstration the other day. Robyn Winfield and that man, what's his name?"

"Steve-something. But they wouldn't have set that trap. They believe in non-violent resistance."

"That's good."

"Ready to order?" The smiling waitress placed their drinks on the table. Paula poured milk into the plastic cup and placed it in front of Beowulf. He glugged it down.

"Have you been to any meetings of the group?" Winters asked, once the business of discussing the menu and deciding what to eat was over.

"No. Nadine went, but I can't always get a babysitter."

"Do you know anything about Robyn and Steve?"

"I'm not a snitch, Mr. Winters. I mean, thanks for the lunch and all, but I don't want to tell on them. They haven't done anything wrong."

He smiled at her. "All I'm asking for is what's public knowledge, Paula. No snitching. Tell you what, let's have a nice lunch. Do you have a phone number for them? If I can talk to them, I'll ask my questions myself."

"That should be okay." She rooted through her bag and came up with a printed flyer, an invitation to a meeting to discuss action against the resort. A phone number had been scribbled on the bottom. "It's Robyn's number. Nadine gave it to me, in case I could arrange to get to the meeting after all."

Winters pulled out his notebook and took down the information. "Thanks, Paula."

Their food arrived. While Beowulf made messy work of his hot dog and fries, Paula chatted happily about Beowulf's adventures at day care and his potential as a soccer star. Winters asked no more about the resort or the protesters.

For the briefest of moments, as Paula wiped the little boy's face and encouraged him to thank Winters for the lunch, John Winters regretted that he and Eliza had never had children.

# Chapter Fifty-four

**BANFF NATIONAL PARK, ALBERTA. TUESDAY AFTERNOON.**

It was a grizzly, brown and silver-tipped, and enormous. Easily seven feet tall on its hind legs, perhaps close to five hundred pounds. It smelled of dirty fur and muddy paws, of fish and rotting meat. Of the wild and the world beyond paved roads and lights and laughter. Smith's hand slid into her pocket. She pulled out the can of bear spray and flipped it open. Her knife would be of absolutely no use here. Probably not her Glock, either. She spread her legs apart and lifted her arms, trying to make herself look equally large and impressive, and submissively lowered her eyes to the animal's chest. "Tracey, I can handle this, but you have to get out of my way. Step backwards, but move slowly. Do not make eye contact, stay calm, and listen to me. If it charges, drop." She raised her voice. She had a tendency to squeak under stress, and was pleased the words came out strong and firm. "Mr. Bear, I need you to go away." She dared a quick look. His eyes were small and black. His teeth were long and sharp. She lowered her eyes again. "Step back, Tracey. Now."

And then, with a huff that had the hair on her arms moving, the animal dropped to the ground. It turned and lumbered into the trees. Soon, not even the shiver of a leaf marked its passing.

Tracey spun around. "Wow. Wasn't that something? I've never seen a bear up close before."

Smith stuffed the can of spray into her pocket. Her legs shook, but she didn't dare collapse, not yet. "Let's hope you never do again. If there is a next time, you do exactly what I tell you. Got it?"

"Sure. Come on. We're almost there. I think I recognize this path."

That Smith doubted very much. But Tracey seemed to be invigorated by the encounter with the bear and her pace quickened. An innocent in the wild. Smith wondered if Tracey would have tried to pat the bear or feed it by hand. That had been known to happen. If they were lucky, they lived to tell the tale.

Feeling much like Gretel following breadcrumbs, Smith followed the scraps of red cloth. It was coming up to two o'clock, only one more hour until she'd insist on turning around, when the forest ahead began to thin out, and more sky came into view. A clearing, most likely.

"We're here!" Tracey shouted. Energized, she broke into a run. Smith followed, moving with more caution. They emerged into an alpine meadow. Full of boulders, scrubby bushes, and tiny plants that would make a carpet of riotous color come spring. A scattering of snow clung to the dark underside of rocks and filled crevasses in the ground.

A lake, a perfect small jewel of sapphire and white, sparkled in the sun.

"Matt," Tracey yelled. "I'm here! Matt, you can come out. It's me, Tracey."

Smith's right hand rested on the knife at her hip. Other than the cries of the girl, all was quiet.

"I told you to come alone." A man stepped out from a line of spruce at the edge of the clearing. He was unshaven, his hair lank, his face dirty, his eyes haunted.

"She never would have made it," Smith said. "How you doing, Matt? Not well, by the look of it."

A small grin touched the edges of his mouth. "Moonlight Smith. I was thinking of you the other day."

Tracey ran toward him. Matt wrapped her in a hug that lifted her feet off the ground. They embraced for a long time. Smith shrugged off her pack and searched for a bottle of water. She took a long drink.

Matt let Tracey go, and she dragged him by the hand. "Molly wanted to help. I hope you don't mind too much."

He studied Smith's face. "I don't mind," he said at last. "Nice to see you, Moonlight." He held out his hand. She took it. "You got anything to eat in there?"

She tossed him a granola bar. He caught it easily and tore the wrapping off. The food disappeared in two quick bites. She found chocolate bars and nuts and passed them over. While he ate, she walked to the edge of the lake to give him some privacy. The water was perfectly clear. Gray and white stones lining the bottom swayed as light passed through the water. Small fish nibbled at unseen plants. Tracey told Matt how worried she'd been and that everyone was looking for him. Matt said nothing.

Finally, Smith turned around. "You have to come back to town with me."

He shook his head. "No. I appreciate you helping Tracey, but you can leave now. We'll manage."

"What do you think you're going to do?"

He had his arm around Tracey's shoulder. He looked down at her, his smile soft and intimate. "We'll manage."

Tracey beamed.

"Hardly," Smith said. "The police like you for the murder of Barry Caseman. You must know that."

"I didn't kill him."

"Tell them then. What are they supposed to think, you running off?"

"I guess your mom called you, eh?"

"Of course she did. She's worried about you."

"Tell her I'm sorry for what happened. Sorrier that I can say."

"Tell her yourself. She's still here. So's the ch…your dad. He's worried sick. So's your mom."

"My mom's here?"

"Matt. Do you not understand how serious this is? You. Are. Wanted. For murder."

"But he didn't do it."

Smith threw up her hands. "The both of you can keep saying that till the cows come home, but it won't make any difference. You have to turn yourself in and tell your side of the story. You don't actually think you're going to run, do you? Run where? To the States? You think the border guards haven't been alerted? Are you going to walk to Ontario? You can't rent a car. Your driver's license has a flag on it. There's a bus, but it costs money and you can't use your credit cards. Even if you manage to get there, they have police in Ontario, you know."

Matt released Tracey. He walked in circles, eyes on the ground, rubbing at the stubble on his face. "This is such a mess, such a fucking mess."

"Start cleaning it up. Come back to town."

"I can't. There's a cabin, back in the woods. An old abandoned trapper's place. We can stay there for a while."

Tracey nodded.

"Listen to yourself, will you?" Smith said. "Do you think we're at the end of the world? This is a national park. The rangers have been told to look out for you. How long before one of them thinks, oh, yeah, that old trapper's cabin would be a nice place to hide out.

"You know I'm right. Otherwise, why have you hung around? You must know you could have hitched a ride out of here before your face got on the news."

He looked at Tracey. "I started to. But then I realized I couldn't leave you behind."

Tracey burst into tears.

Smith groaned. She zipped up her pack. "I'm not going to stand around here arguing. You can come with me. I'll drive you to town. We'll call your dad and he'll take you to the police station and wait with you while you make a statement. Or you can play mountain man and try to hide out and possibly get shot—or get Tracey shot—in a shootout as a dangerous fugitive. Your choice."

"I don't want to see my dad."

"Geez. I'll go with you then. While we walk, I'll brief you on what to do and what not to do at the police station. You want to ask for a lawyer straight up."

"How do you know what I should do? Have you been arrested?"

She swallowed. No more prevaricating. He'd asked. She had to answer. "No, I have not been arrested. I have, however, been the arresting officer. I'm with the Trafalgar City Police. Constable Third Class."

"Hey," Tracey said, "you never told me that. You pretended you were trying to help."

"I was trying…I am trying to help."

Matt started at Smith for a moment. Then, to her surprise, he burst out laughing. "Of all things. You, the wilderness kid with the hippie parents and the funny name, a cop. Me, the cop's kid, a waste-of-space, wanted for murder. Makes about as much sense, I suppose, as Lucky Smith sleeping with my dad. Your mom said you still ski."

"Whenever I can."

"Me, too. I was planning on teaching Tracey this year. Guess that won't happen, eh?"

"It still can."

"Okay, Constable Smith. You win. I'll come with you and hand myself over to good old dad. Probably be a feather in your cap, eh?"

More likely a stern talking to for not immediately reporting Matt's contact with Tracey. Smith kept the thought to herself.

"I'm running out of freeze-dried food anyway. Never could stand that stuff. Got anything else to eat in there?"

She handed him two granola bars. "Where's your things?"

He jerked his head toward the trees, as he unwrapped one bar. The second he stuffed into his pocket.

"Matt," Tracey said. "Are you sure?"

"No. But it's what I gotta do. I guess I knew that all along."

# Chapter Fifty-five

**BIG EDDIE'S COFFEE EMPORIUM. TRAFALGAR, BRITISH COLUMBIA. TUESDAY AFTERNOON.**

As soon as lunch was over and Paula and Beowulf had waved good-bye, John Winters made a phone call. Robyn Winfield answered on the first ring.

He thought he might have to persuade her to meet with him. Instead she sounded almost eager. She suggested Big Eddie's in ten minutes.

The last thing Winters wanted was another coffee. But they had to meet somewhere, and he wasn't ready—yet—to request she come into the station. Sometimes, such was the policeman's lot.

Robyn told him she was shocked, shocked to hear about the setting of the trap. Then she shrugged and said, "Some people take the protection of the planet very seriously indeed. I'll mention it at the next meeting of the action committee. Remind everyone we don't want to put lives in danger. Although, *some people* don't seem to think the lives of wild animals are of any importance."

"You are aware that the trap was illegal, in the first place, and secondly, it was a deliberate attempt to injure someone? We will be investigating, and charges will be laid."

"If you find the person who did it. If I have any information I'll be more than happy to share it with you."

"Tell me about Steve McNally."

"What about him?"

No denial at the name. So, it was McNally at the demonstration. "Might he...know someone...who'd set the trap?"

"Steve's committed to the protection of the planet. As am I. Other than that, I don't account for him, and he doesn't account for me."

"He has a reputation, you must know that, of going beyond non-violence."

She shrugged. "Man's gotta do what a man's gotta do. I've heard the talk. If it's true, no one was hurt."

"Lucky maybe."

"He's never been charged with anything."

"Lucky then."

She had fabulous blue eyes, the deep turquoise of the Caribbean Sea. Winters suspected she used colored lenses. Her red hair was cut very short. Her skin was tanned and lightly freckled, and she used no makeup. She wore jeans, well-worn but not tattered, and a Save the Whales t-shirt under a black leather jacket. As she sipped her coffee, she focused those lovely eyes on him.

She made him very uncomfortable, and he wasn't sure why. He suspected she was laughing at him.

"This is a serious matter," he said.

"And I take it seriously. We are talking about nothing more than the survival of our planet..."

"Save me the lecture. All we're talking about is a handful of people from Vancouver or Calgary who want to spend their vacation time in the mountains."

"It grows, you know. One little development here, one small hotel there. What's the harm? A couple of luxury lodges. Soon you have a multi-lane highway and a nice new Walmart for all those people to shop at. Dam the rivers, cut down the forest, starve the bears, kill the fish." Her eyes flashed with anger. "It has to stop somewhere. It will stop here. One way or another." She downed her drink and shoved her chair back. She studied the scattering of people in the room. Early afternoon on a Tuesday, the clientele mostly consisted of young people, the sort who had jobs in restaurants or shops, not in business offices or city hall. A few teenagers off school early, a group of gray-haired women dressed in lululemon relaxing after yoga class.

"People." Robyn lifted her arms in the air. "Please, can I have your attention?"

The clatter of cups and buzz of chatter stopped. Eddie looked up from the cash register and Jolene stopped halfway across the floor, a tray of quiches and salads in her arms.

Robyn, Winters had to admit, had a commanding presence. She paused, long enough to ensure every eye was on her. Her arms were outstretched, inviting them all into her circle.

He could do nothing but sit and fume.

"There will be a demonstration tomorrow morning. Eight o'clock at the Grizzly Resort. I'm going to protect that wilderness with my body. With my life if necessary. We have to stop those bulldozers and diggers. Is anyone with me?"

"Yes!" a young man, long hair tied back under a blue bandanna, shouted.

"How about you?" Robyn pointed to the yoga women.

They glanced at each other, hesitating. One of them leapt to her feet. "We'll be there." Her friends nodded, not entirely enthusiastically.

Winters stood up. "That's enough."

Robyn pumped her fist into the air. "Eight o'clock. Spread the word. We'll show them what the people of Trafalgar can do."

The teenagers cheered.

"This is over," Winters said. "Let's go."

"Or what, you'll arrest me?" She focused her intense sapphire eyes on his. Her voice dropped to a whisper only he could hear. "Washed-up, small-town cop, you have no idea what you are dealing with. Get your hands off me," she shouted, although he had made no attempt to touch her. She spun back to face the room. "This isn't a police state, not yet."

Winters knew when to make a strategic retreat. He walked out. Jolene threw him a strained smile as he passed.

What the hell was Robyn playing at? She'd pretty much invited him to show up tomorrow with a full complement of officers and arrest her. In full view, of course, of as many townspeople as she could gather. No doubt she'd be giving the media plenty of notice.

Media. Attention. Make a big enough scene, she might get some national focus. Nothing like attractive young people courageously lying in the mud or fastening themselves to trees in defiance of a row of bulldozers to make the front page of the major papers. Add police stepping in to move them, and she might even get herself on the CBC national news.

Winters marched back to the station, fury rising. He'd been played like a cat played a particularly stupid mouse. No more friendly chats in coffee shops. Next time he spoke to Robyn Winfield, it would be in interview room number one. Was it possible Paula had been in on it? Setting him up?

Probably not. Paula had no guile in her. She seemed to genuinely like him and had been happy to help.

Robyn would have known he'd be wanting to talk to her. All she had to do was sit back and wait for him to stick his head out of the mouse hole.

For the first time, John Winters wondered if the trap had been set, after all, for him.

# Chapter Fifty-six

**BANFF NATIONAL PARK, ALBERTA. TUESDAY AFTERNOON.**

"Do you want to tell me what happened?" Smith asked. "We've got a long walk ahead of us."

After an initial burst of exuberant energy, Tracey had begun dropping back. Matt Keller and Molly Smith were forced to slow their pace so she could keep up. Matt took Tracey's hand.

"First, how'd you get a phone to call Tracey?"

"I went down the trail, closer to town. Sat on a log and put on a sad face. A couple came by and I told them I'd lost my phone and needed to contact my pal who was meeting me. I figured even if I was on the news, tourists wouldn't have paid any attention."

"True enough. Tell me what happened that night. You called your dad. Said you'd found your friend dead when you got home. Was that the truth?"

"Yup."

She studied his face. She saw no cunning. No attempt to lie or to excuse himself. Then again, she was a lousy judge of character. "Why'd you take off?"

He slowed. "Tracey, you walk ahead."

"Why?"

"Please?"

"Okay." She let go of his hand and skipped down the trail. Tracey, Smith thought, did not seem to realize how serious this still was. She was happy, just to know Matt loved her so much he couldn't leave without her.

Sometimes, that's enough.

But not often.

"I recognized him."

"Recognized who?"

"The guy who killed Barry."

"Geez, Matt. Are you sure?"

"Sure I recognized him, or sure he killed Barry? Both."

"All the more reason to tell the police."

"I don't…I can't."

"Why not?"

"Barry was a scumball, pure and simple. Always looking for the main chance. Not smart enough to be a big-time crook, dumb enough to keep stepping into the shit and thinking it was his big break." Matt snorted. He studied the path beneath his feet. "Takes one to know one, I guess."

"Barry was into something criminal and his partner got mad at him. Is that what you're saying?"

"Not partner. But yeah, he screwed up, probably got greedy and had to be taken out of the picture."

"You're involved in this business too, are you? What is it? Drugs probably."

"Not me. I'm no genius, but I like to think I'm smart enough to stay out of that sort of trouble."

"Why then are you so reluctant to go to the police? If this guy is after you, trying to shut you up, you're better with the police than hiding behind trees."

"Maybe. Moonlight…"

"Call me Molly. I hate that stupid name."

"Molly." Matt lifted his head. He watched Tracey, trudging up the trail. They were keeping their voices low and every once in a while she looked over her shoulder, checking that Matt was really there. "She's a good girl. A great girl. A lot better than I deserve."

"Do the right thing for her. The right thing is not leading the life of a fugitive."

"Hard to know, sometimes, what's the right thing. How many lives can I ruin?"

"You're not making any sense."

"*Au contraire*, I am finally coming to my senses. I don't know what I'm going to do, Molly. I guess I'll find out when I find out."

"You know who killed Barry. Tell me. You'll be telling the Mounties soon enough."

They started at a squeal from up ahead. Tracey stumbled over a tree root. She pitched forward, arms windmilling. She hit the ground with a yelp of pain.

Matt reached her in two quick strides. "You okay?"

She flipped onto her rump, and gave her head a good shake. "I think so." She held out her hand, and he pulled her to her feet. She turned to him with a smile that would light up the night woods. He did not release her hand, and they walked on together.

Smith glanced at her watch. Three-thirty. They'd be back at the car before dark. She'd hand Matt over to his father, and then head out of town. She'd have to drive through the night, but she wanted… she needed… to be home.

# Chapter Fifty-seven

**BANFF SPRINGS HOTEL. BANFF, ALBERTA. TUESDAY AFTERNOON.**

Lucky spent the day doing nothing. Nothing but worrying.

She'd hoped that after their talk yesterday, Karen would want to be, if not exactly friends, at least no longer enemies, but when Lucky suggested lunch, she'd been brushed off with an abruptness verging on rude. Karen was regretting her confessions.

Lucky ate lunch alone, once again not tasting the food and barely registering a word of the novel she'd brought to keep her company.

She'd expected Moonlight to call, to say she was leaving and were there any last-minute updates. But she hadn't.

It hadn't been fair of Lucky to ask Moonlight to come. The girl had her own life to live.

Adam seemed like—he was—a good man. He adored Moonlight, as well he should, without being overly protective or possessive. In the early days of their relationship Moonlight told her mother she worried that when they were on the job, Adam would feel he had to look out for her, rather than treat her like any other officer. But they didn't work for the same force, so didn't usually find themselves working together. And when they did, he was learning to keep a professional distance.

Lucky hadn't liked Moonlight's late fiancé, Graham Buckingham. She thought they were too young to get married; she thought Moonlight needed to see more of the world first, to get some experience before settling down. On one occasion, she'd seen a flash of the bully in Graham's attitude toward Moonlight. And, worse, the girl had submissively rushed to do his bidding.

When Graham died, Moonlight had been inconsolable for a long time. Deep in her heart, where she would never confess even to herself, Lucky had been glad her daughter was free of him.

Five years later Moonlight hadn't seen much more of the world in terms of geography, but she had certainly seen human nature in all its permutations.

Lucky, the old-time hippie, had initially been horrified when Moonlight pulled herself out of her grief and announced that she intended to become a police officer. Lucky was happy to admit she'd been wrong. The job was a good fit for Moonlight. It might put her in some moral dilemmas at times, but wasn't that part of life?

Lucky and Paul had deliberately not brought their laptops on their vacation. They didn't want to find themselves constantly checking e-mail, and Paul said if he needed to be contacted his staff could phone him. With nothing more interesting to do, Lucky popped into the hotel business center. She settled down at a computer and logged on. She was astonished at the amount of activity on Facebook in the short time she'd been away. Some of her friends had been to a demonstration in front of the Grizzly Resort offices on Sunday. All the chatter was about meetings and organizing protests.

Oh, dear. Precisely the sort of dilemma she'd been thinking about Moonlight facing. Moonlight was opposed to the resort, as befitted a wilderness adventurer. But she was charged with keeping the peace, and if the demonstrations got out of control Moonlight might well find herself dragging friends, even her own mother, off to jail.

No, not her mother. This time, Lucky decided, she'd have to stay out of it. For Moonlight, but also for Paul. Poor Paul, if one of his officers had to arrest his lover. Perhaps Lucky would volunteer for a behind-the-scenes job. Designing pamphlets or making phone calls.

Better not. She'd only chafe at her inactivity and find herself on the streets after all.

She moved to shut down the computer as a new message popped up on Facebook. A demonstration was being called for tomorrow morning at the resort. Passive non-violent resistance. Her friends began liking the post or saying they'd be there. Someone commented that her husband had a construction job at the site and he needed the work.

The flame wars began.

Lucky closed the Internet browser. As she went back to her room to put on a better pair of walking shoes she reminded herself that every cloud had a silver lining. This might be enough to make Paul decide to head back to Trafalgar.

Her cell phone rang. Paul.

"I've had a call from John. Trouble's brewing over that damned Grizzly Resort. It's going to need a lot of PR, so I have to get back."

Lucky refrained from mentioning that she knew all about it.

"It's too late to leave now. I don't want to drive over the passes at night. First light tomorrow, will that be okay with you?"

"Yes. Where are you?"

"At the station. I'm with Jonathan. We've finished up a meeting with Blechta."

"Has something happened? Did he have something to tell you?"

"Forensic results are coming in. Didn't tell us much we didn't know. There've been no further credible reports of any sightings of Matt. Only the mysterious stranger stuff we get with every missing person. Jonathan's here to report back to Karen." Paul didn't sound all that pleased at the idea, but he would make the effort to be accommodating to his ex-wife. To Matt's mother. "Jonathan suggests we meet for a drink at the hotel. Go over what we've learned and decide if there's anything he can do after I've gone. Gotta run, Blechta's waving at me."

"Okay."

Home. At last they were going home. When they arrived in Banff, was it only four days ago, Lucky thought that she could live here, in this wonderful hotel, forever.

Now, all she wanted was to go home.

# Chapter Fifty-eight

**BANFF NATIONAL PARK, ALBERTA. TUESDAY EVENING.**

The sun was touching the mountains to the west when they finally arrived back at Smith's car.

Sylvester was delighted to see her. Smith held the back door open for the dog while Matt threw his stuff into the trunk. She followed Sylvester around the parking lot for a few minutes, letting Matt and Tracey have a precious moment of privacy.

Their last for a long time. Perhaps, if things did not go well for Matt, the last they'd ever have.

When she got back to the car, Matt had his arm around Tracey's shoulders and her face was buried into his chest. They pulled apart. Smith typed in the password, and then held out her phone. "You wanna make the call. Or shall I?"

Matt held out his free hand and she gave it to him. "Your dad's in the contact list under CC."

He kept one arm around Tracey's shoulder and punched buttons with the other. He hesitated, his finger hovering. He buried his face in Tracey's hair. Smith waited. Sylvester waited.

A long time passed. Finally, Matt pulled away. He looked at Smith, and then he took a deep breath and made the call.

"Hi, Dad."

She was standing a few feet away, but Smith could hear the shout from the other end.

"I'm with Molly. We're coming back to town. I'd rather talk to you first. Please. How about the parking lot behind the Lighthouse Keeper? Ten minutes. Hear what I have to say first and then I'll go with you to the police station. Ten minutes. See you then."

Paul said something more, and all the color drained from Matt's face. "Fuck, no!" He ended the call, threw the phone at Smith.

She grabbed it out of the air. "What's the matter?"

"You bitch, you set me up."

"What the hell are you talking about? You must have known your dad would do nothing other than take you to the police station."

Matt whirled around. He faced Tracey. He grabbed her face in his hands. "I'm going, kid. I won't be back."

"What do you mean? What happened?"

The trunk was still open. Matt gave Tracey a quick kiss and moved to get his backpack. Smith's phone rang. She ignored it, stuffed it into her hip pocket. She stepped in front of Matt, blocking his path. "I don't know what's changed, but I can't let you go."

"You can't stop me."

"I can try." He wasn't a large man, but he was fit, and he was a man. Smith bent her knees and flexed her fingers. She touched the knife attached to her belt.

"Get out of my way."

"No."

"I'm truly sorry, Moonlight." He moved. He swung at her face, but she had read the intention in his eyes. She ducked, slipped aside, pulled the knife out of its sheath. Matt's fist connected with only air. Tracey screamed. Sylvester barked.

Matt faced her, his eyes narrow, a vein pulsing in his neck. Smith held up the knife. It wasn't much of a knife, not intended for fighting. It was small, but it was sharp. It would do the job, if it had to. She had no idea what the chief could possibly have said to Matt in that short phone call that would have him on the run again. Right now, that didn't matter.

"You won't use that on me, will you, Moonlight?"

"I will if it becomes necessary." She took a deep breath. "Matthew Allen Keller, I am arresting you for the murder of Barry Caseman."

"No!" Tracey screamed.

Sylvester jumped against Smith's leg. She staggered, and instinctively, glanced down.

Matt leapt at her. He grabbed her knife hand by the wrist. He twisted. Pain shot up her arm. She gripped the weapon, refusing to give it up. His breath, sour from days in the wilderness, was on her face. His brown eyes narrow with anger. She brought up her left knee. Jammed it into his groin. Too close to have much strength behind it, but enough that he grunted and relaxed his hold. She twisted her arm free and stepped back. "Don't do this Matt. You're resisting arrest. Stop now and I won't charge you with assault."

But rage was in his eyes and it was unlikely he even heard her. He came at her again, ducking low. She held the knife out in front of her, knees bent, heart pounding, blood rushing. She slashed empty air. She tried to think. She needed time to think. Would she use the knife on Matthew Keller?

No.

She didn't have any equipment on her. Without handcuffs she couldn't control him even if she won the fight; she couldn't secure him in the back of the car while she drove. All she could do would be to let him go. Or to injure him severely enough that he couldn't escape.

And that, she wasn't prepared to do.

# Chapter Fifty-nine

**BANFF SPRINGS HOTEL. BANFF, ALBERTA. TUESDAY EVENING.**

They had just ordered a round of drinks and appetizers when Paul's phone rang. He pulled it out of his pocket. When he saw the display, he glanced at Lucky, his eyebrows lifted in a question. "Molly. Hello."

Lucky only had time to hope her daughter hadn't run into a problem on the highway, when Paul leapt to his feet. His chair crashed to the floor. "Matt! Where are you?"

Karen Keller clutched her hands to her chest. Tears pooled in her eyes. "Oh, thank heavens," she breathed.

"Where is he?" Jonathan Burgess shouted.

"You can trust Molly," Paul said into the phone. His eyes were fixed on Lucky, and a small smile touched the edges of his mouth. Lucky fell back into her chair, overwhelmed with relief. It was over. It was all over. Karen wept softly. A waiter hurried over to pick up the chair.

"I'll meet you at the police station in Banff," Paul said. "You know you have to turn yourself in, son. Okay, I guess that'll be all right. Where? Ten minutes? We'll be there. Your mother's here. Yes, I understand. Jonathan'll come instead. Matt? Matt? What the hell?" Paul took the phone away from his ear. He looked at it, not understanding. He gave it a shake. Held it to his ear. Punched buttons.

He was still on his feet. The lounge was full of before-dinner drinkers, every one of them watching the drama unfolding at their table. The waiter continued to hold the chair, not quite sure where to put it.

"Did he hang up?" Jonathan said.

"As if something had interrupted him." Paul punched more buttons. "Keller here. I need a trace on this phone. He rattled off Smith's numbers. "It's urgent. One of my officers, and I believe she might be in trouble. No don't do anything. Just find it for me.

"He said the parking lot behind the Lighthouse Keeper in ten minutes. I suspect something's happened to prevent that meeting, but it's the only thing I have right now. Lucky, will you take Karen upstairs?"

Karen was still weeping. Her arms were wrapped around herself and her eyes were closed. She didn't appear to have realized things had suddenly gone very wrong.

"I want to come with you," Lucky said.

"No."

"But Moonlight…"

"Is more than capable of taking care of herself without her mother's help. Look after Karen."

Lucky nodded.

"Keep trying to get her. Tell her we're going to the Lighthouse Keeper as arranged."

The two men ran out of the restaurant. The wait staff stood back and watched them go. The patrons returned to their drinks and nibbles. Lucky got to her feet and bent over Karen. "Why don't we go upstairs, dear, and wait?"

Wait. What else was there to do but wait?

# Chapter Sixty

**BANFF NATIONAL PARK, ALBERTA. TUESDAY EVENING.**

Let him go. She knew where he was; she could have search parties in the woods before Matt was so much as out of sight. Her phone kept ringing, vibrating against her hip. Almost certainly the chief trying to get Matt back.

Matt circled, fists up, lips tight, eyes focused. He feigned coming in from the right. She swung to her left, realized her mistake, back to center. He danced away, out of her reach. His breath came in short sharp bursts.

"Okay, Matt," she said, lowering the knife. "You…"

Her right leg collapsed in a wave of pain. She fell to the ground, landing hard on her rear. The knife flew out of her hand.

Tracey was on her. Screaming. Pounding her fists into Smith's chest and face. Screaming, screaming.

Stupid, stupid, stupid. First rule of a fight: know where *all* your opponents are. Smith had turned her back on Tracey. Thinking the girl was harmless. Forgetting that any animal, no matter how small and defenseless, will fight to protect its mate.

Sylvester lunged at Tracey, growling, teeth bared. He wanted to help, but he wasn't a guard dog, just a family pet. Tracey scarcely seemed to notice the dog's grip on her arm, as she pummeled Smith. More in anger than with skill or strength. Smith lifted her hands to protect her face and at the same time tried to scoot back on her butt, get herself out of range. Sylvester jumped on her arm, sharp claws ripping into her jacket. She had no idea where the knife had gone.

Suddenly, the blows stopped and Tracey was out of Smith's space. Bodily lifted to her feet. Matt's arms were tight around her, and she wept into his chest.

Matt stroked the girl's hair. "I've done enough damage, Molly. I won't have Tracey sent to jail because of me. If you forget what Tracey did, I'll come with you. I give up."

Smith wiped at her nose and her hand came away streaked with blood. Her butt ached where she'd landed on a rock and she could still feel the pressure of Tracey's fists in her chest. Blood leaked through torn fabric on her sleeve.

Fuckin' lunatics the both of them. "You'll come with me all right." She got to her feet, swallowing a gasp from a knee full of pain. She spat blood from a torn lip. "I might think about not mentioning your girlfriend's temper." Keeping her eyes fixed on Matt, she bent, scooped up the knife, and shoved it into her belt. Sylvester rubbed against her leg.

"You drive." Smith threw the keys to Tracey. "Let's go."

Smith put Matt in the back, beside the dog. Sylvester whined, confused. *No more confused,* Smith thought, *than I am.* She climbed in beside Tracey. Smith shifted in her seat, pulled the phone out of her rear pocket. The casing was cracked, the face shattered. She'd have a phone-shaped bruise on her butt tomorrow. "Fuck!" She punched buttons. Silence. She twisted in her seat, spoke to Matt. "My phone's not working. You can buy me another. We have ten minutes until we get to town. You wanna tell me what brought on that little display?"

Matt leaned forward. He laid his hand on the back of Tracey's neck. Sylvester, who never bore a grudge, licked it.

"My mother's boyfriend, Jonathan Burgess."

"What about him?"

"Did he send you after me?"

"No, he didn't send me after you. He's here with your mom, trying to help. Like I am. For whatever that's worth."

Matt studied her face.

"We don't have all day here, you know."

"Sorry. I believe you. I guess I overreacted."

"You think?"

"Don't leave me alone with Burgess, okay?"

It would be a long time before Matt was alone with anyone. Except maybe his cell mate. "Why?"

"I told you I saw the guy who killed Barry. I was coming up the stairs after work when he came down. He was hurrying, head down, hood up. But he passed under a light, and I recognized him straight off. He didn't know me. Otherwise, he would have killed me right there."

"You're telling me Burgess killed your friend? I find that hard to believe."

"No. Jonathan wouldn't get his hands dirty. The guy I saw worked for him."

"Are you sure?"

"I'm sure. I went to Calgary about two weeks ago. My car died on me, needed a lot of work. I was broke. I needed money. I'd met Jonathan once, when my mom brought him to Banff."

"We had lunch," Tracey said, "at the hotel."

"Yeah. Big spender, liked to flash his cash around. Have you seen that rock my mom's wearing? She sure as hell didn't buy it herself. Nor did my dad. I did some checking up on Burgess. Easy to do. He owns his own company. They're into property development, resource exploration. Big projects. Big pay-offs. He owns some smaller companies as well. Bit of this, bit of that. He's been divorced twice, no kids. I wondered what he saw in my mom. There are pictures on the Net of him at charity functions with glamorous women. The sort of low-level model or wannabe actress, twenty years old, a hundred pounds, who attach themselves to men with money. Eye candy."

"Your mom's pretty," Tracey said. "She's thin."

"I guess so, but she is my mom. And that's the point. She's old enough to be a grandmother. I figured Burgess must be seriously in love with her, you know. Not to mind her age."

Smith kept her opinion of a man in his sixties who didn't *mind* dating a woman in her fifties to herself. She looked out the window. They were on the highway. The dark forest spread out to her right, surrounded by fencing. To the left, a steady stream of transport trucks and cars. Overpasses had been built at regular intervals to allow wildlife to move from one side to the other. "So you figured you'd touch Burgess for a loan?"

"Why not? He has the money. He wants my mom to be happy."

"And?"

Tracey slowed, took the exit ramp off the highway.

"Mom had told me they were going out to dinner that night, so I figured he'd be in the office in the afternoon. I didn't want to phone ahead. I dropped in. He gave me a thousand bucks, enough to get the car fixed. Told me to get lost."

Smith wasn't looking at Matt, but she heard the shrug in his voice. "We're almost there. Get to the point. I don't see what any of this has to do with what happened to Barry."

"I arrived around noon. Figured Burgess would be at lunch. I didn't want to be turned away if he was, so I hung around outside. It was a nice day, and there's a park in front of the building. I saw Burgess. He was walking with a guy. Expensive suit. Expensive but tacky, I thought. Flash ring. Big guy. Lots of muscle. Sharp eyes. I figured him for a private detective or something like that. The next time I saw the guy he was coming out of my apartment. And Barry was dead."

"You think he killed Barry. Good assumption. But I don't see what that has to do with Burgess. Everyone talks to plenty of people. I talk to the scum-of-the-earth all the time. No one arrests me for it."

"I did some more checking after I got home. Found a couple of pictures of Burgess with this guy. He works for one of Burgess' companies. Meaning, Jonathan's his boss."

"That's quite the accusation."

"You'll understand why I wasn't happy to hear Burgess is coming with my dad to pick me up."

"Your dad and I'll be there. He's not going to do anything."

"I doubt he's gotten where he is by being stupid. Or hasty."

"You're still leaping, though. Why would Burgess, if he did order this guy to do his dirty work, kill your pal Barry?"

"I went into the apartment. First thing I saw when I switched on the light: Barry dead. I called Dad right away. I figured he'd know what to do. I threw my phone onto the table and went out to the landing to wait for him. Only then did I have time to think about it. I figured the hit was meant for me. Burgess probably figured I'd keep coming back for money, causing trouble with my mom if I didn't get it. He has a lot of money. Money buys things. So I ran. I keep my camping stuff ready so I can get outta town fast if I get the chance. I guess I panicked."

"You tend to do that," Smith muttered. "I saw a picture of Barry on TV. You don't look remotely alike. If Burgess does have the wherewithal to order one of his employees to make a hit, he's not going to be so sloppy as to get the wrong guy."

"It was night. The apartment's dark. He made a mistake."

"I don't think so. The question then is, why would Burgess want to kill your pal?"

The car began to slow. They were entering town. Tracey pulled up to the side of the road.

Smith glanced at the gas tank. Half-full. "Why have you stopped? We're going to the Lighthouse Keeper."

Tracey switched off the engine. She turned and faced Smith. "I might know something about that."

# Chapter Sixty-one

**BANFF, ALBERTA. TUESDAY EVENING.**

"You told the guys about your mom's new boyfriend, didn't you?" Tracey asked Matt.

"Sure. Why not? Looks good on me, having a sugar daddy for a stepdad."

"You're not the only one who can use the Internet to find out things." She faced Smith. "I've known for a while that shady stuff's going on at the car rental where I work. They think I'm stupid. I'm not stupid, but I know when to mind my own business."

"What sort of shady stuff?"

"Charging for repairs that aren't made. Charging several different people for one lot of repairs. Fix a chip in a window, make the renter pay for a full windshield replacement. Scratch nicks and cracks into the car when checking it over and charge for a door replacement. That sort of thing. Barry worked at the garage where the cars were serviced. He had to be in on it. I'm pretty sure they're also smuggling marijuana into the States in rental cars."

"How's that possible? You don't know where the cars are going. Cars rented in Canada can't be dropped off in the States, and vice versa, right? They'd just bring the drugs back home."

"Tom makes friendly, finds out they'll be in Glacier Park, say, and asks the renter to run him an errand of some sort. The errand involves dropping off a book or delivering a message. Nothing anyone would think twice about. But the cars are packed with drugs. The border guards aren't going to be suspicious; the people in the car aren't trying to hide anything. If they do get stopped and searched, hey, it's the renter's fault, isn't it?"

"You knew about this?" Smith asked Matt.

"I suspected Tom and Barry were into something illegal, yeah. None of my business."

"That certainly puts a new slant on the killing of Barry. But it still says nothing about Jonathan Burgess."

"Maybe it does," Tracey said. "Mr. Simpson, who owns the car rental franchise, also owns Kramp's Auto Repair. At least on paper he does. No one knows that."

"But you do?" Smith said.

"Like I said, people think I'm stupid. I was good with computers in school. Real good. But my mom wouldn't buy me one for homework and stuff, so I fell behind. One of my teachers offered to help me get into university. She wanted me to get a degree in computer science." Tracey laughed. "As if. I quit school at sixteen. Didn't see the point, really."

"I didn't know that," Matt said. "Maybe we can get a loan and you can still…"

"Let's stick to the problem at hand, why don't we?"

"There's a lot of spare time at the car rental place. Slow nights, not much to do in the office. So I hacked into the company's books."

Matt whistled.

"Don't be too impressed," Tracey said. "It was easy. Global Car Rental and Kramp's Auto Repair are owned by a company in Simpson's name, which is, in turn, owned by Burgess Enterprises."

Pieces of the puzzle began coming together. Smith glanced at Matt. He nodded.

"Barry came to Calgary with me that day. He wasn't working, my car was in the shop, and I needed a lift. He didn't come up to the offices. He was, however, with me when we saw Burgess talking to the guy in the flashy suit.

"It's possible Barry approached Burgess later. Maybe he also knew about the company ownership, maybe he recognized Burgess, and figured he wouldn't want word to get out that he was involved in shady dealings."

"Blackmail? Was Barry the sort to do that?"

"If it would net him a buck, Barry was the sort to do anything at all."

"I need a phone," Smith said.

"Why?"

"I'm not going to meet the chief and Burgess in a dark parking lot. Who knows if Burgess made a couple of calls of his own. Tracey?"

"I don't have mine with me. Sorry."

"My mom tells me there used to be public phone booths on every corner."

"Like Superman changed in," Tracey said.

"Whatever. I could use one now." Smith's purse had been kicked under the seat. She dug it out, scrambled around and found her ID. She got out of the car.

The streetlights had come on while they talked, but it wasn't yet dark. Condos and hotels lined the street. Cars drove past, and people were out walking. A man with two miniature dachshunds trotting at his heels approached.

Smith stepped in front of him. She lifted her badge. "I'm sorry, sir, but I need to use your phone. Won't be a minute."

He blinked in surprise. He reached into his pocket and pulled out a small flip phone.

"Wait here." She didn't know the chief's number. Her mom had also told her that people used to be able to remember the numbers of all their friends. Smith did remember one number though. Sergeant Winters' cell phone number was the same as Graham's birthday.

"John Winters."

"Hi, Sarge. It's Molly."

"Molly, I…"

"Sorry, but this is urgent. I need you to contact the chief ASAP. Tell him the meet at the Lighthouse is off. He has to ditch Burgess fast. We'll be parked in the street next to the library. He is not, repeat NOT, to inform Burgess or Karen of that location."

"Got it."

"Thanks, John. Any problems, have him call me at this number. It's not my regular one." She hung up. Turned to the dog owner. "Sorry, sir, I am taking possession of your phone."

"Can you do that?"

"Yes. You can pick it up tomorrow morning at the RCMP detachment. Thanks."

She got back into the car. Told Tracey to drive. She glanced in the side mirror. The man's mouth was hanging open as he watched them pull away.

Sylvester barked good-bye.

# Chapter Sixty-two

**THE WINTERS HOME OUTSIDE TRAFALGAR, BRITISH COLUMBIA. TUESDAY EVENING.**

"You look puzzled," Eliza Winters said.

"I am puzzled. That was a strange phone call. I feel as though I've walked into a James Bond movie when it was almost over." He made the call.

Keller answered. "This isn't a good time, John. I've a situation here. I'll call you back."

"That's what I'm calling about. Don't say any names, but are you with someone named Burgess?"

"Yes."

"I've had a call from Molly."

"Go ahead."

"She lost her phone, but has a message for you. You have to ditch Burgess. Fast. The location of the meet has changed. They'll be beside the library. Do not, repeat not, inform Burgess."

"Is Blechta aware of this development?"

"She didn't say anything about that."

"I can be at the station in a couple of minutes."

"I'm here if you need anything."

Keller hung up.

"I wonder," John Winters said to his wife, "if I should have said, the eagle flies at midnight."

# Chapter Sixty-three

**BANFF PUBLIC LIBRARY. BANFF, ALBERTA. TUESDAY EVENING.**

The car slid into the nearly empty street outside the public library. Smith told Tracey to park in a dark spot, then to switch off the engine and kill the lights.

They sat, listening to the quiet and watching the night move in. Tall trees surrounding the property covered them in shadow. In the library, lights were being switched off. Two women came out the door. They called good night, climbed into their respective cars and drove away.

Smith glanced at her watch. Five minutes since she'd called Winters.

Sylvester whined in the backseat. She ignored him. Her phone rang.

"John here. I called the chief. Gave him your message."

"Did he understand?"

"I think so. What's happening there, Molly?"

Headlights lit up the dark. A car turned in. Keller's car.

"Gotta go. The boss is here."

Keller pulled up behind them. To Smith's infinite relief, he was alone.

He got out of the car. Smith, Matt, and Tracey did also. Sylvester tried to made a run for it, but Smith shoved him back inside.

Tracey and Smith hung back. Paul and his son looked at each other for a long time. Cars drove past and they heard a woman's laugh. Then Matt said, "Dad," and Paul embraced him. When they separated both men's eyes were wet.

Keller turned to Smith. "Good job, Constable. Now what's this about Jonathan?"

"I suspect he ordered the hit on Barry Caseman," Smith said. She kept her eyes moving, scanning the thick foliage surrounding the building, checking pedestrians, passing vehicles.

Burgess would have to be a fool to order an attack on two police officers and two civilians in a public place in a small, busy town.

Still, no telling what people would do when their well-laid plans began to unravel.

"You can't be serious," Keller said.

"She's perfectly serious, Dad. I'm ready to go to the police. I want you to be with me. I saw who killed Barry. I know he works for Burgess. I was scared, I ran. I wasn't thinking straight. Mom, oh god, Mom will never forgive me."

"This is a lot to take in," Keller said. "But if Burgess is responsible for this, then the last thing your mother will do is blame you."

"I suggest we get going," Smith said. "I'll drop you both at the station. Matt can fill you in on the way, and then I'll take Tracey home."

"I want…"

"I don't care what you want. You can't stay with Matt. He has a long night ahead of him." Longer than that if Blechta didn't buy his story.

Smith wasn't entirely sure she bought it herself. "The Mounties will want to hear all about this car-rental scam, but that can wait. I suggest you quit that job. Don't bother giving notice."

"I'll take Matt," Keller said. He glanced at Sylvester, trying to push his way through the back window of Smith's car. "You look a bit cramped for space. Blechta will want a full report from you, but he'll want to talk to Matt first. Check on your mother. And

Karen. Karen should go back to Calgary immediately, but she won't leave without seeing Matt. Burgess will suspect something's up. Try and stay out of his way."

"Will do."

Matt gathered Tracey into his arms. He held her for a long time. When he stepped away she was crying. "It's all okay, now. It'll all be okay. My dad says so. Right, Dad?"

"Right, son."

Smith and Tracey watched them drive away before getting into their car. Smith drove through town. Tracey sniffed. "I'm sorry about...about your face." She wiped her nose on her sleeve.

"I'll live."

Smith pulled up in front of Matt's building. "I suggest you try to get some sleep. Blechta will be calling you soon. You have to tell him what you told me about the car-rental scam. You won't see me again, Tracey. I'm going to tell my mom what's happening and then go to the station. Soon as I've made my report, I'm leaving town."

"Thanks for everything, Molly."

"Take care, eh? Tell Matt to trust his dad from now on."

"I will."

A beige Corolla pulled up in front of them. They watched the driver struggle to parallel park.

"That's the same sort of car that was parked in the lot for a couple of days. You might want to tell the police about that. It made Tom really jumpy. More jumpy than usual. I thought he'd have kittens when the cops arrived to ask about Barry. Soon as they left he rushed out to check on it."

"You think it was carrying drugs?"

"Probably."

"Did you get the plate?"

"No, but the office will have it."

"Tell the Mounties about it, will you?"

"Should I call now?"

"It'll wait until tomorrow. Blectha'll be too busy tonight to care."

Tracey opened the car door. Light flooded in. "You're from Trafalgar, right?"

"Yes."

"I learned something about Trafalgar when I was crawling around the web of Burgess' companies."

"Yes?"

"There's some land there he wants to buy. But it's owned by someone else, who plans to put in a resort. Burgess is trying to get it. I thought, well, if he wants it real bad, he'd be willing to pay a lot. So if you have some money to invest, you might want to know that. He seemed like such a nice guy, too. Goes to show, eh? You can't trust people. Bye."

And Tracey was gone.

Smith didn't know anything more about computers than she needed to do her job or play music on her iPad. It sounded as if Tracey had been doing a lot more than just hacking into the books of the rental car company.

It wouldn't hurt to tell the chief. Have him drop a few hints Tracey's way that that sort of thing was frowned upon by the law and if she kept it up she could get into some real trouble.

Tracey was probably talking about the Grizzly Resort. Smith didn't have money to invest, and in any event, if she did, she'd hardly buy a piece of the Grizzly. That would see her run out of town on a rail, not to mention banned from her mother's dinner table.

# Chapter Sixty-four

**BANFF SPRINGS HOTEL. BANFF, ALBERTA.
TUESDAY NIGHT.**

Lucky was with Karen in her room, sitting in armchairs in the near-dark. The TV was on but neither woman could have told anyone what was playing. Karen was no longer crying, but the tissue she twisted between her fingers was soaked and torn to shreds.

Lucky was about to call room service to order tea, when the door flew open. Jonathan Burgess stormed in. Karen leapt to her feet.

"What's the matter? What's happened? Where's Matt?"

"Damned if I know. Your husband ordered me out of his car and told me to take a taxi."

"Why?"

Burgess crossed the room. A bottle of Glenlivet was on the dressing table, beside two glasses and an ice bucket full of water. He poured himself a hefty slug. "Ice has melted. Get me some."

Karen stood. Lucky grabbed her arm. "Ice can wait. And so can a drink. Tell us what's happening."

"I don't know. Paul got a call from the police. They told him Blechta needed to see him at the station immediately. He was to come alone. He wouldn't tell me why. Dumped me on the street like a hooker who's worn out her welcome." Not waiting for ice, he downed the drink. Poured another.

In front of Lucky's eyes, Jonathan visibly pulled himself together. His back and neck straightened, and he moved his shoulders. He turned to Karen with a strained smile. "Sorry to bark at you, darling. I couldn't get a cab for ages. Like police, they're never around when you want them."

Karen sat back down, her eyes cautious.

"We know Matt's made contact, so that's one good thing. Have you heard from your daughter again, Lucky?"

"No."

"I'm sure she's fine. Probably ran out of power to her phone. Now, if you'll excuse us, Karen would like to lie down for a while. She's finding this very stressful, you know."

*No,* Lucky thought, *I didn't know. I'm selfish that way.* "I'll be in my room, if you need to talk, Karen. Good night." Before she could move, her phone rang. She didn't recognize the number. "Hello?"

"Hi, Mom, it's me. I'm in the lobby. Are you in your room?"

"No, I'm with Karen and Jonathan."

"Isn't that handy? I'll be right there. What's the number?"

Lucky gave it and hung up. "Moonlight's coming up."

Karen ran to the door. She was standing in the hallway when they heard the ping of the arriving elevator.

The woman who came into the room had a torn lip with a streak of blood running down her chin, the skin around her right eye was swelling, the front of her t-shirt was spattered with blood, her sleeve was torn and bloody. She walked as if she were in pain.

Karen gasped. Lucky almost screamed. "What on earth happened to you?"

Moonlight put her hand to her face. "I almost forgot what with the adrenaline high. This is going to hurt like heck when I come down. Now I know why I got such funny looks in the lobby."

"Matthew?" Karen asked. "Surely, Matthew didn't do that to you?"

Lucky rushed to the bathroom. She pulled a towel off the rack and ran warm water over it.

"No, Mrs. Keller, in all honesty I can say Matt didn't lay a finger on me. Thanks, Mom." She took the towel and began wiping at her face and hands. She looked at Jonathan Burgess. "Matt and Chief Keller are at the RCMP station. Matt can identify the man who killed Barry Caseman. Turns out he ran because he thought it was a case of mistaken identity and the killer was after him."

Karen burst into another round of tears. Lucky's legs gave way and she dropped onto the bed.

"I wonder why he'd think that?" Moonlight continued. "You'll be interested to know Matt's pretty sure he knows who sent the killer. Seems he saw the guy with his employer in Calgary recently. Fascinating, eh, Mr. Burgess?"

Jonathan headed for the closet. He pulled out his suitcase and began throwing clothes into it. "In that case, I'll be heading home. I've missed important meetings dealing with this situation."

Lucky's head spun. She glanced at Karen, watching Jonathan in confusion. "This isn't over," Lucky said. "I think you should stay…"

"That's an excellent idea," Moonlight said. "You might want to call your lawyer on the way."

"When you're ready to come home, Karen, rent a car." Jonathan snapped his suitcase shut, scooped his keys off the table. He threw Moonlight a look of pure rage. Then he opened the door and left.

Moonlight sat down. She let out a long painful breath, and put one hand against her chest.

"What was that all about?" Lucky said.

"I'm sure we'll find out. Eventually. I have to go to the station. Why don't you come with me, Mrs. Keller? They'll let you see Matt for a few minutes."

# Chapter Sixty-five

**GRIZZLY RESORT. OUTSIDE TRAFALGAR, BRITISH COLUMBIA. WEDNESDAY MORNING.**

John Winters' alarm shrilled and he slapped it before it could disturb Eliza. He laid in the dark, listening to the steady drumbeat of rain pounding on the roof. Whipped by unusually high winds, branches moaned and scratched against the window.

Perfect.

He touched his lips lightly to Eliza's sleeping face. She murmured softly and rolled over. He got out of bed. He pulled back the curtains and peered out into the night. Rain ran in torrents down the windows.

He would have preferred a good old-fashioned snowstorm, but this would do as well as if he'd ordered it himself. The rain should help reduce the number of people heading to the Grizzly Resort for today's demonstration.

He made coffee and toast to eat in the car and was making his way slowly down the mountain before seven. Not a glimmer of moon or stars broke the cloud cover, and the forest was shrouded in deep darkness. His headlights caught the rump of an elk disappearing into the trees. As he joined the highway, traffic thickened, heading into town for the day, but moving slowly against the rain and wind. In places, the road clung to the side of the mountain, steep cliffs on one side, an intimidating drop into the river on the other. Makeshift waterfalls had formed in the night, spilling rainwater onto the highway.

He hadn't heard again from Paul Keller or Molly Smith. No news was, hopefully, good news. They'd contact him when they could.

He dropped into the station to see if there had been any fresh developments overnight about the demonstration. He'd alerted the Mounties to Robyn's impromptu protest, and they said they'd have officers on-site.

Not that he needed to inform anyone. As if by magic, by the time he left the office the previous evening, posters had popped up around town, nailed to telephone poles, in the windows of the environmental shops or activist-owned businesses. Posters with the now-familiar logo proclaiming "This is what a Grizzly looks like" with details about today's protest hastily scrawled across. Ray Lopez told him Facebook had notified his daughters about the demonstration and they'd asked if they could take the morning off school.

Needless to say, Ray turned that request down flat.

At seven-thirty, John Winters arrived at the Grizzly Resort site. So far, there were more police vehicles than others—RCMP and a TCP car with Dawn Solway behind the wheel. Adam Tocek was there, sipping a coffee. Norman waited in the truck, where he would stay. He would not be used for crowd-control, that wasn't his job.

"Heard from Molly?" Winters asked Adam.

"A quick call last night, to say Matt had been found and was going with his dad to the police station. She had a report to make, needed some sleep, should be home later today."

"I'm glad that's over then."

"Tell me about it. I have twenty pounds of defrosted turkey in the fridge and don't want to have to eat it all myself. She started to make a pecan pie before she left. I finished it off. Keep this to yourself, Sarge, but I'm glad I didn't have to eat it with her watching."

Winters laughed. Dawn Solway wandered over to say hi.

The security barrier was down across the construction road, and four uniformed Mounties stood in front of it, intending to keep protesters off the property. The rain had turned the unpaved road into a morass. Behind the barrier, Darren Fernhaugh paced a rut in the muddy track. His workers drank coffee and leaned against trees, watching.

Everyone waited.

Promptly at eight o'clock, a beige Corolla slowed, pulled off the highway, and turned onto the construction road. Robyn Winfield was behind the wheel. She drove as far as she could, moving slowly through the mud, bringing the car to a halt with its bumper inches from the security barrier. The car was packed with young women. They spilled out, opened the trunk, began collecting signs. To Winters' considerable dismay, Paula was with them. At least she'd had the sense not to bring Beowulf.

"Show time," Adam said.

As they watched, a handful more cars arrived and parked along the edge of the highway. A few women Winters recognized from around town, a vanload of modern-day hippies. A couple of Vietnam-era hippies, probably wanting to relive their lost youth. Uniformed Mounties shifted in front of the security barrier; hard-faced men in overalls tossed aside coffee cups. Darren Fernhaugh continued to pace. A rain-proof poncho was thrown over his shoulders, and the hood dripped water onto his nose.

He saw John Winters watching him and approached. "Can't you get rid of these people?"

"We will if they block the highway or attempt to come onto your property."

"That one," Fernhaugh pointed to Robyn, moving from group to group, slapping backs, talking loud, "is the ringleader. She's been talking about physically stopping work here. Can you take away that backpack she's carrying?"

"I'll check it out," Adam said.

Fernhaugh groaned. "I can't afford this, I just can't afford it. More delays, more protests. What's going to happen when prospective buyers see these signs all over town saying they aren't welcome? If this gets national exposure, John, it'll finish me."

So far the only media Winters could see was one sodden young man from the *Trafalgar Daily Gazette* interviewing Robyn Winfield. Adam Tocek stood beside her, shifting uncomfortably from one foot to another. Clearly he didn't want to ask to search her bag in front of a reporter. Dawn Solway adjusted the weight of her equipment belt.

The crowd lifted their signs and began to march in a circle. There couldn't have been more than a dozen people in all. Much less than Robyn would have been hoping for.

Steve McNally was noticeably absent. Smart enough to know when to stay out of the rain.

His phone rang. "John Winters."

"It's Molly. I've broken my cell so I've borrowed the boss'. Figured you'd want an update on what's happening here, but first there's something that's been bothering me all night."

"Can we talk about this later? I'm at a demonstration in front of the Grizzly Resort."

"Mom told me one was forming. I think you might want to hear this. It's about the resort."

"Go ahead."

"We believe Barry Caseman was killed on the orders of a Calgary businessman by the name of Jonathan Burgess. The killer, the alleged killer, has been identified, but cannot be located at this time. Burgess is in Calgary, surrounded by lawyers, so whether or not anything can be proved, remains to be seen. I found out that this Burgess has an interest in the Grizzly Resort. I don't mean interest in the business sense as owning part of it, but interested as in wanting it. I didn't think much of it, at first, doesn't matter to me one way or the other who develops the property. Then I remembered Mom telling me the Grizzly people are worried about keeping their heads above water until they can get the units sold and cash coming in."

Winters glanced around. Darren Fernhaugh's secretary was arguing with a stern-faced woman in her late sixties. Much waving of arms and shouting. The construction workers were still behind the police line, but hurling abuse about tree huggers and job-killers. Robyn Winfield was being interviewed, while Adam Tocek eyed her backpack. Fernhaugh marched over to her car and began pounding on the hood, ordering her to get it out of the way, he was expecting deliveries this morning.

Rain continued to fall.

"I don't have anything but a bad feeling that kept me awake when I finally got to bed," Smith said. "Burgess owns a car rental company, Global, that's definitely into criminal activity, including moving drugs. I was told last night about a vehicle of his that might be involved in a major deal, thought it might be going to Trafalgar. No one would be bringing marijuana *into* the Kootenays so it could be full of the white stuff. Trying to finance a takeover of the Grizzly site, maybe? It's a stretch, probably nothing. Sorry to bother you."

"Not a bother. I'll check into it. You have a description, plate number?"

"I'll try and get the tags for you. The car description isn't worth much. A beige Corolla is the most common car in the world."

"A what?"

"Corollas are the world's most common car, or so I've heard, and beige is the most common color."

The interviewer had moved on to talk to someone else, and Adam Tocek was asking Robyn to let him check her backpack. She had her hands on her hips, her legs parted, and a determined set to her chin as she looked up him. A uniform was trying to get Morris Jennings, the bulldozer operator, to stay behind the security barrier, but by the look of it, Jennings was rapidly running out of patience. He'd told Winters what he'd do if he ever found the person who'd set the trap he almost put his foot into.

Darren Fernhaugh continued to pound on Robyn's car, yelling for someone to move it.

Robyn's car. A beige Corolla.

When he'd run a check on her, he'd found no record of her owning a vehicle. In one of her blog posts, she'd called the fossil-fueled automobile modern transportation for the horsemen of the apocalypse.

Steve McNally had not shown up.

"Molly, tell me something about this Burgess. Is he a property developer?"

"Yeah, I think so. Also in oil and gas exploration. High risk, high return."

"I've got to go." He cut the call. Punched the single button that brought up the TCP dispatcher. "Jim, give me a check on this plate. It's from Alberta." He read off the numbers. "Fast."

The seconds ticked by.

Paula and some of the women were chanting, "Forests for bears," waving their placards, and forming into a line, putting the Mounties between them and the workers. Paula was about two feet from the front bumper of the Corolla, lifting her protest sign up and down. She was small and wet, but determined.

"It's a rental vehicle owned by Global Car Rental."

"I need a bomb squad at the Grizzly Resort. ASAP."

Denton was good at his job. He didn't even ask why. "I'm on it."

Winters stuffed his phone into his pocket. He waved to the Mountie in charge, walked over to join him. "I have reason to believe there might be an explosive device in that car." He kept his voice low.

"Are you fuckin' kidding me?"

"We need to get this area cleared. Immediately. I've called for the bomb guys, but they'll be a long time getting here."'

The Mountie studied the chanting protesters, stern-faced police, angry workers. "No one's going to move because we ask them to."

"We're done with asking. We tell them. I want everyone, including cops, out of this area in five minutes. If they have to go onto the property, so be it."

He ran toward the mass of people. "Clear this area. Now!"

They stared at him. One old guy, gray beard halfway down his chest shouted, "Hell, no. We won't go!"

The others took up the chant. "Hell, no. We won't go."

"Get back. Everyone, get back."

Robyn saw him coming. She reached into her backpack and pulled out a length of chain. She darted around Adam Tocek and headed into the woods, intending to circle around the men and barriers.

"Adam," Winters shouted, "let her go. Everyone, get away from that car. Darren, get your men back. Move these people."

A woman stepped in front of him. She bristled with indignation, the effect ruined by the steady drip drip of water from the brim of her hat. "You have no right…"

"I have every right. Constable, move this person. I want every one of you as far away as you can get. Now! Now! Now!"

Tocek swept the woman up. She squealed as he wrapped his arms around her from behind and simply carried her into the woods, her legs kicking at air.

The chanting began to die down. People glanced at each other in confusion.

Solway called to him, "What's up?"

"There might be a bomb in that car."

*Bomb.*

The word spread. Protesters dropped their signs and ran. Some into the woods, some down the construction road. Some moved quickly but calmly, a few were screaming or crying. The Mounties had stopped trying to hold them back, and were guiding people through the line. The workers disappeared in a rush.

"Are you sure?" Solway asked Winters.

"Not in the least. I'm not prepared to stand around and find out, though."

She went to help an elderly woman pick her way across the muddy truck depressions.

Paula stood beside the Corolla. Still clutching her sign. She watched him, her eyes wide. Winters waved his arms. "Get away from there. Run."

She didn't move.

He sprinted toward her. He grabbed her and lifted her off her feet. He wrenched the sign out of her hands, and threw it down. Without breaking stride he rounded the security barrier. She was a small woman, but still a weight, and he wasn't as young as he used to be. His feet sank into the mud, the wet earth clawed at him, slowing him down.

They reached the bend in the road. He could see the construction equipment up ahead, and the trailer that housed the offices. Rain fell onto discarded protest signs. Robyn Winfield had used the chain to fasten herself to the undercarriage of a bulldozer. The look on her face, when she realized no one was the least bit interested in her, would have been funny in other circumstances. People milled about, some were running, disappearing into the woods. A Mountie had slipped in the mud and another officer was helping him to his feet.

The forest exploded. The pressure punched him solidly in the back, propelling him forward. He dropped Paula, lost his footing, collapsed on top of her. He felt heat on his back, a roaring in his ears. He wrapped his arms tightly around Paula's head and buried his face into her hair. Spots of pain sprung up all across his back and the back of his legs. He kicked out, trying to throw the fire off.

He knew he was burning.

# Chapter Sixty-six

**GRIZZLY RESORT. OUTSIDE TRAFALGAR, BRITISH COLUMBIA. WEDNESDAY MORNING.**

John Winters felt hands on him, slapping at his clothes. He rolled off Paula, flopped onto his back. Adam Tocek was crouched beside him, hands and face black. "You're okay, Sarge. Some flaming debris. That's all." He sounded like he was talking from the bottom of the river. Then he jumped to his feet. "The truck. Norman." He ran.

Winters shook his head. His ears rang. Paula laid where he'd dropped her, sobbing. Winters rubbed his back into the mud, and then he got to his feet, moving carefully, checking for pain. In front of him, in the direction of the highway, the forest was on fire. Pieces of metal that had once made up a car were burning lumps haphazardly tossed round the clearing and into the line of trees. Tocek skirted the flaming wreck that had been the beige Corolla. Arms over his head, he kept to the center of the road where there was nothing to burn.

Winters turned. People lay on the ground or stood in shock. Some were crying, some were simply staring. There appeared to be no damage to the buildings or equipment. For a moment Winters wondered why everyone, police, construction workers, protesters, started to dance. Comprehension came slowly: they were stomping on fiery debris littering the yard. The job made considerably easier by the rain-soaked ground. A woman was bleeding profusely from a gash in her head. The old guy with the long beard pulled a tissue out of his pocket and gently, uselessly, began dabbing at it. One of the Mounties was sitting on the ground, his face white, his teeth clenched, his right leg at a bad angle.

It had been, as these things go, a small bomb.

But enough to kill or maim anyone standing within a few yards of the car.

Winters helped the weeping Paula to her feet. He ran his eyes down her. Her front was caked in mud, but she appeared unharmed. He guided her to a group of women. They gathered her into their arms.

Robyn Winfield was sitting on the ground, tied to a bulldozer by a length of chain wrapped around her waist. She was screaming, pulling at the chain as if trying to break it. With a pop, Winters' hearing came back.

"What the hell do you think you're doing?" he yelled.

"I didn't do it. I didn't know anything about that. I'd never…" She jerked at the chain, "Get this Goddamned thing off me."

"Don't you have a key?"

"No, I don't have a key, you fool. It needs to be cut away."

"I have people to see to first. You can wait. Constable, stay with Ms. Winfield. Not that she's going anywhere, but some folks might have an argument with her."

Dawn Solway nodded.

"McNally. That criminal bastard. He set me up. He brought me the car. Said he'd be following with a bunch of friends." Robyn put all her rage into the chain. It didn't give. Winters noticed with some satisfaction that her hands were beginning to bleed. "I demand you take me to the police station. Immediately."

"You demand? You are in no position to demand anything."

He turned at the sound of a bark. Adam Tocek trotted down the road, Norman leading the way. The dog was unharmed, and very interested in the chaos all around him.

In the distance, sirens approached.

# Chapter Sixty-seven

**BANFF SPRINGS HOTEL. BANFF, ALBERTA. WEDNESDAY MORNING.**

Paul Keller's face was a picture of shock. "Of all things. I'm leaving now. I'll come to the office soon as I arrive. Keep me posted."

He put away his phone.

"What?" Lucky and Smith said in unison.

Keller glanced around. They were in the lobby, preparing to check out. Karen paced by the door, waiting for her rental car to arrive. Her hair hung around her face in lank strands, and the remains of tears streaked through her hastily applied makeup like a dried-up river bed.

Keller walked to a quiet alcove. Smith and her mother followed.

"A car bomb."

"In Trafalgar!"

"No one killed. No injuries other than a couple of scratches, minor burns from debris. One broken leg."

"Oh, my God," Lucky said.

"People could have been killed," Keller said, "including John and Adam, if it wasn't for you, Molly."

"Me? I wasn't even there."

Keller glanced toward the door. Karen continued to pace. "That beige Corolla? It had the bomb."

Smith stared at him. Speechless. When she found her voice, she said, "I thought it was delivering hard drugs. I had no idea."

"Where did it go off?" Lucky asked.

"At the Grizzly Resort. During the demonstration."

"I cannot believe environmentalists would do anything…"

"That's all I know, Lucky. John has arrested one of the demonstration organizers on suspicion, and he's taking her in now. The other, conveniently, seems to have disappeared."

"The car that was used for the bomb. It belonged to Global Car Rental. Burgess' company." Smith's knees felt weak. A car bomb. If she hadn't suspected it was being used to smuggle drugs… She didn't finish the thought.

"Molly, help your mother get her things in the car, will you? I need to make a couple of calls. Blechta's working on a warrant for Global Car Rental and Kramp's Auto Repair now, based on what Tracey had to tell him. Matt gave a pretty good description of the man he saw leaving the apartment immediately following Caseman's death, and once he's picked up, we're hoping he'll squeal on his boss. This business this morning will strengthen Blechta's hand."

"Speak of the devil." Lucky nodded toward the doors.

Ed Blechta came in, followed by Matt and Tracey, holding hands and looking exceedingly happy. Matt stopped and gave his mother a long hard hug.

"They let him go," Keller said. Judging by the overwhelming relief in his voice, Smith understood how worried he'd been. He'd taken Matt to the station last night, and then been told to leave.

The arrivals joined the group in the alcove. Keller nodded to Blechta and the two men moved further away.

"Thank you, Molly," Matt said. He held out his hand. She took it.

"I mean it. I did a lot of thinking last night, courtesy of the Royal Canadian Mounted Police and their fine facilities. Nothing like a night in the cells to make a man think about his life. I've been a fuck-up for too long." He turned to Lucky. "I cannot apologize enough for the way we met, Mrs. Smith."

Lucky wrapped her arms around him in a hug. “You don’t have to. Just look after that girl of yours.”

“That I will do.” He beamed at Tracey. Her smile lit up her whole face.

“How’s my mom handling it?” Matt asked Lucky.

“Not well. She’s in shock. Disbelief. Anger. Not sure who she’s angry at. Jonathan for betraying her… and you. Herself for believing in him. Moonlight for exposing him. Paul most of all, for moving on without her. She’s been calling Jonathan all morning. He’s not answering.”

Smith snorted. “Huddled with his PR people and lawyers, I’d suspect. Making travel arrangements, probably. I hear the weather’s nice in Brazil this time of year.” Guys like Burgess, nothing ever touched them. The company’s affairs would be so convoluted no wrongdoing could be traced back to him. The only hope of nailing him was finding Barry’s killer and getting him to outright say Burgess had ordered the hit. That might well never happen. Burgess would make sure the guy knew that his family, if he had one, would be taken care of—one way or the other—while he was in prison. Burgess had dumped Karen Keller fast enough. Smith wondered if he’d taken up with Karen precisely because she was the ex-wife of the chief constable of Trafalgar. Might have hoped for some inside knowledge or influence there. Although, she had to admit, it seemed like one hell of a lot of trouble to go to just to get his hands on a piece of resort property.

“Matt,” Karen called across the lobby. “My car’s here. I’m leaving.” She hadn’t said a word to Paul or Lucky since last night. And when Lucky attempted to say good morning, Karen had turned her back. She had a lot to deal with, a lot of pain ahead of her.

Matt and Tracey joined her. Matt took her suitcase and they went outside.

Blechta and Paul reappeared.

“We picked up Tom Dunning last night,” Blechta said. “From what Chief Keller and Tracey have told me we have enough to charge Dunning with something major. Conspiracy to commit an act of terrorism would be a nice start. Should be enough to scare him into spilling all the dirt. Dunning's description, by the way, of the guy who dropped off that Corolla, is pretty much a dead match to the man Matt saw at his apartment. We've issued a Canada-wide warrant for him. As for who picked it up and drove it to Trafalgar, the driver's license used was a fake one, but thanks to your Sergeant Winters, we're looking for a known eco-terrorist name of Steve McNally."

"Let's go home, Paul," Lucky said. "I've had enough vacation."

He put his arm around her, and they walked together to the front desk.

Smith moved to follow.

"One minute, Ms. Smith, if you please."

"Yes?"

To her considerable surprise, Ed Blechta thrust out his hand. "You did good work here, Constable. You've got good instincts and you're like a rabid dog with a bone. If you're ever looking for another job," he cleared his throat, "I'd be happy to give you a recommendation."

"Thanks. But as for a new job, I think I'm pretty good right where I am."

# Chapter Sixty-eight

**TRAFALGAR CITY POLICE STATION. TRAFALGAR, BRITISH COLUMBIA. WEDNESDAY MORNING.**

John Winters put Robyn Winfield into interview room one. His hands had shaken all the way back into town, and his heart refused to stop pounding. Whether from the aftershock of the bombing or in pure rage, he didn't know.

Fire trucks had arrived and, with the help of the rain and the wet condition of the forest, put the fire out before it had a chance to spread. The few injured were loaded into ambulances. Ray Gavin had been called to begin the initial forensics examination of the now-demolished Corolla. Darren Fernhaugh ordered his secretary and his men to stop gawking and get back to work. The protesters left, but not before letting Robyn Winfield know what they thought of being used to stage a violent protest. Before leaving, Paula, covered in mud from head to toe, kissed Winters on the cheek. "You saved my life."

Around a knot in his throat, he told her to say hi to Beowulf.

Robyn had sat on the wet ground, fuming so hard Winters was surprised her clothes weren't drying. Finally, once everything was back to some semblance of normal, Winters asked Fernhaugh for a bolt-cutter.

The chain broke. Adam Tocek took one arm, Dawn Solway the other, and Robyn was lifted to her feet.

Winters formally arrested her and snapped on handcuffs. Tocek and Solway marched her off the property, while construction workers cheered and catcalled, and police and firefighters watched. She was loaded into the back of Solway's cruiser, and Winters followed them to town in his van.

He took Ray Lopez into the interview with him. Lopez removed the cuffs and Winters handed Robyn a glass of water.

She drank deeply and then said. "I'm going to get something out of my shirt, okay?"

"Go ahead."

She reached, not into a pocket, but into her bra. She brought out a piece of paper, and handed it to him. Her eyes glittered and the edges of her mouth turned up.

He read the paper. "What the hell?"

"Make the call, Sarge. They'll tell you. And make it fast, I've places to go."

He stormed into the hallway, a confused Lopez following.

"RCMP."

"What?"

"She's an undercover cop."

"You're kidding me."

"I really, really wish I was. Make the call, will you? I've no doubt they'll confirm what she says. In the meantime, I want to know what the hell kind of game she's playing."

When Winters returned, Robyn was leaning back in her chair. Her eyes were closed. She opened them very slowly. If she were a cat, she would have licked her paws.

He did not sit down. "People were almost killed out there today."

"That," she said, "had nothing to do with me. If you forget, I was standing right there. I would have been the first one to go up."

"I saw you running away, seconds before the explosion."

Her eyes darkened. "Pure luck. McNally set me up. I didn't realize how dangerous he had become. I trust you people are looking for him."

"We are. Although I'm sure he's long gone by now. Tell me about the car."

"He disappeared day before yesterday, came back with that vehicle. Said it was his, and I could use it to transport the demonstrators."

"It was a rental car. You didn't check?"

"No, I didn't check. I was undercover, if you don't know what that means."

The door opened. Lopez. He nodded to Winters.

"Told ya," Robyn said. She started to get to her feet. "My work here is done."

"It's done when I say it's done. I want answers."

"I did not know he'd planted a fucking bomb in the car. We talked about how to get more media exposure than that pathetic small-town newspaper. I guess he decided not to share his idea with me. I would have put a stop to it, if he had."

"Maybe. What about the trap? The leghold trap at the resort."

She shrugged. "It wouldn't have hurt anyone. McNally wanted to hide it, use it like a real trap but I put it out in the open. Even if someone stepped in it, they wear construction boots there. No harm done."

"This whole thing. You orchestrated it all. The protests, the demonstrations. You weren't just an observer, you set everything in motion."

"I didn't start anything, Sergeant. The ball was rolling; I gave it a little push. That was my job. These people, these so-called environmentalists, they're a threat to our country. Oh, yeah, some of them are nice ladies who bring along their knitting to demonstrations. Some are terrorists, pure and simple. I proved that, didn't I? Flushed them out of their caves into the open. We can put McNally away for a long time. You might not like my methods, but I got results. And that's all that counts."

"Are you really that stupid? Results? You could have gotten us all killed. You've been played like a violin. You think this was about terrorist groups? What do you call them? Eco-terrorists? Get real. It was about money. Land for resource-extraction. Pure and simple. There's gas under that land, and there are people who want it bad enough to kill for it. They must have been absolutely delighted when some stupid, brain-dead undercover cop wandered in and suggested escalating everything."

"I…"

"I wouldn't be at all surprised if they knew all along who you are. The people of Trafalgar care about the environment, very much, but they believe above all in legal peaceful protest. Guys like McNally wouldn't have had a hope in hell of getting in with them. That's why he kept to the sidelines. Let you, the smiling woman with the blog, the following, the *passion*, suck them in.

"I have absolutely no doubt you were intended to go up along with the car. Imagine the headlines. Courageous fighter for the environment murdered by… It probably doesn't even matter who they intended to pin the bombing on. No one would be able to do anything to build homes on that land. Not ever. It would be a shrine. For a while, until a shell company bought it, and handed it off to an oil and gas company for fracking. You don't need people wanting to be part of a community, to get along with their new neighbors, for fracking. They'd probably leave the roadside untouched. Maybe put up a nice monument to you. You think McNally's an eco-terrorist? He's a common criminal, in the pay of bigger criminals. And you're his patsy."

"You know nothing about this. Nothing about playing in the big leagues. Sometimes, we have to take chances, risks, throw the dice. You're a small-town cop, sitting behind your desk chasing down pickpockets and jaywalkers and going home to have dinner with your wife every night at five o'clock."

"Get the hell out of here, and get out of my town. If I see you here again, I'll find some pretext to arrest you. Ray, escort this *officer* to get her things. And then drop her at the bus station."

John Winters slammed the door on his way out.

# Chapter Sixty-nine

**TOCEK-SMITH HOME. OUTSIDE TRAFALGAR, BRITISH COLUMBIA. ONE WEEK LATER.**

The extensions on the hand-carved wood table had been laid, the good wineglasses taken out of the cabinet, additional china and silverware borrowed from Molly Smith's mom. Adam Tocek made a huge pot of turkey tetrazzini with the Thanksgiving bird; Madeline Lopez threw together an enormous salad; Lucky Smith dug pumpkin and apple pie out of her freezer. John Winters brought the wine, and Paul Keller provided the beer.

"What I want to know," Lucky said, as the steaming casserole was passed around, "is what's going to happen to Jonathan."

Keller shook his head. "We can only hope we can convince one of his men to roll over on him. Even then, he's surrounded by lawyers, buried in a maze of interconnected companies, protected by middlemen."

"You mean he's going to get off?" Matt served himself a generous helping.

Tracey sat beside him, sipping at a glass of wine. "Tom's going to testify, isn't he? Won't that help?"

"It'll help," Keller said. "Against Simpson and McIntosh, about drug running and fake car repairs."

"Mr. Simpson was arrested," Tracey said. "Jody's out of a job, but she's finally ditched Tom. I'm glad of that." She rubbed her jaw absentmindedly.

"Blechta has brought in computer experts and they're ripping the company computers, as well as their personal ones, apart. Finding, I might add, further evidence of what you, Tracey, came up with on your own. Nothing, however, on the murder of Barry Caseman or the bomb in the Corolla. Facing a charge of assisting in an act of terrorism, Simpson copped quickly enough to trafficking and fraud. He claims he was never told what was in the Corolla, just that it was to be left alone until picked up."

"What I'd like to know," Eliza said, twirling her fork through her pasta without ever lifting it to her mouth. "is how that bomb works. The car was driven to Banff from Calgary. Sat in a parking lot for a couple of days, then driven to Trafalgar. Isn't that incredibly dangerous? Surely this Steve McNally wouldn't have taken such a risk. Suppose he'd hit something, or been in an accident?"

Smith reached across the table and grabbed the bottle of white. In the four years she'd been working with John Winters, this was the first time she'd properly met his wife. Eliza didn't come to police functions; she didn't pop into the station to say hi or bring the lunch he'd left in the fridge. She was beautiful and elegant and distant, still scarcely seemed to belong in Trafalgar at all.

She'd brought a huge bunch of flowers, yellow roses and baby's breath, artfully arranged in a cut-glass vase as a hostess gift, and thanked Molly and Adam, in a sexy, almost-breathless voice, for inviting her to their home.

Smith guessed that Eliza had been dragged along to make Tracey feel more at ease at what was essentially a party for cops and partners, all of whom knew each other well. When they arrived, Tracey had stared at Eliza with her mouth practically gaping open. Eliza greeted her warmly, drew her causally aside, and asked questions about living in Banff. Smith suspected Mrs. Winters had been primed before arriving.

Over drinks, they talked about generalities, the weather, the potential for an early opening of the ski hills, Matt and Tracey's plans for the future. Once they sat down and the food was brought out, conversation inevitably drifted to the one topic on everyone's mind.

"Not dangerous, no," Gavin said. "No matter how big an explosion, and this was a small one as these things go, trace evidence remains. He used a component called C-4. It's used by the military but available on the black market for those who know where to look. C-4 is useful precisely because it isn't unstable. It can't detonate on its own, not even if lit by a small flame or shot with a bullet."

"How much do you need?" Tracey asked.

"About the size of a brick," Gavin said. "In this case it was fastened to the undercarriage."

Madeline Lopez shuddered. "Scary."

"That it is. It's soft, like dough. McNally drove the car to Trafalgar, allegedly, and before he handed it over to Robyn…"

Smith was looking at John Winters at that moment, about to ask if he wanted a top off to his wine. His lips twisted in disapproval at the mention of Robyn Winfield, and he gave her a dark look.

"… he crawled under the car, and simply pressed a detonator into the compound. Primed to go off at a cell phone signal. Easy."

"Too easy," Lucky said.

"At eight-thirty that morning we got a report of a stolen motorbike," Lopez said. "We found the bike a couple of hours later in an alley behind Front Street. Its tracks match those found on an access road about a kilometer from the Grizzly Resort site. We believe McNally stole the bike overnight, hid himself in the woods, and at the right time, made the call to the detonator. Then, back to town, dumped the bike, and leapt on a Greyhound bus."

"Never to be seen again," Smith said.

John Winters lifted his glass. "About that, I have news." He couldn't hide the grin that spread across his face. "I got a call just before we got here. Steve McNally was picked up by the Mounties in Kelowna, getting on a plane for Fort McMurray."

"I'll drink to that," Gavin said. And he did so.

"Cheers," said Lopez. Everyone drank.

"He'll testify against Jonathan, then?" Lucky asked.

"Don't get your hopes up," Winters said. "McNally's unlikely to know who ultimately ordered the attack. He's just muscle-for-hire. They're charging him with committing an act of terrorism, attempted murder, and various other charges. He'll go down for a long time. The people behind him? That remains to be seen."

"Makes me so mad," Lucky said with a determined huff. Keller smiled at her. "It'll be all over the news that he was an activist. By the time his real motivation comes out, they'll have gone on to another story and environmentalists will be stuck with the blame."

"What's happening about Barry?" Tracey said. "I didn't like him, but he didn't deserve to die. What about the guy who killed him?"

"These things take time, Tracey," Keller said. "Blechta's building a case. They'll find him."

"But it's been a whole week!"

*A whole week,* Smith thought. They'd consider themselves lucky if it was over in a whole year. The man Matt had seen leaving his apartment had disappeared. If Matt had gone to the police immediately, they might have had a chance of finding him. But two days had passed. Plenty of time to get himself to just about any place in the world. Or, more likely, to get himself dead and buried in an unmarked grave, his reward for being so careless as to be seen.

Police in Alberta and B.C. were only beginning to work their way through the network of drug dealers and shady businessmen. Forensic computer searches found that Global Car Rental and Kramp's Auto Repair were, indeed, owned ultimately by Burgess Enterprises. Company vice-presidents were shocked to hear of the wrongdoing of their employees. Steps would be taken to ensure such didn't happen again.

"It's only speculation on my part," Keller said, "and mustn't go beyond this room, but I'd guess Jonathan ordered the hit on Barry because of the timing. Barry Caseman was a greedy man, greedy but strictly small-time. He figured he could shake down

Jonathan. Make some extra money by threatening to expose him for being behind the car rental scam. Any other time, Jonathan would have laughed him off. But with C-4 coming to Banff, and then to Trafalgar, he didn't want any attention on him, or on Global Car Rental. So Barry had to go. There was little risk on Jonathan's part. If not for you, Matt, coming home when you did, the police in Banff wouldn't have gotten anywhere. A hired killer, gone before the body was discovered. No clues, no motive, no suspects."

"Have you heard from your mother?" Lucky asked Matt.

"I called her yesterday. She's not doing too well. She's staying at Aunt Pat's place for a while. She wasn't living with Burgess, thank God, but some of her stuff was there. He had it packed up and sent around without a word. Hasn't bothered to call her or get in touch."

"She'll need your support."

"We're going to Calgary tomorrow," Tracey said.

"And so," Eliza said slowly, "the small players are caught in the net, and the big ones swim away."

"The world we live in," Adam said. "Burgess will get off without a scratch."

"Not entirely," Lucky said. "Karen and I had a drink one night in the hotel. Karen told me, bragged about it, that Jonathan had big plans. He was about to be offered a post as a special advisor to the prime minister. Something about encouraging foreign investment in resource-extraction. What other people call selling out and..."

"Get to the point, Lucky," Keller said.

"If I must. He'd been handpicked by the prime minister for the job. Dare I suggest no politician will now want to touch him with the proverbial ten-foot pole? The bombing is news nationally, and Burgess Enterprises has been mentioned in the papers. No accusations, of course, but mud's flying, and I'd say Jonathan's political dreams are dead."

"I'll drink to that," Molly Smith said.

"Anyone for pie?" Lucky said.

To receive a free catalog of Poisoned Pen Press titles, please contact us in one of the following ways:

Phone: 1-800-421-3976
Facsimile: 1-480-949-1707
Email: info@poisonedpenpress.com
Website: www.poisonedpenpress.com

Poisoned Pen Press
6962 E. First Ave. Ste 103
Scottsdale, AZ 85251